"I have to find out the truth,"

Allison said.

"I suppose you're right." Gabe smiled grimly. "No matter who gets hurt."

"You must think I'm a monster! I'd never willingly add to anyone's misery."

"I wasn't referring to anyone else. I was thinking of you," Gabe said quietly. "You've had a lot of disappointment in your life. I wouldn't like to see you go through any more."

His husky voice warmed Allison. Very few people had ever been concerned about her—certainly no one like Gabe. Was he being sincere? Or was it just a tactic to get rid of her?

"Why should you care what happens to me?" she asked hesitantly.

"I can understand why you don't trust me." He reached over and captured her hand.

Gabe's warm touch sent a tingle up her arm. She tried not to let herself imagine what it would be like if circumstances were different and he really *was* interested in her....

Dear Reader,

Welcome to Silhouette **Special Edition**...welcome to romance. This month of May promises to be one of our best yet!

We begin with this month's THAT SPECIAL WOMAN! title, *A Man for Mom,* by Gina Ferris Wilkins. We're delighted that Gina will be writing under her real name, Gina Wilkins, from now on. And what a way to celebrate— with the first book in her new series, THE FAMILY WAY! Don't miss this emotional, poignant story of family connections and discovery of true love. Also coming your way in May is Andrea Edwards's third book of her series, **This Time Forever.** In *A Secret and a Bridal Pledge* two people afraid of taking chances risk it all for everlasting love.

An orphaned young woman discovers herself, and the love of a lifetime, in Tracy Sinclair's latest, *Does Anybody Know Who Allison Is?* For heart-pounding tension, look no further than Phyllis Halldorson's newest story about a husband and wife whose feelings show them they're still *Truly Married.* In *A Stranger in the Family* by Patricia McLinn, unexpected romance awaits a man who discovers that he's a single father. And rounding out the month is the debut title from new author Caroline Peak, *A Perfect Surprise.*

I hope you enjoy all these wonderful stories from Silhouette **Special Edition,** and have a wonderful month!

Sincerely,

Tara Gavin
Senior Editor

Please address questions and book requests to:
Silhouette Reader Service
U.S.: 3010 Walden Ave., P.O. Box 1325, Buffalo, NY 14269
Canadian: P.O. Box 609, Fort Erie, Ont. L2A 5X3

TRACY SINCLAIR

DOES ANYBODY KNOW WHO ALLISON IS?

Published by Silhouette Books
America's Publisher of Contemporary Romance

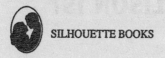

SILHOUETTE BOOKS

ISBN 0-373-09957-6

DOES ANYBODY KNOW WHO ALLISON IS?

Printed in U.S.A.

Books by Tracy Sinclair

TRACY SINCLAIR

author of more than forty Silhouette novels, also contributes to various magazines and newspapers. An extensive traveler and a dedicated volunteer worker, this California resident has accumulated countless fascinating experiences, settings and acquaintances to draw on in plotting her romances.

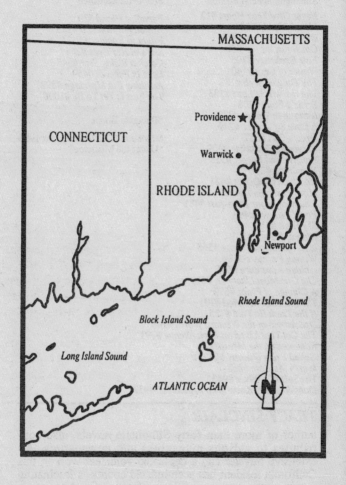

MASSACHUSETTS

CONNECTICUT

Providence ★

Warwick ●

RHODE ISLAND

Newport ●

Rhode Island Sound

Block Island Sound

Long Island Sound

ATLANTIC OCEAN

N

Chapter One

Allison Riley had always wondered who her parents were, like all the other children at the orphanage. It was merely a matter of speculation, however, until she was twenty-five years old and living on her own. Finding out who she was became a top priority the night Bruce broke their engagement.

He'd skirted the issue, but the real reason was her "uncertain background," as his parents so delicately put it. They vigorously opposed what they considered an unsuitable marriage.

"This doesn't mean we have to stop seeing each other," Bruce had said uncomfortably.

"As long as your mommy and daddy don't find out," she'd answered bitterly.

"That isn't fair, Allie! You know I work for my dad. It wouldn't do either of us any good for me to openly defy him. We can't get married if I don't have a job."

"You could get a job with another firm. You're thirty-three years old. Isn't it time you left the nest?"

"Investment banking is in a recession right now. It wouldn't be easy to find a comparable position somewhere else. If you'll just be patient, I'll try to smooth things over with Mother and Dad."

"What if they don't change their minds?"

When Bruce had failed to assure her of their future together, no matter what, Allison's illusions died. He was a spoiled rich man's son, and his parents were shallow social climbers who expected him to marry a debutante—which he would undoubtedly do.

It was a shock to realize, once she started to think rationally rather than emotionally, that she honestly didn't care. Her pride was hurt naturally, but the reason for her rejection was the really crushing blow. Allison vowed at that moment that she'd never again let herself be dismissed as a shadowy figure without a past, or even a name of her own.

The search for her identity had taken her to a hospital in Philadelphia where she was born. And now, here, to a mansion in Newport, Rhode Island.

Butterflies were beating their wings in Allison's stomach as she stood outside the imposing double doors of Rosewood Manor. Was the missing piece of the puzzle within reach? If so, would she be welcome? Or would her mother be horrified that the daughter she gave away so many years ago had suddenly turned up to intrude on her life?

There was only one way to find out. Allison drew a deep breath and rang the bell.

A butler with an impassive face answered the door. His carefully blank expression was replaced by startled surprise when she asked to see Monica Van Ruyder. After an instant, his mask descended once more.

"Whom shall I say is calling?"

"She doesn't know...I mean..." Allison paused to compose herself. "My name is Allison Riley."

He allowed her into the entry hall, but no farther. She glanced around in awe at the marble columns and arches below the twenty-foot ceiling. Beyond the pillars was a sweeping staircase with ornate wrought-iron railings that curved on both sides before fanning out to a second floor.

As her dazzled eyes swept over paintings, antique wall sconces and rose-colored damask draperies, the butler returned with a younger man, somewhere in his forties. He had a weak chin and thin lips compressed in a straight line.

The man greeted her with a menacing scowl. "What do you want here?"

It was a startlingly rude reception, but Allison tried not to let it bother her. "I'd like to see Monica Van Ruyder."

"What about?"

"Well, I . . . it's personal."

"I'm her brother, Martin Van Ruyder. You can tell me."

"It's about something that happened a long time ago," Allison said reluctantly.

"I suppose you're going to claim she owed you money. All right, submit an itemized bill and we'll pay it if it isn't too outrageous. Don't be greedy. I'm sure she doesn't owe you a cent, but we'll write it off to nuisance value."

"I didn't come here for money! I'd just like to talk to her. I'm sure she'll want to hear what I have to say." Allison lied out of desperation.

A nasty smile curved his mouth. "That proves you don't know the first thing about Monica. Women never interested her."

Allison hadn't come this far to be turned away. Her nails made crescent marks in her damp palms. "I really must insist on seeing your sister."

"Okay, that's it! I don't know what your game is, but if you're not out of here in two seconds, I'm going to call the police."

Allison stared at him in bewilderment. "Why won't you let me see her? You don't even know why I came."

"I'm sure you have a very plausible story prepared—one involving money. You scam artists come out of the woodwork when somebody wealthy dies."

Allison's first reaction was incredulity. "You mean she's—I don't believe you! You're just saying that to get rid of me. She can't be dead!"

"What difference does it make to *you?* You couldn't have been on very close terms if you didn't even know she died."

Allison felt a crushing sense of defeat as the news sank in. It wasn't fair to have arrived too late. "Was it an accident?" she whispered.

"What difference does it make?" he asked curtly.

"Please, I'd like to know."

"Why?"

"I think Monica Van Ruyder was my mother."

"What?" Martin's face flushed with anger. "You're really going for the gold, aren't you? Which marriage is supposed to have produced you? My sister had three husbands. That was written up in the newspaper. It's a funny thing, though, nobody ever heard of her having any children."

Allison was instantly sorry for her bald statement. She never would have blurted out her suspicion if she hadn't been so upset over the news of Monica's death.

"I suppose you've concocted some wild story to get around the facts," he taunted. "All right, try it out on me. Why am I supposed to believe Monica was your mother?"

"I'm not sure she was," Allison answered slowly. "That's what I came to find out."

"Oh, so now you're having second thoughts about getting away with it. At least you realize your scheme won't work. If you're smart, you'll go back to wherever you came from and try to fleece an easier mark."

"I'm not trying to deceive anybody. All I want is information. I was raised in an orphanage and I never knew who my parents were."

"That's very touching." He sneered. "How did you arrive at Monica?"

"I spent a lot of time going through the records at the hospital in Philadelphia where I was born. There were two other possibilities, but she seemed the most likely."

"And as long as you had a choice, why not pick the richest one?" Martin's voice was heavy with irony.

"No! I didn't want anything from her."

"Then you won't be disappointed, because that's exactly what you're going to get. You'd better leave now."

"Could I just see a picture of her?" Allison pleaded.

His teeth clicked together. "No, you may not! I want you out of this house. If you try to pursue your outrageous fraud I'll have you thrown in jail. Is that quite clear?" Without waiting for an answer, he strode to the door and flung it open.

She had no choice. In all fairness, Allison could see why Monica's brother would think she was a fortune hunter. The family was unimaginably rich. If only he realized that she didn't want a cent from them, just confirmation, one way or the other.

An attractive older woman was coming down the staircase as Allison went out the door. "Who was that pretty girl, Martin?"

"Nobody, Mother," he answered briefly.

Mary Louise Van Ruyder gazed at her son with raised eyebrows. She was in her sixties, but her figure was still trim and her face relatively unlined. She obviously took good care of herself, yet she wasn't one of those foolish women who try to deny the passage of time by following fashion's dictates, however unsuitable. Her short gray hair was simply styled, and her navy linen dress was elegantly understated.

"My eyesight is still excellent," she remarked dryly. "I distinctly saw a young woman in the hallway. What did she want?"

"Nothing to concern yourself over," he answered dismissively.

"If you're trying to whet my curiosity, you've succeeded. How many more times must I ask you?"

"It was just some woman with a wild story about Monica. I didn't want you to be upset by it, that's all. She won't be back, I guarantee you," Martin said grimly.

"How did she know Monica?"

"She didn't. That's what makes her visit so outrageous. The whole thing is really quite absurd, not worth repeating." When Mary Louise gave him a level stare, he continued reluctantly, "She had some weird idea that Monica might have been her mother. You see, I told you it was all a lot of rubbish."

"What made her think that? She must have had a reason."

"These scam artists make up their own reasons. I knew she was a phony when she claimed to have tracked Monica to a hospital in Philadelphia. Remember how Monica hated that town? She wouldn't even go with us to Aunt Jane's funeral. Father was furious."

An unreadable expression crossed Mary Louise's face. "I'd like to talk to the girl," she said quietly.

"That would be very foolish. Haven't you been through enough grief?"

"I'm not a delicate flower, Martin. You don't have to shield me from the hard facts of life."

"Father always did. I'm only trying to do what he would have wanted me to," Martin said righteously.

"Your father was a good husband, but he was somewhat overly protective. Since he's been gone, I've learned to think for myself. Kindly permit me to continue to do so."

"Excuse me for saying this, Mother, but you aren't always astute about people. You've been sheltered all your life so it's understandable that you take everybody at face value. You don't know how devious fortune hunters can be."

"Are we still speaking about that young woman?"

"The same applies to anyone who tries to take advantage of a credulous woman," Martin answered primly.

"You make me sound like a doddering old lady."

"I didn't say that. But you *are* in your sixties."

"That doesn't automatically affect the mind," Mary Louise said ironically.

"You have to be realistic, Mother. You're a very wealthy woman. All sorts of people are attracted by your money, and you aren't even aware of it. You've already proved how gullible you are."

"I assume you're referring to Sergei. I do wish you weren't so close minded about him."

"I'm sorry, but I can't help feeling that your friendship is quite unsuitable. Besides being five years younger than you, the man is a decorator, for heaven's sake! That's a hobby, not a job."

"Sergei is an interior designer, and a very successful one. It happens to be a profession requiring intensive training. Members of the association have to meet rigid standards."

"Then he has less excuse for trying to use you than that girl who was just here."

"I'm capable of making up my own mind about her. Ask her to come back."

"I couldn't if I wanted to. She didn't give me her name."

"It's Allison Riley, madam." The butler, who had been lurking unobtrusively in the background informed her.

"Thank you, Jordan." She ignored the baleful look her son shot at the butler. "Invite her to tea tomorrow, Martin."

"How am I supposed to find her?"

"You might try phoning all the hotels in town. There aren't that many."

"What if she's staying at one of those bed and breakfast places?"

"That will take a little longer, so I suggest you get started." Mary Louise smiled pleasantly. "Will you have the car brought around, Jordan? I'm going out."

After his mother left, Martin stalked into the library and slammed the door. He pulled up a chair to the exquisite

Louis XVI desk and dialed the phone, but the call wasn't to a hotel.

Burton Rockford sat in his plush office high in a Manhattan skyscraper, having a quiet talk with his son, Gabriel. It was a pleasure that didn't occur often enough in the older man's opinion. He enjoyed his son's company.

As head of the venerable law firm of Rockford, Rockford, Collingsworth and Strand, Burton handled only the most prestigious clients. But Gabe had a full caseload, in addition to an active social life.

"Your mother would like you to come over for dinner sometime before your fortieth birthday," Burton remarked mildly.

"That gives me five years." Gabe's gray eyes sparkled with merriment as he laughed, showing even white teeth in a tanned face.

Burton regarded his tall, athletic son with the pride he always felt. Even sprawled in a chair with his long legs outstretched, Gabe had a natural grace. The lithe body coupled with a ruggedly handsome face worked like catnip on women, his father reflected. Maybe that was the reason Gabe was taking so long to settle down. His mother kept dropping not-so-subtle hints about grandchildren, but so far he hadn't shown any signs of cooperating.

"Is that why you asked me into your inner sanctum today?" Gabe grinned. "To find out how I'm spending my nights?"

"I have a pretty fair idea." Burton smiled. "I was young once, myself, although you might find that hard to believe."

"You could still give me a run for my money," Gabe said fondly.

"Thank heaven I'm too old for those games. There's a lot to be said for marriage."

"And you've said it all," Gabe teased.

"It doesn't seem to have fallen on fertile ground," Burton commented dryly. "What are you looking for in a wife?"

"Who said I was looking?" Gabe's laughing face sobered. "That isn't strictly true. I'd like to get married. The problem is, I've never met the right girl."

"You must be very hard to please. All the young ladies I've seen you with have been real beauties."

"The chemistry always seems to be missing." Gabe got up to stand by the window, jingling coins in his pocket as he looked down at the traffic far below. "Maybe I'm being unrealistic. What if I never meet the one who makes bells ring?"

"I don't think you have to worry. Sometimes when you least—" Burton broke off as his buzzer sounded. He switched on the intercom, saying irritably, "I told you I didn't want to be disturbed."

His private secretary's voice sounded slightly harried. "I'm sorry, Mr. Rockford. Mr. Van Ruyder is on the line. He's calling from Newport. I told him you were in conference, but he insists on speaking to you."

"All right, put him on. Pompous little ass," Burton said before picking up the receiver. "God save me from rich men's sons who couldn't get a job if their daddies didn't give them one."

"Careful there." Gabe chuckled. "I might have to go to work for another law firm to prove I didn't make partner through nepotism."

"You're not putting yourself in the same class with that little twit?" Burton picked up the receiver. "Hello Martin, what can I do for you?" he asked smoothly.

"You can catch the first plane to Newport and talk some sense into my mother!" Martin's voice was high and strained.

"What seems to be the problem?"

"I swear, she's getting senile! Any slick con artist can sell her a bill of goods."

"I think you're being a little hard on her."

"Am I? That man, Sergei Yousitoff is proof enough. He got Mother to introduce him to all her friends, and now he's the toast of Newport. She refuses to see how he's using her."

Burton suppressed a sigh. "I understand Mr. Yousitoff was an established designer here in New York City before he took Newport by storm. You might not care for the chap, but I've always found him to be quite pleasant."

"Do you consider it proper for him to be staying here as a guest in the house? The man is little better than a tradesman! What do you think her friends are saying?"

"I imagine some of them are quite envious. Now, if you'll excuse me, Martin, you caught me in the middle of a conference."

"I haven't told you why I called yet!" Martin exclaimed indignantly.

"I'm glad to hear you had a more compelling reason."

"Wait until you hear!" Martin was too wound up to hear the irony in the older man's voice. "Some woman came to the house today claiming to be Monica's long lost daughter."

"You're not serious?"

"Why do you think I'm in such a stew? Can you believe the nerve of some people? Before I threw her out, she practically admitted she was a fraud."

"I realize these incidents are upsetting, but unfortunately there are unscrupulous people in the world who prey on the grief of others. My advice is to put it out of your mind."

"That's exactly what I would have done, but Mother insists on listening to her story. She's making me scour the town until I find the wretched woman and invite her here for tea tomorrow afternoon."

"I don't quite understand. The girl was at your house, but Mary Louise didn't speak to her?"

"I wouldn't permit it. I was afraid something like this would happen. You know how Mother feels about not having any grandchildren. You'd think Monica and I deprived her of them on purpose! It isn't *my* fault that Laura can't have children. God knows we've tried everything." Martin's voice rose to an unpleasant whine.

"It's natural for a parent to want grandchildren." Burton slanted a glance at Gabe. "But I'm sure Mary Louise doesn't blame either you or your wife."

"That doesn't mean she's resigned to the fact. You should have seen her face when I told her this perfect stranger was claiming to be Monica's daughter. Any sensible person would know it couldn't possibly be true, but Mother wants to believe in fairy tales."

"I think you're underestimating her. There must be more to this than you're telling me. Surely the girl offered some kind of proof to back up her claim."

"Absolutely nothing except a theory. She claims a woman named Monica Van Ruyder had a baby at a hospital in Philadelphia on the same date as this Allison person was born. There were probably a dozen other babies born that day, but you can bet none of the other mothers were as rich as Monica. The woman is clearly an opportunist!"

Burton was lost in thought. "Most likely," he said finally.

"You can't believe there's any truth to her story!" Martin exclaimed. "Look at the facts. Can you see our Monica with a baby? She couldn't stand the little ankle biters. That's what she always called them. And then there's another thing. Even if you were willing to suspend credulity, why on earth would she go to Philadelphia to have the kid?"

"Your father had a sister who lived there, didn't he?"

"Aunt Jane. All the more reason why Monica would have avoided the place like poison. She didn't get along with the old girl."

"Well, if that's all this young woman has to go on, I don't believe you have anything to worry about."

"Still, I don't like the idea of letting her come here to tea. Who knows what sob story she'll give Mother?"

"You'll be there, too, I assume?"

"You better believe it! I wouldn't leave those two alone for an instant. Fraud or no fraud, this could be serious. If Mother was convinced she had a granddaughter, she'd start thinking about a new will!"

"Mary Louise is too sensible to do anything that precipitous, but I do think it's a good idea for the entire family to be present for moral support. This is bound to be painful for your mother."

"I tried to shield her from it," Martin said piously. "I try to be the man of the house now that father is gone, but she treats me like an adolescent. That's why you have to be here to expose the woman. Tea isn't until three. You'll have plenty of time to make it by then."

"I'm sure you can handle the situation without my help. I work mainly on corporate matters these days."

"I need action, and I want it fast! May I remind you that the Van Ruyder family is one of your biggest clients," Martin said imperiously. "I'd hate to see you blow the account—to put it succinctly."

The older man's eyes cooled, but his tone remained cordial. "We pride ourselves on having only satisfied clients. If you're no longer comfortable here, I'll be glad to supply you with a list of capable attorneys. I'll have it delivered to you by messenger."

Martin backed down hastily. "Don't fly off the handle, Burton. I'm sorry if I was out of line, but this thing has got me crazy! Please come and help me out. I don't know what that woman might have up her sleeve, or how Mother might react. There's a lot at stake here."

"That's true, but you don't need me. It shouldn't be difficult to expose the woman. All you have to do is point out the discrepancies in her story. She'll discredit herself."

"Only if Mother listens to logic instead of her emotions. The hell of it is, this girl looks like Monica. Well, no, maybe that's not entirely true, but she has Monica's coloring. You know, long black hair and big blue eyes with those thick black lashes. Except that Allison's don't look fake.''

"She sounds like a real beauty," Burton commented. "Does she have Monica's figure?"

Gabe's rather bored expression changed to interest as he glanced up from the magazine he was leafing through.

"She isn't as well endowed, if you know what I mean. But I guess she has a pretty good figure," Martin said unenthusiastically. "She's also clever enough not to come on too strong, which is another thing that worries me. I voiced my suspicions in no uncertain terms, but if I tear into her to prove them, Mother's sympathies might be aroused.''

"That would be a mistake, I agree." Burton glanced over at his son. "I'll tell you what I'll do, Martin. I'll send Gabriel there to help you out. He's quite good at sensing when witnesses are lying.''

"What are you volunteering me for?" Gabe asked suspiciously. "I can't go anywhere right now. I have—" He stopped in midsentence when his father waved him to silence.

"That's great!" Martin exclaimed. "I'll have a room made up for him. How soon can he get here?''

"I'll ask my secretary to look up the airline schedule and call you back.''

As soon as his father hung up, Gabe said, "Whatever it is, I can't do it.''

"Don't be so negative. I thought you'd like a nice vacation in Newport. The weather is beautiful at this time of year, and you can indulge in all those sports you pursue so tirelessly.''

"If it's such a rare treat, why didn't *you* jump at the chance?''

"The most strenuous sport I engage in these days is chasing clues in a mystery novel." Burton smiled.

"As much as I appreciate your generous offer, I'll have to pass. I really can't get away right now. I just got stuck with the Beckwith divorce case." Gabe made a wry face. "I can't say I'm looking forward to it. They're an unappetizing pair."

"Then you'll be pleased to have an excuse to get out of it. I'll have Farnsworth take over for you."

Gabe gave his father a curious look. "Why the sudden rush to accommodate that little pip-squeak, Martin? You got a bit testy with him there for a minute. What did he do, threaten to take his business elsewhere?"

"The boy doesn't have the authority to fire a gardener's helper," Burton said disgustedly. "I suppose I should be more understanding. Martin blusters to make up for his own ineptitude. But sometimes I can't help getting impatient."

"Then why are you sending me to smooth the heir apparent's path? If Mary Louise is smart, she'll leave her fortune to a home for wayward poodles."

"I want to make sure she doesn't do something equally foolish with it." Burton relayed to his son what Martin had told him. "Your job is to see that this young woman doesn't get away with it."

"She sounds like an amateur," Gabe said dismissively.

"Perhaps, but this is an emotional issue. Monica caused her parents a lot of heartache. She could be captivating one moment and a little witch the next."

"You can speak plainer than that." Gabe joked.

Burton barely heard him. His mind was focused on the past. "She was very beautiful and high spirited, so people tended to make allowances for her escapades. Everyone except her father. Peter and I got along well, but he was a strange duck in many ways—almost mid-Victorian in his thinking. He was very strict with his children, yet he treated Mary Louise like a pampered pet, shielding her from anything that might upset her."

"She doesn't strike me as a shrinking violet."

"She's really emerged from her cocoon since Peter isn't here to do her thinking for her anymore. The lasting damage was to the children. I can't help wondering if they might have turned out differently if their father hadn't been so rigid with them."

"Or maybe they were just bad seeds. I can't say I really knew Monica, because she was ten years older than I, but I remember she had a reputation for being wild."

Burton nodded. "I helped Peter get her out of many a scrape."

"Is there any chance this girl's story is true? *Could* Monica have had an illegitimate child somewhere down the line?"

After an almost imperceptible pause, Burton said, "You're an attorney. You know there has to be evidence to prove any allegation."

Gabe's gaze sharpened. "That doesn't answer my question. Do you know something I don't know?"

The older man smiled. "I like to think I've acquired a little more knowledge through the years."

"In other words, you aren't going to tell me. Why not? It would make my job a lot easier."

"I want you to go there without any preconceived ideas."

"So you do think it's a possibility," Gabe said slowly.

"If you insist on having my opinion, I'd say the girl is probably a fraud. It seems too coincidental for her to come forward just a short time after Monica's death. Where has she been all these years? Undoubtedly she's prepared to answer that. It will be up to you to decide if her story is credible or not."

"From your end of the conversation I gather that she's very attractive. Aren't you afraid that will color my judgment?" Gabe grinned mischievously.

"You haven't let a beautiful woman talk you into anything so far," his father answered dryly.

"I should have quit while I was ahead." Gabe laughed. Then his face sobered. "If this girl *is* on the up-and-up, I feel sorry for her. It's going to be quite a shock to find out what her mother was really like."

"Unfortunately we don't get to pick our relatives. I'll have someone check the records at the hospital in Philadelphia. That part of her story should be easy to verify. The rest is up to you. Stop on the way out and have Eleanor make a plane reservation for you. Plan to be at the Van Ruyder's by three o'clock tomorrow."

"It might take me several days to make up my mind about the girl," Gabe said with an innocent expression. "I don't want to make any snap judgments."

Burton smiled. "You can take the entire week—and your tennis racket. You deserve a little vacation."

"I might prefer one that doesn't include Martin, but I suppose nothing in life is perfect."

Burton's eyes twinkled. "As you young people say, you've got that right. Keep me informed."

Allison's spirits were at low ebb when she left the Van Ruyder house. She hadn't expected to be welcomed with open arms, but Martin's aggressive hostility was hurtful. The worst part, however, was learning of Monica's death. That the woman had died such a short time ago, seemed like a very cruel twist of fate.

Would Monica's reception have been any different than her brother's, though? She'd succeeded in keeping her baby a secret from the family all these years. It would have been a shock to be confronted by a past she'd thought was safely buried.

Maybe it was wrong to have come here. What right did she have to disrupt the lives of these strangers—even if they *were* family. But were they? The question would always nag her if she didn't resolve her own doubts.

What would be the harm in trying to find out, as long as she did it discreetly and didn't bother the Van Ruyders again? They were prominent members of the community, and Newport was a little town, except for the yearly influx of summer tourists. People in a small community usually knew everybody's secrets. A little prudent questioning of the natives might uncover something. It was certainly worth a shot.

Allison knew just where to start. The proprietor of her hotel was born in Newport and had lived there all of his life. He'd told her that—and much more—while she was checking in. If anyone knew about Monica's earlier life, it would be Mr. Jensen.

John Jensen was at the front desk, reading the postcards left by the hotel's guests for him to mail. When Allison entered the lobby, he gathered them together hastily and pushed them into a drawer.

"Back so soon?" he asked.

"I just went for a little ride today," she replied. "Tomorrow I intend to get up early and do some serious sightseeing, starting with The Breakers. I can't wait to see those fabulous old mansions."

"That's the most famous one, but if you ask me, Marble House is more elegant. It was built by another one of the Vanderbilts, back in the late eighteen hundreds. They called their summer homes cottages. Some cottage! Marble House was modeled after the Petit Trianon at Versailles and cost eleven million to build in *those* days. Can you imagine what that would mean in today's dollars?"

"It boggles the mind," Allison murmured obediently.

"You can't believe how those people lived. The family only stayed at Marble House for six or seven weeks a year. They brought a regular staff of thirty-six when they came to town, but for big parties they hired extra help."

Allison made appropriate sounds of amazement as John Jensen related tidbits of information about the illustrious former inhabitants of Newport. Under different circumstances her interest would have been genuine, but for now she was more concerned with his knowledge of present-day residents.

"You certainly know a lot about Newport's history. It must have been very glamorous in those days. Too bad none of the big old homes are occupied anymore," she remarked artlessly.

"Well now, that's not exactly true. The eight most famous houses are maintained by the Preservation Society, but some of the old line families still live on the smaller estates. They aren't quite as grand as The Elms or Rosecliff, but they're pretty posh all the same."

"Who can afford the upkeep on even a smaller version?"

"The Van Ruyders for one. Peter Van Ruyder is dead now, but his family still comes to Rosewood Manor every summer—what's left of them, that is. Peter's great grandfather was a big banking tycoon. That's where the family fortune came from originally, then his grandfather branched out into all kinds of other things. By now the money just comes rolling in. Martin won't have to do a lick of work for the rest of his life, which is just as well. The boy can't even bait a fishhook," Jensen said disdainfully.

"I seem to remember reading about a Monica Van Ruyder in the society columns," Allison remarked casually. "Would she be a relative of this family?"

"That was Martin's sister. She died about a month ago."

"How sad. She must have been quite young."

"Monica would have been in her middle forties by now, although it's hard to believe. I still think of her as a pretty little teenager, screeching around town in her red convertible and driving the boys wild. She was a proper little hellion in those days, always getting into one scrape or other. It made her father furious, but she was the one person he couldn't control."

"She sounds very... colorful."

He chuckled. "She was that, all right. But don't get me wrong. She wasn't a bad kid, just full of the devil. Monica lit up a room when she came into it, and everybody crowded around her. Naturally she was spoiled. It's my personal opinion that Peter was too strict with her—or at least he tried to be. I think that's why she ran off and got married so young the first time. Still in her teens she was.''

Allison's breath caught in her throat. "Who did she marry?''

"A local boy. The name wouldn't mean anything to you.''

She wondered if Monica was married here in Newport, but that wouldn't be something that would interest a tourist. Maybe there were records at City Hall. "Was she—did she have any children with him?''

"It might have settled her down a mite if she had, but three marriages didn't produce any offspring. Poor Mary Louise didn't have much luck with her children. Monica never had any, and neither did Martin.''

"Is he married?''

"He's on his second marriage, but give him time," Jensen said dryly. "He's young yet.''

"Younger than Monica?''

"No, a couple of years older. He's all Mary Louise has left now. We all thought when Peter died a couple of years ago she'd sell the old place. Monica didn't come home much and Mary Louise rattled around in that big house with only Martin and his wife Laura for company. But she's been coming back every summer, as regular as clockwork. Of course we're all happy to have her here. Mary Louise is a nice lady—no airs at all. She does a lot of work for charity, too.''

"It must have been a great shock when her daughter died. Was it an accident?''

"Funny thing, but nobody knows exactly how Monica died.''

"That seems strange. The family is so prominent.''

"When you've got their kind of money, you can hush things up.''

"You mean there's some kind of scandal connected with her death?''

"If there was, it never came out.''

"You must have some theory about how she died," Allison persisted.

John Jensen looked at her speculatively. "You seem mighty curious. Did you happen to know Monica?"

"No, I . . . I guess I just got caught up in your story." She forced a smile. "It's like reading a book and wanting to know the ending. You make the Van Ruyders sound so interesting. You really should be a writer."

He looked mollified. "They're tame compared to some of the people around here. I can't mention any names this time, but there's a certain family that spends every summer here. They bring a nanny along to take care of the children. At least that's what she's supposed to do, but I happen to know—" The telephone rang cutting him off in midsentence. Allison had gotten all the information she could safely probe for, but as she turned away, Jensen held out the receiver to her. "It's for you."

She looked at him blankly. "Are you sure? Nobody knows I'm here."

"Somebody does," he answered laconically.

Allison took the receiver from Mr. Jensen and said tentatively, "Hello?"

"Miss Riley, this is Martin Van Ruyder. I've been phoning all over town looking for you." His voice managed to sound cold and petulant at the same time.

"Why?" she asked in bewilderment.

"It wasn't *my* idea, it was my mother's. She wants to meet you."

"You told her about me? She believes my story?"

"I didn't say that. I'm still convinced that you're a fraud."

"But your mother doesn't think so." Allison was filled with excitement. She wasn't wrong after all!

"My mother is grasping at straws. She wants to believe her daughter isn't really gone, that she left behind something of herself. But you and I know that isn't true. You're perpetrating a cruel hoax."

"If you really believe that, why did you call me?"

"Because she insists on seeing you. I can't prevent it, but you can. If you have any decency at all you'll go away and leave us alone. I'll tell her you realized you were mistaken."

"But I don't know that! All I want is a chance to find out for sure."

"I could make it worth your while. Just name your price—anything within reason," he added prudently. "I'll write you a check and you can pick up a nice little profit without any hassle."

"I wish I could convince you that I don't want anything from you or your family."

"Yeah, sure," he answered sardonically. "You'd better reconsider. You're passing up a good thing."

"The answer is no," she said firmly.

"All right, we'll play out your little charade, but don't think you're going to get away with it. When our lawyers get through with you, you'll wish you'd taken the money and run."

Allison felt a slight chill. "You didn't need to call a lawyer. I'm not asking for anything."

"I thought that would shake you up." Martin gave a nasty laugh. "We have the best legal advice money can buy, so be prepared. If you still insist on going through with your shakedown, come to the house at three o'clock tomorrow afternoon for tea—but don't expect any sympathy," he added mockingly.

John Jensen stared curiously at Allison as she slowly replaced the receiver. "Is everything all right?"

"I don't know," she answered in a muted voice. "I have a feeling I just opened Pandora's box."

Chapter Two

Allison paused for a long moment outside the imposing front door of Rosewood Manor. This was the last chance to change her mind. Should she take Martin's advice and leave the Van Ruyders alone? Maybe he was right. If she was mistaken about Monica, it would cause his mother further pain for no good reason.

Allison's indecision changed to determination. She'd lived too long as a non-person, somebody without parents or a past. The Van Ruyders might not want to accept her—in fact, from what she'd seen of Martin, she wasn't too thrilled with *them*—but she had to know the truth.

The butler opened the door with the same impassive countenance he'd worn the day before. It was impossible to tell if he shared his employer's opinion of her. Not that it mattered, Allison told herself. She didn't expect to find any friends here.

Jordon preceded her down a long hall, past a huge drawing room and a paneled den to a charming sitting room filled with bowls and vases of flowers. Tall French windows looked out on a manicured lawn that stretched out beyond a flagstone terrace.

Allison had only a fleeting impression of luxury. Her attention immediately focused on the four people in the room, who were regarding her with the same keen interest. She braced herself for hostility, needlessly as it turned out.

The older woman rose from a down-filled, floral patterned couch and smiled pleasantly. "I'm so glad you could join us for tea, Miss Riley. I'm Mary Louise Van Ruyder."

"It was very kind of you to invite me," Allison murmured.

"You've met my son, Martin. This is his wife, Laura."

Allison exchanged polite greetings with a very thin, very chic blond woman wearing a deceptively simple green cotton dress. Everything about her spelled money, from her perfect hairstyle and long polished nails to her aloof manner. Or maybe that was an echo of her husband's disapproval, although she hid it better than he did. Martin was having trouble masking his dislike. He had merely nodded curtly.

She didn't have time to dwell on it because Mary Louise was introducing her to the fourth occupant of the room, the most dazzling specimen of manhood Allison had ever seen. His features were rugged rather than conventionally handsome, but they made his face more interesting. Perfection was reserved for his tall, athletic physique, which couldn't have been improved upon. That should have been enough good fortune for any man, but this one was more than just a centerfold. Intelligence shone out of his penetrating gray eyes.

"And this is Gabriel Rockford, a dear friend of the family," Mary Louise concluded.

"He's our attorney," Martin said tersely.

Gabe stood and took Allison's hand, smiling charmingly. "I hope you won't hold that against me. Everybody has to do something."

She wasn't fooled by his easy manner or the male admiration in his eyes. Gabe had been brought in to prove she was a fraud. He was more polished about it than Martin, but he was the enemy, nonetheless. She withdrew her hand, realizing he could tell by her icy fingers how nervous she was. In his eyes that probably made her automatically guilty.

"Okay, we're all here," Martin said. "Let's get down to business."

"Where are your manners?" his mother asked. "Miss Riley was invited to tea." She looked inquiringly at Allison over the exquisite antique tea service on the table in front of her. "Do you take lemon or cream?"

"Neither, thank you," Allison replied.

A uniformed maid brought the delicate teacup and saucer after Mary Louise had poured. She placed it along with a monogrammed linen napkin on a table next to Allison, then passed a tray of small tea sandwiches.

"Is this your first visit to Newport?" Mary Louise asked.

"Yes, I've always wanted to visit Cape Cod, but somehow I never got around to it."

"Aren't we lucky that you finally found time," Martin commented sarcastically.

"Where is your home?" Gabe cut in smoothly.

"I live in New York City," Allison answered.

"That gives us all something in common," Mary Louise said pleasantly. "Gabriel's office is there, and our family home is on Park Avenue."

"I'm sure she's aware of *that*," Martin remarked.

His mother continued as though she hadn't heard him. "I do love New York, although not necessarily in the summer. When it gets hot and humid in the city I escape to Cape Cod."

"You're very fortunate. It was stifling when I left." Allison wondered when they were going to get past polite generalities.

Laura joined the conversation for the first time. "Do you have a job in the city, Miss Riley?"

"Yes, I'm a buyer in the better sportswear department at Maison Blanc." It was an upscale women's store.

"Really! I buy quite a few things there. Mrs. Frasier takes care of me. Perhaps you know her?"

"Oh, yes. She's been with us for many years. Her customers won't let anyone else wait on them."

"That's because she isn't pushy. So many saleswomen tell you everything looks good on you because they're only interested in making a sale. Mrs. Frasier never does that." Laura had become almost animated.

"Oh, for—!" Martin swore pungently under his breath. "How much longer are we going to keep up this charade?" He turned on Gabe. "Why aren't you asking her some questions? That's what you're here for!"

Mary Louise's pleasant expression didn't waver as she gazed at her son. "Much as we're enjoying your company, Martin dear, your presence here isn't required. Why don't you and Laura drive over to the tennis club? I'm sure Gabriel and Miss Riley will excuse you."

Martin wilted under his mother's calm scrutiny. "No, I'll stay," he muttered.

"Then perhaps you'll offer our guest some cake." She held out an antique china serving platter filled with several kinds of cookies, slices of poppyseed cake and assorted petit fours. He took the plate reluctantly as Mary Louise said to the maid, "We can manage by ourselves now, Florence."

When Allison refused the pastries, Gabe said, "You really should try those little chocolate things. They're fantastic."

"And a million calories in every bite," Laura remarked.

"None of you ladies have to worry about your figures," he answered gallantly, but his gray eyes were on Allison.

She steeled herself against the rush of pleasure his attention gave her. Gabe had the faculty of making a woman feel special, as if he couldn't wait to be alone with her. What female wouldn't be flattered? But she mustn't be fooled by his potent male appeal. Behind that beguiling manner was a keen legal mind that had already judged her and found her guilty.

When the maid had left them alone, Mary Louise said to Allison, "Martin tells me that you came to Newport to see my daughter, Monica."

"Yes, but I didn't know she was...that she had passed away. I hope my unexpected visit didn't cause you more pain. That wasn't my intention," Allison said earnestly.

"I'm sure that's true. You seem like a very nice young woman. Had you ever met my daughter?"

"No, I was hoping to."

"Because you think she was your mother?"

Allison took a deep breath. "I think it's a possibility, yes."

"Can you give us some reason why you believe that?" Unlike Martin, Mary Louise's tone wasn't challenging. She sounded as if she honestly wanted to know. "To my knowledge, Monica never had any children."

"This is very difficult. The last thing I want to do is hurt you." Allison was tempted to give it up. How could she disillusion this poor woman who had just lost her daughter? As unlikely as it seemed, Mary Louise didn't seem to know Monica had been pregnant and borne a child.

"I loved my daughter very much, but we didn't have as close a relationship as I would have liked. Monica didn't allow anyone into her confidence completely. If you have information on the part of her life I didn't share, I would like very much to hear it." When Allison continued to hesitate, Mary Louise said, "You've made a serious assertion. You can't simply leave it at that. Unless of course, you're having second thoughts about the validity of your claim."

"I can tell what you're thinking, but you're wrong. I didn't come here to try to get money from you, or intrude on your lives in any way. I'm sorry if this comes as a shock, but your daughter had a baby when she was eighteen. I just want to find out if I was that child."

"I assume you have some kind of proof that Monica was the person involved?" Gabe asked. "Couldn't you have made an honest mistake?" He was giving her a chance to recant gracefully.

"I saw the records at Our Lady of Mercy Hospital in Philadelphia. Monica Van Ruyder had a baby girl on May 27, the year I was born. She was eighteen at the time."

"Either you're lying, or it was somebody else by the same name," Martin said.

"Her address was listed as Park Avenue, New York," Allison answered simply.

"What was the father's name?" Gabe asked.

"It was left blank."

"I think you'd better start at the beginning," Mary Louise said. "What led you to Philadelphia in the first place?"

"I recently decided to look for my parents," Allison began. "I'm an orphan and I never knew who they were."

"You didn't feel the need to know before now?" Gabe asked.

"I was curious, naturally. It's something an orphan always wonders about."

"But you never did anything about it until recently. Why is that?"

"Good question," Martin said with satisfaction.

"My reasons are personal," Allison said firmly. "What matters is that I did start to search for them. I'd been told I was born in Philadelphia. That's all the information I had."

"The orphanage told you that, but not your mother's name?" Gabe asked.

"They didn't have any records on me. I was told by my mother—or I should say, the woman I thought was my mother."

"Wait a minute!" Martin exclaimed. "What kind of nonsense is this? You decided you didn't like the mother you had, so you chose Monica instead?"

"Let me explain. For the first nine years of my life I lived with a family named Riley. I always thought they were my parents and their five younger children were my brothers and sisters. We were a typical working-class family, although it was always a struggle to make ends meet. Tim Riley was a construction worker—a laborer actually—and Nora, his wife had been a cook at a big duplex on Fifth Avenue. But after the children started to come along, she had to quit."

"Do we have to sit through this soap opera?" Martin sneered. "What does any of this have to do with Monica?"

"Stop interrupting, Martin," Mary Louise ordered impatiently. "Go on, Miss Riley."

"I suppose it does sound like a bad movie," Allison said wryly. "I'll try to speed it up."

"No, I want to hear everything," Mary Louise said.

"There isn't much more to tell. The construction industry hit a slump and Tim was out of work for a long time. Money got really tight with so many mouths to feed and, well..." Allison stared down at her tightly clasped hands as the old hurt surfaced. "That's when they told me I wasn't really their child and they couldn't keep me any longer."

"They raised you from infancy and then just dumped you in an orphanage when the going got rough?" Gabe asked incredulously.

"Our situation was really grim. I didn't realize it at the time, but I do now. It took me a while to get over feeling abandoned although as I got older I understood that their own children had to come first. I wasn't their flesh and blood."

"It must have been quite a shock to find out you were adopted," Mary Louise said gently.

"Yes, but children are resilient. And the orphanage wasn't like something out of *Oliver Twist*. After I stopped feeling sorry for myself I made a lot of friends, and the people who ran the place were very decent."

"Did your family—the Rileys, that is—come to visit you?" Mary Louise asked.

"It was discouraged during the first couple of months. After that they phoned a few times, but we were never really close again."

"They probably felt guilty about what they'd done," Gabe said. "If they didn't, they should have!"

"Don't judge them too harshly. None of us knows what we might do in a similar situation. If Monica was my mother, she chose to give me up, too." Allison tried to diffuse the emotional atmosphere. "I guess I'm not much of a prize." Her laughter had a catch in it.

After assessing his mother's misty eyes and Gabe's touched expression, Martin whispered rapidly to his wife.

Laura obediently followed his instructions. "I'm sure we're very sorry for your unhappy life," she began.

"I appreciate your sympathy, but it's misplaced," Allison cut in. "I have a great life. I went to night school and got a college degree, which led to an excellent job. My standard of living isn't anything like yours, but I have a nice apartment and lots of friends. I'm really a very happy person."

"Then why do you want to disrupt other people's lives?" Martin burst out.

"I don't. Whether I'm right or wrong about your sister, I won't ever bother you again after I leave here."

"That's very noble, but you know Mother wouldn't permit that."

"We're being a trifle premature," Gabe said. "Let's go back a little. Do you have a copy of Monica's hospital record, including the reason for her stay there?" he asked Allison.

"No, but you can ask to see it," she answered. "They have everything on microfilm."

"That kind of information is usually confidential. You just asked for it and they gave it to you?"

"Not exactly. I telephoned first, but they wouldn't tell me anything, so I became a hospital volunteer."

Gabe stared at her. "But you live in New York."

"Philadelphia is only a short train ride away. I did volunteer work on the weekends. They're shorthanded on Saturdays and Sundays, so they were glad to get me."

Martin frowned at her disapprovingly. "You're admitting you lied to the hospital authorities so you could break into their secret files. Besides being a criminal act, it shows what kind of a person you are. If you lied to the hospital, why should we believe you're telling the truth now?"

"I didn't lie to anybody," Allison protested. "I was a very competent worker. I did all sorts of things the nurses didn't have time for. And I didn't break into any files. I became friendly with a woman in the office. I told her my story and she looked up the information for me."

"That doesn't make it any better. It just shows how you use people for your own devious purposes."

"I don't think that's the issue right now." Mary Louise frowned. She turned to Allison. "I assume the Rileys told you the date of your birth, but there must have been more than one baby born on that date. Why are you so sure you were Monica's?"

"By the process of elimination. Nora Riley told me my mother was an unmarried teenager. That's why she had to give me up. There were three women who had baby girls that day, but one was married, and the other was twenty-two."

"One could have been lying about being married, for appearance sake, and the other might have passed for a teenager," Gabe said pointedly. "Your foster mother could have made an honest mistake."

"I realize that, so I looked for further indications. Another reason that seemed to point to Monica, was her address. I told you Nora worked for a very social family on Fifth Avenue—the Charlton Langerfelds. Did you know them?" she asked Mary Louise.

"I might have heard the name, but even if I knew them, why would that be significant?"

Allison hesitated. "Giving up a baby for adoption must be very traumatic for everyone involved, even if keeping the infant isn't an acceptable alternative. It would be only natural to want to keep track of the child, to see how it turned out."

"I see," Mary Louise said thoughtfully. "And what better way than placing the baby with somebody you knew—not personally, but someone you could keep in touch with, in a casual way, like an acquaintance's household help. Yes, I can understand your reasoning."

"Well, *I* can't," Martin stated. "If Monica *had* given birth to a baby, she wouldn't have given it to somebody's cook!"

"What if no debutantes were available?" Gabe asked sardonically.

Allison ignored them and appealed to Mary Louise. "Now you can see why I said I wasn't sure. Can you think of anything that might tip the balance one way or the other? Do I look like your daughter? Can you see anything of her in me?"

"You're asking my mother to prove your case for you?" Martin asked incredulously.

"Or to disprove it," Allison answered despairingly.

"Judge for yourself." Mary Louise picked up a photograph in a silver frame and handed it to her.

Allison's breath caught in her throat. "Is this my—your daughter?"

The picture showed a laughing woman with dark hair and blue eyes. She was wearing a brief white bathing suit and had her arm around the waist of a very handsome man.

"I prefer this snapshot to the more formal studio portraits," Mary Louise said. "It captures her vitality and zest for living."

Allison studied the picture avidly. The woman's coloring was similar to hers, but it was difficult to tell from the candid snap if they actually looked alike. Monica's nose was short and straight like her own, her eyes were wide and thickly lashed. But something about her expression indicated a difference between them, an attitude perhaps. There was a challenging quality in the bold way she faced the camera with her head thrown back, almost as if she were inviting criticism. Was there also something a little dissatisfied in her expression? The photographer must have caught her at a bad angle. By all accounts, Monica had had everything.

"Is this a recent photo?" Allison asked.

"It was taken last summer."

"Is that her husband with her?"

"No, she was divorced. He couldn't be your father, in case you're wondering," Mary Louise said quietly. "She'd only known him a few weeks."

"That didn't occur to me. I was just...I don't know, maybe trying to gather all the information I could about her. So I could tell if we were anything alike."

"It might be interesting to find out." Mary Louise looked at her reflectively. "I have an idea. Newport is so dreadfully crowded at this time of year. I don't know what your accommodations are like, but I'm sure you'd be more comfortable here. Why don't you stay with us for a few days?"

"Have you lost your mind, Mother?" Martin said thunderously. "We already know the woman is a con artist. This might be what she's been angling for all along. If you let her in this house she could steal us blind!"

"Martin is only thinking of you," Laura said nervously, with a somewhat apologetic glance at Allison. "What you're considering is rather rash."

"It pains me to have to remind both of you that this is my home," Mary Louise replied evenly. "If either of you feels it would be too crowded to have another houseguest in residence, my feelings won't be hurt if you make other arrangements for yourselves."

"I don't believe this! Gabe!" Martin appealed to his lawyer.

"Your mother does have a point. She can invite anyone she likes. Besides, if I cross her, she might send me packing, too." Gabe grinned.

"A lot of good *you* are," Martin muttered.

"I'm sure we'll all have a lovely time getting to know one another." Mary Louise's face was imperturbable. "I hope I'm not being premature, Miss Riley. You will join us, won't you?"

Allison was slightly dazed at this turn of events. So many emotions coursed through her that it would take time to sort them all out. But that could come later. Right now she seized the opportunity presented to her.

"I'd be delighted to accept your kind invitation. And please call me Allison."

"That would be a lot more friendly. And do call me Mary Louise. I'll tell Florence to prepare a room for you."

After his mother had left, Martin confronted Allison furiously. "I suppose you're pretty proud of yourself, worming your way in here. But it won't do you any good. You'll never get a red cent out of Mother if I can prevent it."

Allison knew it was useless to argue with him. "I'm sure you'll be able to. I don't expect to leave here any richer than when I came. Now if you'll excuse me, I'm going back to the hotel for my things."

Gabe followed her outside. "I'm sorry about Martin's rudeness."

"You aren't responsible for his behavior," she answered curtly. "Anyway, you probably agree with him. Your manners are merely better."

"That's no compliment." He smiled. "Anybody could fit that description."

"I don't know why it's so difficult to convince him that I'm not a fortune hunter. His mother is willing to keep an open mind. That's all I ask."

"Don't be fooled by Mary Louise. Under that old world charm is a very shrewd lady."

"Is that a warning?" Allison thrust her chin out pugnaciously. "Perhaps you'd better go inside and inventory the silver before I get back."

"I'm not your enemy," Gabe said gently.

"Am I supposed to consider you a friend? Martin brought you here to discredit me. He was quite open about it."

"That might have been *his* purpose. Mine is to discover the truth. You, yourself, admit you have doubts. There's a lot at stake here, and not only monetarily. I would hate to see Mary Louise hurt needlessly."

Allison's animosity drained away. "I would, too. She's a really nice person. I wonder how she ever produced a son like Martin."

"Mary Louise didn't have much say in her childrens' upbringing. Her husband was a very strong man with rigid convictions. That could be why both kids grew up with problems."

"Monica, too?"

Gabe shrugged. "She went through three husbands. That indicates a certain restlessness, if nothing else."

"It's hard to believe. She and her brother had every advantage. What was Monica looking for?"

"The same thing everyone else is, I presume. True love."

"If such a thing exists."

Gabe's eyes wandered over her delicate face, lingering on her soft mouth. "You're very young to be so cynical."

Allison was suddenly aware of him as a man, rather than an adversary. A man to beware of, she reminded herself. The glow in his eyes was part of the act he was putting on to win her confidence so he could trip her up.

"Girls learn at an early age that love means something entirely different to women than it does to men," she said tersely.

"Obviously you've met the wrong men."

"Possibly, but I'm not interested in finding out. So if you're going to suggest furthering my education, you can save your energy. It won't get you anywhere."

"You should never challenge a man unless you're prepared for the consequences," he said softly.

"It wasn't a challenge, merely a statement of fact."

"You never expect to fall in love again?"

"I didn't say I ever was in love."

"You didn't have to. What happened, Allison, did he leave you for another woman? Although I can't conceive of it."

"How many women have you fed that line to?" she asked derisively.

"I don't believe in playing games," he answered quietly. "I've always been truthful in my relationships."

"That's hard to believe. Men make extravagant promises to get what they want—and foolish women believe them. It's standard operating procedure."

Gabe's sober expression changed to amusement. "If you're referring to sex, I assure you I've never made any promises to entice a woman into bed."

He wouldn't have to. That hard body must have given great pleasure to a lot of women. Allison's cheeks warmed as she had a sudden, vivid picture of what it would be like to lie naked in his arms.

"I'm sure you lead a very active sex life, but I'd prefer not to discuss it," she said primly.

"We'll have to do something about those inhibitions of yours," he teased. "Sex is a normal, healthy part of life."

"But not a subject for discussion."

His eyes sparkled with laughter. "I didn't intend to supply details."

"Will you tell me how we got on the subject of sex?" she demanded. "We hardly know each other."

"I hope to become a lot better acquainted," he murmured.

"You've just proved my point about men being different from women," she said angrily. "You wouldn't hesitate to make love to me for the sake of your clients. It's all part of the job."

"Have you ever looked in a mirror?"

"Please don't add insult to injury by telling me how beautiful I am! I'm not as gullible as your girlfriends."

Gabe gazed at her with an unreadable expression. "I guess I've met my match. Since you've figured out my game plan, I'm no danger to you."

"Exactly." Allison hoped she sounded more confident than she felt.

"Does this mean there won't be any romantic kisses in the moonlight?"

"You've got *that* right."

"And I suppose skinny-dipping in the pool at three in the morning is out. Too bad." A little smile curved his firm mouth as his eyes swept over her curved body. "You'd be enchanting by starlight."

Her pulse rate speeded up—as he knew it would. Gabe *wanted* her to picture their nude bodies linked together while the cool water gently rocked them against each other. Their lips would meet and then part. Until he gathered her close for the ultimate embrace.

"I have to get my things from the hotel," she said abruptly, getting into her car and slamming the door.

Gabe's face was enigmatic as he watched the car disappear down the driveway.

"Well, what did you think of her?" Mary Louise asked when Gabe returned to the house.

"She's very lovely."

"That much is evident. You know what I'm asking. Do you agree with Martin that she's an opportunist?"

"You evidently don't think so, or you wouldn't have invited her to be a guest."

"Lawyers!" Mary Louise exclaimed. "They will never give you a straightforward answer."

"That's because there isn't one. I can't make a judgment without knowing her better, any more than you can."

"It's the reason I invited her here." Mary Louise frowned thoughtfully. "She does bear a resemblance to Monica— that beautiful glossy black hair and porcelain skin. She has Monica's deep blue eyes, too."

"There must be thousands of girls with the same coloring. All it takes is an Irish ancestor somewhere in the family tree."

"Then you don't think it's significant?"

"I didn't say that. I was only playing devil's advocate. There are other things that are more significant. I don't see how Monica could have had a baby without your knowledge."

Mary Louise's eyes were sad. "It displays a lack of trust on her part. That's difficult to live with."

Gabe's gaze sharpened. "Are you saying it's possible?"

"How can I be certain? Monica went away to school, she went to summer camp. My generation turned their children over to other people to raise, because we were told it was the thing to do. It was called providing them with every advantage."

"Then Allison's story could be true," he mused.

"That's what I want you to help me find out. Do you know what it would mean to me to have a grandchild?" Mary Louise's face was radiant. "This time I wouldn't let anyone come between us. We'd have the kind of relationship I've always wanted."

"You mustn't substitute wishful thinking for common sense," Gabe said gently. "You're too intelligent for that."

Mary Louise sighed. "You agree with Martin. You think I'm an addled old woman."

"On the contrary. I think what you did was remarkably astute. We should have an interesting few days, if nothing else." After a look at her downcast face Gabe added, "And who knows? They may change our entire lives."

A man appeared in the doorway of the sitting room. Sergei Yousitoff was around sixty, tall and distinguished looking, with a full head of dark hair sprinkled with gray. He was wearing casual clothes, but he would have looked equally at home in white tie and tails. He had the self-confidence and sophistication of an ambassador, or perhaps a captain of industry.

"Am I interrupting anything?" he asked.

"No, do come in," Mary Louise said. "How was your meeting with Nancy Buffington?"

"Long," Sergei answered tersely. "I feel the urgent need for a drink."

"I'll make you one." Gabe walked over to an inlaid rosewood cabinet where a silver tray held Baccarat decanters filled with a variety of spirits.

"Make it a double," Sergei called. "I know Nancy is a friend of yours, Mary Louise, but I can't take her job, even for you. Besides having more money than taste, she's the kind of idle, empty-headed woman I can't abide."

"I always had a feeling you were prejudiced against the rich," Mary Louise teased.

"Not at all. I find money very useful when it isn't excessive. If you had a few less millions I'd ask you to marry me."

"Doesn't that prove you're prejudiced?"

"No, it simply means I have an aversion to being considered a fortune hunter."

Her smile faltered. "I must apologize for my son's behavior last night. I really don't know why you put up with it."

He touched her hair lightly, gazing into her eyes. "Don't you?"

Gabe strolled over and handed Sergei a glass. "Would you like to offer me a dollar to go to the movies?" he asked with a grin.

"Gladly. How much more would it cost for you to take Martin with you?"

"Now you're getting up into big money." Gabe laughed, then slanted a chagrined glance at Mary Louise. "Martin is just a little overly protective. I'm sure it's nothing personal."

"You're probably right," Sergei answered politely.

"Well, at least you won't be the primary target for the next few days," Mary Louise said brightly. "We have a new houseguest. I'll be interested in your opinion of her."

"Not another potential client?" Sergei asked warily.

"I wish I could afford to turn away clients like you do," Gabe joked. "You're pretty exclusive."

"I've reached the stage of life where I can afford to be. I have more than enough money, a successful career and good friends."

"You're a lucky man."

"It would seem that way, wouldn't it?" Sergei glanced at Mary Louise, suppressing a sigh.

"Allison should be back soon," she said. "I want you to meet her."

"Who is Allison? Tell me about her."

As Mary Louise started to, Florence came into the room. "You have a telephone call, Mr. Rockford," she said.

"Thanks, Florence. I'll take it in the library."

"What do you have to report?" Burton Rockford asked his son.

"You haven't given me much time," Gabe protested. "I just met the girl a couple of hours ago."

"I know what a fast worker you are," his father answered dryly.

"The circumstances are a little different in this case."

"Granted. So, what did you think of her?"

"I honestly don't know what to tell you. She's either very clever, or incredibly naive. She admitted to having doubts about Monica being her mother."

"That sounds like she has very little proof, so she's playing on the family's sympathy instead."

"Not successfully with Martin. He never passes up an opportunity to bully her, which of course enlists Mary Louise's sympathy. How can he be so stupid?"

"Through long practice. Other than being sympathetic, how does Mary Louise feel about the girl? Does she believe her story?"

"She'd like to. She invited Allison to stay here."

Burton gave a startled exclamation. "Didn't you try to dissuade her?"

"Martin did, needless to say. Actually I think it's a good idea. If Allison is a phony, she's apt to reveal the fact in some way. Like referring to incidents in Monica's past that she'd have no reason to know about unless she'd been reading up on her. Monica's exploits were widely covered in the society columns. Like the time she fed caviar canapés to the chimps in the Central Park Zoo."

"As a matter of fact, she wasn't responsible for that. It was her style, but she was in Jamaica at the time," Burton said.

"That's the point I'm making. It's just the kind of colorful story that could trip Allison up."

"Then you're inclined to believe she's a fraud."

"What really nudges me in that direction is the improbability of Monica being able to have a baby without her parents' knowledge. How could they not know she was pregnant? It's not something that's easy to hide. Mary Louise said Monica was away from home a lot, but *somebody* must have known."

"Perhaps they didn't see fit to tell Mary Louise," Burton remarked.

"Monica went to exclusive schools and camps. They'd be out of business if they helped her conceal a serious thing like that."

"Only if the secret got out."

"So *you* think Allison is on the up-and-up?"

"Not necessarily. I just want you to consider all of the possibilities."

"It's a heavy responsibility," Gabe answered soberly. "Mary Louise is a levelheaded lady, but she desperately wants to believe Allison's story."

"She's tougher than she looks. If it's not true, she'll survive."

"That's remarkably insensitive of you!" Gabe exclaimed. "Whatever happened to compassion and fair play? In spite of my loyalties being with Mary Louise, I don't relish the prospect of trying to trap Allison. You evidently wouldn't have any problem with that."

Burton chuckled. "At my age I'm fairly immune to big blue eyes. I gather this Allison is your type, although I always thought you were partial to blondes."

"She makes them pale by comparison."

"Perhaps I should have handled the situation myself. Remember that you're representing a client. Just tell yourself the girl is a hostile witness and treat her accordingly."

"If I ever faced a witness like Allison I'd lose the case," Gabe said wryly. "When I look into those big blue eyes you're immune to, I see Snow White, not the Wicked Witch."

"I've known some very cold-blooded criminals who were also beautiful women. Although I'm not saying it's necessarily so in this case, Mary Louise doesn't deserve to be exploited," Burton said quietly.

"I'm just afraid her hopes are already too high. The trouble is, she's a woman with a lot of love to give, and nobody worthwhile to give it to." Gabe paused for a moment. "How do you feel about Sergei Yousitoff? He's another houseguest."

"I've always found him to be a very nice fellow."

"I think he's in love with Mary Louise. He was joking about marrying her, but I got the impression that he was serious."

"If she's smart, she'll snap him up. Sergei is intelligent, well educated and amusing. He even moves in the same circles that she does, through his business connections. They could have a good life together."

"Maybe he's concerned that people would think he married her for her money."

"That's nonsense. Sergei is independently wealthy. He doesn't have the kind of money Mary Louise does, but few people do."

"Another obstacle is Martin. He guards the family fortune as zealously as if he made it himself."

"There's plenty to go around. Your job is to see that it goes to people who deserve it."

"Using that yardstick, Allison has already worked harder for it than Martin ever did," Gabe said derisively.

"I'm becoming concerned, Gabriel. Are you sure you can remain impartial?"

"Not to worry. What does Allison have besides a beautiful face, an enticing body and a way of looking at a man that makes him want to carry her off to bed." Gabe laughed at the sudden silence on the line. "I'm only pulling your leg, Dad. She's all of that and more, but I don't approve of people who try to profit from the tragedy of others. If that's what Allison is aiming to do, I won't hesitate to nail her."

"I certainly hope so."

"Relax, I won't let you down."

Long after he'd hung up the phone, Burton Rockford continued to look grave.

Chapter Three

Allison was excited by the prospect of staying at Rosewood Manor. Who wouldn't be? It was the most elegant, still privately owned and occupied mansion in Newport.

She entered a different world when she returned with her luggage and was shown to a luxurious guest room on the second floor. It was spacious and airy, with French doors leading to a balcony large enough for a round glass table and a couple of white wrought-iron chairs.

The balcony overlooked an oval swimming pool that sparkled like an aquamarine set in green velvet. The pool area and tennis court took up only a fraction of the spacious grounds. Extensive, carefully tended lawns bordered flower beds and surrounded a white gazebo whose latticed walls were covered with climbing roses.

Allison was gazing at everything with delight when there was a light tap at the door. The maid who'd shown her to her room had come to tell her the family was having cocktails in the library. Allison ran a comb through her hair and freshened her lipstick before going downstairs.

She was dismayed to find her hostess and Laura had changed for dinner. Mary Louise wore a jade green silk dress with a magnificent diamond and emerald pin on the shoulder, and Laura was wearing a red faille cocktail suit. The men had on suits and ties. Allison felt terribly out of place in the same white linen skirt and navy-and-white striped blouse she'd worn all day.

With supreme tact, Mary Louise didn't appear to notice. "Were you provided with everything you need?"

"Yes, my room is lovely, thank you," Allison answered.

"We want you to be comfortable here. I'd like you to meet my good friend, Sergei Yousitoff."

If he was curious about her, Sergei concealed it well. He was as charming as he would have been to any other guest.

After they'd exchanged pleasantries, Allison felt some apology was due her hostess. "I didn't know you dressed for dinner. I'm sorry."

"It's quite all right, my dear," Mary Louise said graciously. "We're fairly casual usually, but tonight Sergei and I have to go to a charity bazaar. It's something I simply couldn't get out of."

"I wouldn't want you to," Allison said. "Please don't change any of your plans for me. I don't expect to be entertained."

"You're very understanding. Unfortunately Martin and Laura have a previous engagement, too, but Gabriel will dine with you."

Allison's nerves knotted at the prospect of an intimate dinner for two. "I'm sure you have other plans," she told him. "I'll be quite all right on my own."

"I planned to spend the evening with you." He gave her a melting smile. "I didn't expect to be lucky enough to have you all to myself."

"That's settled then," Mary Louise said. "Fix Allison a drink, Sergei."

"I envy you and Gabe," he told Allison as he mixed her drink. "I wish we could stay home and have a quiet dinner and some interesting conversation, but Mary Louise has this compulsion to do good deeds."

"Stop complaining, you sound like a husband," Mary Louise said lightly.

"He doesn't sound anything at all like *Father*." Martin glowered at the older man.

"That's true. Your father didn't argue, he simply refused to go anyplace," she said.

"How can you say that?" Martin protested. "You and Father had a very active social life. He had a world of friends, all very influential people."

"Yes, dear." Mary Louise looked at her watch. "Hadn't you and Laura better be running along? We must go, too. I've told the staff to serve your dinner in the morning room," she told Gabe. "It's so much cozier. You don't want to be shouting to each other down that long table in the dining room."

Allison felt self-conscious with Gabe after everyone had gone. She didn't normally have trouble talking to people, but this man left her tongue-tied. They had nothing in common. His custom-tailored suit, the very costly gold watch on his wrist, his expensively styled hair—these were only superficial things, but they put him in a world that was foreign to her.

"Mary Louise is a very thoughtful hostess," Gabe remarked. "Besides providing me with a lovely dinner companion, she chose congenial surroundings as well."

"There are certainly a lot of rooms in this house," Allison commented brightly. "I don't even know what a morning room is."

"If you're ready for dinner I'll show you."

He led the way to an informal room furnished with wicker furniture and brightly printed cushions. The floor was tiled, and two walls were glass from floor to ceiling. They looked out on floodlit gardens that were echoed inside by pots and tubs of blooming plants.

Despite the informal atmosphere, a glass-topped hexagonal table was set with yellow-and-white organdy place mats, heavy sterling flatware and crystal wineglasses. In a centerpiece of fragrant yellow roses was a thick round candle.

"What a perfectly charming room," Allison exclaimed. "This house is unbelievable."

Gabe nodded. "Not many of us can afford to live like this anymore."

A uniformed maid entered carrying a tray with two delicate soup bowls set on matching saucers. The bowls contained cold avocado soup topped with a dollop of sour cream and a sprig of watercress.

When the woman had served them and left the room, Allison said, "I never saw her before. How many servants are there?"

"I don't know. It takes a large staff to run a place this size. The crew of gardeners and maintenance workers is probably as extensive as the household help."

Allison gazed out at the flower beds drenched in moonlight. "It must be like living in a fairyland. All you have to do is ask and your wish is granted."

"Not every wish. It's a trite saying, but money can't buy love or happiness."

"The Van Ruyders look happy to me."

"Appearances can be deceiving."

"That was insensitive of me," Allison said penitently. "Monica's death must have been devastating to her mother. And to Martin, too. It explains why he's so hostile toward me."

"Rudeness is never excusable."

"It's understandable, though, if he thought I was making baseless accusations his sister couldn't deny. I shouldn't have said anything after he told me she passed away. But at first I thought he was just trying to keep me from seeing her, and then I was so shocked that I didn't realize how my claim would affect the family."

Gabe shrugged. "Martin has always been his own worst enemy."

"That doesn't make me feel any better. I still wish I hadn't come."

He looked at her enigmatically. "You can always call it off. You said you have doubts about your relationship to Monica."

"It's too late to back away now. I've raised questions in her mother's mind as well. For all our sakes, I have to find out the truth."

"I suppose you're right. No matter who gets hurt."

"You must think I'm a monster! I barely know Mary Louise, but I can tell she's a kind, generous person. I'd never willingly add to her misery."

"I wasn't referring to Mary Louise. I was thinking of you," Gabe said quietly. "You've had a lot of disappointment in your life. I wouldn't like to see you go through any more."

His husky voice warmed Allison. Very few people had ever been concerned about her—certainly no one like Gabe. Was he being sincere? Or was it just a tactic to get rid of her? Bruce had left a legacy of distrust along with disillusion.

"Why should you care what happens to me?" she asked hesitantly. "It would be easier for you if I retracted the whole story and left quietly. You could go back to your law office and your debutante girlfriends."

"I'm too old to date debutantes." He smiled. "Besides, I've never cared for women whose main concern was their appearance and where the next party will be."

"You're only interested in women who can hold an intelligent conversation?"

He laughed. "I didn't say that. After all, I'm a healthy adult male. I do appreciate intelligence, but if the woman is as beautiful as you, I might become distracted."

"I don't think so." Allison gave him a level look. "I think you know exactly what you're doing."

"I can understand why you don't trust me." He reached over and captured her hand. "Poor little Allison. You haven't had much reason to trust people."

Gabe's warm hand sent a tingle up her arm. She tried not to let herself imagine what it would be like if circumstances were different and he was really interested in her. That was impossible, of course. Even if Gabe wasn't predisposed against her, he knew women a lot more glamorous than she.

Allison withdrew her hand and sat back. "You don't have to feel sorry for me. I've learned to take care of myself. I don't need anyone."

"No one is completely self sufficient. We all need somebody."

"That's what pets are for," she answered lightly.

"Cuddling with a cocker spaniel doesn't do it."

"They have redeeming features. Dogs are loyal and faithful. They don't question your motives, and they're always there when you need them."

"All very noble qualities, but how about someone to hold you in his arms and kiss away the problems of the day?"

"What good is that? It's only a temporary solution at best."

"You've been even more deprived than I realized," he said in a deep velvet voice. "Obviously you've never known a real man. Someone whose only priority was to make love to you and bring you more pleasure than you've ever known."

Allison could almost feel Gabe's mouth on hers, his hands moving sensuously over her body. Bruce had never stirred her senses this easily. She stared at him, unable to look away.

He leaned toward her, his eyes incandescent in the candlelight. Fortunately there was a distraction.

The maid had removed their soup plates and the salad that followed it. She returned now with the main course, breast of herbed chicken, wild rice and fresh asparagus.

"This looks delicious," Allison said brightly, struggling to regain her poise.

Gabe didn't continue his subtle seduction. "Mary Louise has a great chef. Her invitations are seldom turned down."

"It's nice that she has a lot of company. It would get very lonely in this big house otherwise. Do her son and daughter-in-law visit often?"

"They live here."

"All summer? Doesn't Martin work?"

"He's self-employed." Gabe's lip curled sardonically. "Martin has appointed himself the full-time job of keeping Mary Louise from remarrying."

"Did his father die recently? It's traumatic for the whole family at first. Children are often jealous of anyone taking a parent's place."

"Peter Van Ruyder died years ago."

"Then isn't it rather mean-spirited of Martin to deny his mother companionship? She's a remarkably young-looking woman, and very attractive."

"I doubt if Martin sees her as a person. To him, she's the guardian of his inheritance and he's dedicated to making sure nobody else gets a share of it. You must have noticed how he treated Sergei."

"I didn't realize there was anything going on between Mary Louise and Sergei. I simply thought he was being charming to his hostess."

"He would like their relationship to be a lot closer than that. I believe Sergei is in love with Mary Louise, but he won't ask her to marry him because people would think he married her for her money."

"Are you sure that's not the reason?"

"Great wealth can be a powerful aphrodisiac," Gabe acknowledged. "But he doesn't fit the profile. Besides being independently wealthy, Sergei is an intelligent and interesting man. He's very much in demand. If he didn't truly care about Mary Louise, he wouldn't put up with Martin for five minutes."

"How does she feel about *him?*"

"It's hard to tell. Her generation was taught to hide their emotions. She's pleasant to everybody, but whether it goes deeper with Sergei is anybody's guess. I do know that she enjoys his company. He's a regular visitor here."

"If she does care about him it would be a shame to let Martin spoil things for them. But having lost one child, I suppose she's especially close to her only remaining one."

"That's a possibility," Gabe answered noncommittally.

"I didn't like to ask the family, but you can tell me. How did Monica die?"

"I'm glad you didn't bring it up in front of them. Her death was quite recent. Mary Louise is holding up magnificently, but I'm sure she has some bad moments when she's alone."

"You don't have to warn me. I would never be so insensitive as to ask questions."

"I know you wouldn't." Gabe smiled winningly. "Somebody taught you very good manners."

Allison had the feeling she was getting the runaround. "At the risk of spoiling your good opinion of me, I'm going to be persistent. You didn't answer my question."

The uniformed maid entered at that very inconvenient moment. This time she lingered, pouring coffee from a silver pot into fragile china cups, then passing sugar and cream. After that she served each of them a crystal bowl containing a perfect mound of crème brûlée with a rosette of whipped cream on top.

Gabe smiled at the woman. "That looks delicious, Anita, but I'll have to jog for an hour to work off all the calories."

She returned his smile. "Would you like red raspberries instead? They're very tasty."

"How about in addition to? I can't pass up Armand's crème brûlée."

"I'll bring them right away, Mr. Gabriel."

"I don't know where Mary Louise gets her produce, but it's terrific," he told Allison. "You have to taste the berries."

There was no point in trying to get him back on the subject of Monica, since the maid would return at any moment. "I'm sure they're very good, but I can't eat two desserts. I'm stuffed already."

"Don't make any snap decisions."

Anita returned with a bowl of ripe red berries that did look delicious. On the tray was a pitcher of cream, extra fine sugar and a bowl of whipped cream.

Gabe speared a berry and held it out to Allison. "You have to try one."

She tasted it and licked her lips. "Mmm, you're right, they're heavenly."

"We'll each have some, Anita."

"But no cream on mine," Allison said. "I have to draw the line somewhere."

He looked at her admiringly. "You don't have to worry about your figure."

"I will if I keep eating like this. I wonder how society ladies stay so thin."

"By being on a constant diet."

"It's kind of sad. They can afford anything they want, but they won't let themselves enjoy it."

"Are you sure that's the kind of world you want to move into?" Gabe asked quietly.

Allison sighed. "You're convinced that's why I came here, but you're so wrong. I couldn't fit into this world even if I wanted to."

"What gives you that impression?"

"So many things. I haven't been to the places they've been, I didn't go to fancy schools. I couldn't hold up my end of a conversation."

"You didn't have any trouble tonight."

"That's different. You're being especially nice to gain my confidence."

"Do you honestly think I've been putting on an act?"

"It's all right. You have a job to do. I understand that."

He stared at her in silence for a moment. "You really don't trust anyone, do you? Well, I guess it's understandable. I wasn't talking about dinner tonight, though. I was referring to the cocktail hour earlier. You didn't have any trouble talking to Sergei and Mary Louise, or even Laura, who isn't the easiest person in the world to warm up. Martin was annoyed at how animated she got with you."

Allison laughed. "Aren't you getting a little confused? You're supposed to be arguing for the prosecution, not the defense."

"I wish you didn't regard me as an adversary," he said soberly. "I only want to get at the truth, the same as you do. No matter how this thing is resolved, I'd like to be friends."

"Even if your suspicions about me are correct?"

He hesitated imperceptibly before replying, "I'm a lawyer, not a judge."

"You're also very adept at not answering questions," she said dryly.

"And *you* should have been an attorney. You'd be dynamite at cross-examination. You remind me of a prosecutor I once faced. My client was accused of tax evasion, but by the time she got through with him, the jury was ready to send him to the electric chair. I was no match for that lady." He chuckled.

"That's because you confronted her in a courtroom instead of over a candlelit dinner table."

He smiled wryly. "It hasn't done me much good with *you.*"

"I'm a special case," she said lightly.

"You are indeed."

The now familiar glow in his eyes alerted Allison. She folded her napkin and placed it on the table. "I can't eat another bite."

"Me, either. I need to get physical. How about it?"

She gave him a startled look. Regardless of their differences, Gabe had been a perfect gentleman up until now. It was hard to believe he'd proposition her that crudely.

Before she could react, he said, "There are some dance clubs in town. Just what we need to work off our dinner. How does that sound?"

Allison felt exceedingly foolish. "It sounds great. I'll change clothes and be right down."

"You look fine just as you are."

"We aren't exactly a matched pair. You have on a suit and tie."

"Which I'll be happy to take off—the tie, that is." He grinned, removing his tie and unbuttoning the top few buttons of his shirt. "There, is that better? Instant casual."

Hardly, Allison thought. Gabe still looked elegant and assured, like one of those men in the ads selling expensive cars or luxury cruises. He also looked wildly masculine. The opening in his shirt revealed a wedge of tanned chest covered with a sprinkling of dark, crisp hair.

"Nobody will be dressed up," he assured her. "You'll fit in perfectly."

Gabe didn't mislead her. Everyone in the crowded, noisy disco was dressed casually, most a lot more so than Allison. The younger patrons wore jeans and T-shirts printed with flip sayings.

They were the tourists, mostly college kids on vacation from New York, Boston and Philadelphia. The rest of the crowd were summer people whose families had homes in Newport.

Gabe was familiar with all of them. He was stopped and greeted repeatedly as they made their way to one of the small tables that ringed the room.

Allison commented on the fact. "You certainly know a lot of people."

"My parents used to have a home in Newport. We spent the summers here when I was growing up, and so did the people I just said hello to. The regulars made up a small, tight-knit community. All the families knew each other."

"Did you have an estate like the Van Ruyder's?"

"Nothing that grand," he said dismissively.

"This must be a wonderful place to spend the summer. Why did your parents stop coming here?"

Gabe shrugged. "Mother got tired of the hassle. Summer help became increasingly difficult to get, both household and gardening, and she had to deal with it on her own. Dad was often tied up in the city all week. She decided it wasn't worth it, once I was off on my own."

So their house wasn't exactly modest, Allison speculated. She'd suspected as much, since they belonged to Mary Louise's crowd.

"The property is still in the family, so to speak," Gabe continued. "They sold it to Dad's brother, my uncle Herb. We all have a standing invitation to visit anytime. I even have a key to the place. I'll show it to you if you like."

Before Allison could answer, a young blond waitress appeared to take their orders. Gabe had to shout to make himself heard over the sudden blast of noise. The combo had returned from their break to resume playing.

When the waitress left, Allison remarked, "This is certainly a popular place."

"What?" Gabe put his arm around her shoulder and leaned forward to speak into her ear. "I can't hear you."

When she turned her head to repeat the remark, their faces were so close that her lips brushed his. Gabe's arm tightened reflexively. Allison's heart started to race as she stared into his gray eyes. The clean masculine scent of his after-shave was like an aphrodisiac, heightened by the close proximity to his hard body. Her lips parted unconsciously as his face lowered to hers, almost in slow motion.

Suddenly one of the wildly gyrating couples spun off the dance floor and collided with their table, bringing Allison to her senses. She drew away, avoiding Gabe's eyes as the youngsters made a laughing apology before dancing away. Gabe seemed uncharacteristically disconcerted, too.

Luckily a group of his friends stopped by. After chatting for a few moments they pulled up chairs for a more lengthy visit. Gabe introduced Allison and her tension lessened as the conversation became general.

When one of the couples got up to dance a little later, Gabe turned to Allison. "I haven't asked you to dance yet. Shall we give it a go?"

"Sure. We came for some exercise." She was completely relaxed with him now. Besides, nobody could get romantic to rock music.

They joined the crowd of uninhibited couples writhing on the dance floor. Allison loved to dance, and the compelling beat dispelled any remaining tension. She was sorry when the music stopped and the guitarist took the microphone for an announcement.

"Okay, kids, here comes a slow one to cool you off. Just one for the older folks," he said over a chorus of protests.

"There *is* a God who looks after us older folk," Gabe groaned, taking her in his arms. "That was more strenuous than racquetball."

"Don't tell me you never go dancing. You're too good at it."

"Memories of my youth."

She smiled. "You're not over-the-hill yet."

"I'm glad you noticed," he murmured, drawing her closer.

Suddenly Allison's tension was back. This time she didn't have to imagine how it would feel to be in Gabe's arms. His taut body was as seductive as she'd known it would be. The broad shoulders, hard chest and muscular thighs brushing against hers created a feverish need that ignored all reason.

When she tried to put distance between them, Gabe's embrace tightened. "We have a problem," he said in a husky voice.

"I don't know what you mean," she answered, holding herself stiffly.

"In case you haven't noticed, there's an awesome chemistry between us."

"You're really incredible! Isn't there *anything* you won't do for a client?" she asked angrily.

"Denying it won't change the facts, Allison. We might as well be honest with each other."

"Is this where I'm supposed to say, you're right, darling, I want you, let's go home and make love?"

"I don't expect to be that fortunate. While I'm convinced the desire between us is mutual, I don't think you'll allow yourself to satisfy it."

"Well, at least we agree on *one* thing."

He smoothed the silky hair off her forehead with caressing fingers. "Nothing is written in stone. You just might change your mind."

"Don't bank on it. I'm sure you've had great success with women, but if I *were* attracted to you, it still wouldn't change my decision. I have a deep aversion to being used. Why don't you just put all your energies into proving I'm a fraud? It would be a lot more honorable."

"At this moment, I don't give a damn who or what you are."

"You'll come to your senses when you remember the fat retainer Martin is paying you to expose me," she said derisively.

The slow number ended and the combo switched to a raucous beat. Allison moved out of Gabe's arms.

"I'd like to leave now," she said.

Allison overslept the next morning after lying awake half the night fuming over Gabe. He was as bad as Bruce—just a little smoother at it, that's all. How long after they made love would it have taken until Gabe started urging her to drop her claim? Men were all alike. Not one of them could be trusted!

After she'd showered and dressed in white pants and a sky blue pullover that matched her eyes, Allison went downstairs to breakfast, hoping she wasn't terribly late. Nobody had told her what time meals were served. It would be embarrassing if everyone else had finished and the staff was waiting to serve her. She'd never been a houseguest before, and certainly never in a place this grand.

The formal dining room was empty, so she went to the morning room, which proved to be the correct place. A long buffet was filled with covered silver dishes, pitchers of fruit juice and baskets of muffins and toast. The room was deserted except for Gabe, who was sipping coffee and reading a newspaper.

Allison hovered uncertainly in the doorway. She desperately wanted a cup of coffee, but was another confrontation with Gabe worth it?

He looked up and smiled at her. "Good morning. Did you sleep well?"

"Very well, thank you." She glanced at the table that held only one other place setting besides his. "Has everyone else eaten?"

"Mary Louise and Sergei have. Martin and Laura have breakfast in their suite. There are hot dishes on the buffet. Help yourself. I can recommend the French toast. Armand makes it out of sourdough bread."

"It sounds delicious, but I think I'll skip breakfast." Allison couldn't match Gabe's imperturbability. Her blood pressure had shot up the minute she spotted him.

"You can't avoid me completely," he said calmly. "Why not relax and try to enjoy yourself?"

"I didn't come here to enjoy myself."

"Then you're off to a good start." He grinned. "Don't go," he called as she turned away. "I promise not to make any personal remarks again. Sit down and have some breakfast."

"Well, maybe just a quick cup of coffee." What Gabe said was true. She couldn't avoid him for the entire visit.

"You're missing a treat if you don't try the French toast. There's real maple syrup, too."

"I don't know how you can eat like you do and stay so trim," she remarked without thinking.

"A compliment is the last thing I'd expect from you." He smiled.

Allison was annoyed that she was the one who'd gotten personal. Gabe was a magnificent male specimen, though. No doubt about it. A well-tailored suit can conceal a lot of flaws, but he didn't have any. His thin cotton T-shirt showed off broad shoulders that didn't need any additional padding. The rest of him was lean and fit, also. His taut jeans spanned a flat stomach and the impressive legs of an athlete.

"I think I will have something to eat," she said, walking over to the buffet.

Under the silver covers were scrambled eggs and crisp bacon, in addition to the French toast Gabe recommended. There was also cereal and fruit. Everything looked appetizing, but Allison's stomach was tied up in knots. She selected a blueberry muffin and poured herself a cup of coffee from a magnificent Georgian urn.

"Would you like to visit some of the old mansions this morning?" he asked.

"No, thanks. I have things to do, and I'm sure you do, too."

"You're my reason for being here." His mouth curved sardonically. "Whither thou goest..."

"Surely you don't expect to follow me around everywhere I go!" she exclaimed in outrage.

"Why not? You don't have anything to hide, do you?"

"That's not the point. I don't want to spend all of my time arguing with you."

"I'll try not to be offensive. But as you pointed out, I have to earn my retainer."

"Why don't you just go chase an ambulance?" she muttered.

His eyes sparkled with amusement. "Rockford, Rockford, Collingsworth and Strand is a very prestigious law firm. We don't chase ambulances. There isn't enough money in it."

"Seriously, Gabe, can't we call a truce? If you were sincere about being attracted to me, I'm flattered. But you can see we're totally unsuited to each other, even if you didn't have doubts about my motives. We come from different worlds."

His expression softened as he gazed at her lovely, pleading face. The sleepless night had left lavender shadows under her eyes, highlighting the fragility of her clear skin.

"Isn't there room in your world for me?" he asked in a husky voice.

"You know it's the other way around."

"For a scrappy kid who refused to give in to adversity, you have remarkably little self-confidence."

"You couldn't be more off base. I'm simply a realist. I've learned to push hard to get ahead, but I have no desire to go where I'm not wanted. *That's* self-esteem."

"Maybe you just don't realize when someone is sincere about wanting you," he said softly.

"Your kind of acceptance isn't difficult to achieve."

Gabe looked at her searchingly. "Would you have felt the same about me if we'd met under different circumstances?"

"Our paths never would have crossed, so the question is academic."

Before he could answer, Anita entered the room carrying a cordless telephone. "You have a long-distance call, Mr. Gabriel."

After a moment's hesitation he said, "I'll take it in the den."

The maid glanced at the buffet. "Can I get you anything else, Miss Riley?"

"No, thank you. I'm all finished."

As the woman began to clear away the food, Allison rose and went through the French doors into the garden. She didn't want to be there when Gabe returned.

Several paths led from the terrace. Allison took the one away from the pool and tennis court area. It cut through thick green lawns and weed-free flower beds to a fragrant rose garden. Scores of bushes were covered with blooms in glorious, vibrant colors. A little farther up the path, Mary Louise was clipping off dead blossoms and putting them in the straw basket over her arm.

She waved and called, "Good morning. Isn't it a glorious day?"

"Beautiful," Allison answered. "I'm sorry I was late for breakfast."

"We don't have any set time. Everyone eats when he feels like it. That's why we serve buffet." Mary Louise took off her gardening gloves. "Did you and Gabriel have a good time last night? He said you went into town."

"Yes, it was very nice," Allison answered without enthusiasm.

"Isn't he a charmer? I wonder why some lucky girl hasn't snapped him up by now. I'm sure it isn't from lack of trying."

"Maybe he's just a confirmed bachelor," Allison remarked, since some kind of reply seemed indicated.

Mary Louise smiled mischievously. "All men are until we change their minds for them. Gabriel is wily, though, he dates a number of girls. If one of them does have the edge it would be Hester. From what I hear from his mother, he sees her more often than the others."

"Hester?"

"The granddaughter of friends of ours. Hester Danville. She's a photographic model."

Allison didn't need to hear anymore. She had a mental image of a tall, sexy blonde with a drop-dead figure and a vocabulary that didn't include the word no. That would be just his type, she thought waspishly.

Mary Louise was looking at her quizzically. "How about you? Why isn't a pretty girl like you married? I realize that's a dreadfully sexist remark nowadays. You'll have to excuse me, my dear. I'm hopelessly old-fashioned."

"You're not at all," Allison protested.

"You don't have to be polite. I've accepted the fact that I'm a dinosaur. In my day, marriage was every girl's goal. To achieve that admirable state we were taught to be submissive." The older woman's voice had a mocking undertone. "When we married, our husbands shielded us from the harsher realities of life. They thought we were too delicate to face them."

"Times really *have* changed. Now women hold down a job in addition to raising a family. A lot of women do, anyway." Allison added. Not anyone Mary Louise was likely to know.

"They're probably closer to their children than I was. Mine never shared their little disappointments with me. They were told by their father to spare me any unpleasantness."

"He must have loved you very much," Allison said awkwardly, since the older woman was obviously regretting her lost opportunity.

"Yes." Mary Louise turned away. "Let's sit on that bench under the tree. The sun is getting quite warm. I suppose that's why the roses thrive so well. They need a lot of sun."

Allison didn't want her to change the subject now that they'd finally gotten around to Monica. There were so many things she wanted to ask. She paused to frame her questions sensitively.

Mary Louise didn't give her a chance. "Gabriel tells me he met a lot of old friends at the disco last night. We'll have to invite them over for a party. I love having young people around."

"Gabe would thank you for that description." Allison smiled. "He kept referring to himself as being one of the older folks."

"That's patently ridiculous. The man is a heartbreaker."

"I know he's younger than your children, but was Gabe friendly with them?" Allison asked artlessly.

"They knew each other, but there was a good ten years difference in their ages. That's a lot when you're young. What am I saying?" Mary Louise gave a slight laugh. "It's an important difference when you get older, too."

Allison knew she was thinking of Sergei. "I wouldn't say that. I think compatibility and companionship are a lot more important, especially when you get older."

Mary Louise smiled wryly. "Has Gabriel been gossiping?"

"He's very fond of you," Allison answered evasively. "He likes Sergei, too."

Mary Louise sighed. "Everybody but Martin likes Sergei."

"I probably shouldn't say this, but Martin is a grown man with his own life to lead. You deserve to be happy, too."

"It isn't that simple. I've always done what was expected of me. When my husband was alive I gave grand parties for business tycoons and political figures. I was on the board of numerous charities, opened our home for worthy causes and lent my name to cultural organizations. I was a credit to my husband and a responsible citizen." Mary Louise gazed out at the distant water, almost oblivious to Allison's presence.

"I'm sure it was a very rewarding life," Allison said, not at all convinced. "But now you've fulfilled your obligations. You've earned the right to explore a different lifestyle. It would be very foolish to pass up a warm relationship because of a silly thing like age difference. Nobody could even tell there was one. You and Sergei look like you're the same age."

"I'm five years older than he."

"Big deal! Men marry women half their ages, and everybody says, way to go. Why should it be any different for women?"

"I guess we haven't come as far as we think we have."

"Nonsense! Age is a state of mind. You're a vital, caring woman with years of living to do. Take my advice and latch onto him before somebody else does."

"My inhibitions aren't the only problem. Sergei has his own reservations. I have so much more money than he."

"I was told he doesn't exactly have to worry about where his next meal is coming from."

"Most people would consider him rich, but not compared to me. Sergei knows how he would be perceived."

"Your friends wouldn't be influenced by gossip—not if they're true friends. And why would you worry about anyone too mean-spirited to be happy for you?"

"You don't suppose people would think I was a silly old woman?"

"Gabe doesn't, and *I* don't—although my opinion doesn't count for anything." Allison gave a slight laugh, embarrassed that she'd gone too far in her enthusiasm.

"You're wrong, my dear. I value your opinion very much. You're the only one around me who has no reason to be biased."

"I hope I've at least helped to put things into the proper perspective."

"You've given me something to think about, anyway." Mary Louise gazed at her with a slight trace of surprise. "I've never spoken this frankly with anyone before. I'm normally a very private person. I didn't even discuss my feelings with my husband."

"Sometimes it's easier with a stranger. You know you'll never see them again, so you can get it all off your chest."

"Surely you're not thinking of leaving so soon?"

"I don't want to wear out my welcome, but I can stay for a week if you don't mind putting up with me that long."

"It would be my pleasure. I'd really like to know more about you."

"What I'd prefer to talk about is Monica. Unless it would upset you too much," Allison said hesitantly.

Mary Louise smiled faintly. "I've come down from the ivory tower Peter built for me." She reached out to the nearest rosebush and stroked a creamy white blossom with her forefinger. "Monica had skin like this rose petal. She was a beautiful baby, and she grew into an enchanting little girl. Everybody made a fuss over her."

The older woman was silent for so long that Allison murmured, "She must have been an adorable child."

Mary Louise nodded. "I hated to see her grow up, but Monica couldn't wait to do everything—drive a car, go to college, see the world. She wanted to sample everything life had to offer."

"I guess all young people feel that way."

"I suppose so." Mary Louise's expression softened. "I'll never forget her first date. She wore too much lipstick and almost tripped in her first pair of high heels. She looked like a little girl playing dress-up, but her young man was completely dazzled." After a long pause, Mary Louise dragged herself back to the present. "That's how I like to remember her." She looked at her watch and rose. "Goodness, I had no idea it was so late. I have a garden club meeting in half an hour."

Allison felt as if somebody had slammed a door in her face. It was interesting to hear about Monica's childhood, but her early years weren't the ones that counted. Was that all Mary Louise intended to talk about? She hadn't come this far to be put off so easily.

"Could I go to the meeting with you?" Allison asked hastily. "I love flowers."

"You'd be terribly bored, my dear. The name garden club is a misnomer." Mary Louise laughed. "Mostly we discuss fund-raising projects and appoint committees. I guess old habits die hard." She picked up her basket as Gabe sauntered down the path toward them.

"Can I be of any help?" he asked. "I'm looking for something to do."

"You can take Allison sight-seeing," Mary Louise said. "I feel terrible about constantly running out on you," she told her. "But we'll spend the evening together, I promise."

Gabe waited until their hostess was out of hearing before saying mockingly, "I guess you're stuck with me whether you like it or not."

Chapter Four

When Allison didn't snap back after his comment, Gabe
looked at her more closely. "Is anything wrong?"

"No, I'm just disappointed, that's all. I got Mary Louise
to talk to me a little bit this morning, but mostly about when
Monica was a child. She said it was the way she wanted to
remember her."

"That's understandable." He smiled. "Parents are fond-
est of the times when they were in complete control."

"But how am I going to get at the truth if Mary Louise
refuses to face it? Why did she ask me to stay here if she
doesn't want to know?"

"I'm sure she does, but you have to understand that it's
difficult for her to speak about the adult Monica."

"*Why?* What did she do that was so terrible?"

Gabe paused to choose his words carefully. "Monica was
perhaps too blessed. She had everything life had to offer.
There weren't any challenges."

"Mary Louise said she wanted to experience everything, but is that so bad? What's wrong with having a zest for living?"

"It's fine if you don't concentrate solely on your own pleasure. I doubt if Monica ever gave a thought to the people she hurt, the ones who loved her."

"If you're referring to her divorces, they're seldom the fault of only one spouse."

"That's certainly true," he answered neutrally.

"Maybe somebody hurt *her* badly when she was young and impressionable. She was only seventeen when she became pregnant." Gabe's silence wasn't lost on Allison. "I know you won't believe it until you actually see the records, but let's just say I'm right. The father didn't marry her. Perhaps he even claimed he wasn't responsible. Think how traumatic it must have been to have a baby all alone and then have to give it up for adoption."

"Mary Louise would never have turned her out, as you seem to be implying. Nor would she have allowed the baby to be adopted. You know a little about her. Can you see that happening?"

"Obviously she didn't know," Allison said uncertainly. "It's the only explanation."

"How would a seventeen-year-old manage on her own?"

"I don't know. I only know Monica Van Ruyder gave birth to a baby in a Philadelphia hospital. How do you explain *that?*"

"I can't. We seem to be at a stalemate."

"You might be willing to leave it at that, I'm not. I have a lot of questions, and I intend to get answers—starting with who the father was. I'll bet even after all these years, Mary Louise can still remember the names of the boys Monica dated when she was seventeen."

"Possibly, but they could be scattered all over the country by now. And even if you did track them down, do you think the guilty party would admit to having fathered an illegitimate child twenty some years ago?"

Everything Gabe said was true. Dejection weighed Allison down, but she refused to give in to it. "Maybe I can tell by his reaction if he's lying."

"I'm a trained interrogator, and even *I* can't tell when someone is lying."

She squared her shoulders and faced him determinedly. "You can try to discourage me all you want. I'm not giving up."

"I don't want to rain on your parade, honey," he said quietly. "I just want you to be realistic. You're facing a daunting task."

"I know," she said forlornly.

Gabe wanted to hold her and stroke her gently, but he knew better than to make any overt gesture. "Who knows, maybe you'll be lucky and they'll all be visiting Newport this summer."

She flared up immediately, misinterpreting the light tone he used to mask his sympathy. "I didn't say it would be easy, but if everyone had your attitude, we'd all still be riding around in horse-drawn carriages."

"Well, you can't invent the automobile until you get some help from Mary Louise, so let's take her advice and go sightseeing."

"How do you expect me to concentrate on purely frivolous things when I have so much on my mind?"

"The Breakers will make you forget everything else, I guarantee it."

After a little coaxing, Allison let herself be persuaded. There really wasn't anything she could do without some clues from Mary Louise.

The Breakers was a huge Italian Renaissance mansion set on a dozen acres of oceanfront property. A pair of thirty-foot-high wrought-iron gates guarded the entrance. They were open now, and a gravel driveway led through a park filled with giant trees. Squirrels scampered around gathering acorns, adding to the parklike atmosphere.

"It's hard to believe this was a family home," Allison remarked, staring at the arches and pillars and rounded balconies. "It looks like a doge's palace, or some terribly posh hotel."

"It could easily be one of those," Gabe said. "There are seventy rooms inside."

"How could anybody possibly use seventy rooms?"

"Thirty-three of them were set aside for the servants, as well as the maids and valets of guests."

"Now that's what I call considerate houseguests, the kind who bring their own help to clean up after them."

"That wasn't one of their duties." Gabe smiled. "Servants had a strict pecking order in those days. A valet drew the master's bath, but he didn't clean out the tub afterward."

"What do you bet it was considered woman's work?"

"You're not suckering me into *that* controversy." Gabe chuckled. "Come on, let's go inside."

The Grand Entry Hall was forty-five feet tall, roughly five stories. Allison stared up in openmouthed amazement at the ornate gilt cornice surrounding a ceiling painted to represent blue sky. Garlands of carved flowers held by golden cherubs were swagged above marble pillars and curved archways. A stained-glass skylight illuminated a huge Flemish tapestry dominating the stairwell of the red carpeted main staircase.

"I don't know where to look first," Allison said, marveling. "There's so much to see."

"This is only the beginning. Wait until we get to the dining room."

Gabe led her to a room even more embellished than the Great Hall. This room was only two stories high, but the vaulted ceiling rose in carved, painted and gilt stages to an elaborately framed painting on the ceiling of Aurora, goddess of dawn.

"Those people must have spent a lot of time staring at the ceiling," Allison remarked.

"Maybe they wanted to be sure the chandeliers didn't fall on their heads."

Two massive Baccarat chandeliers strung with thousands of crystal prisms and beads illuminated a carved oak table inlaid with lemon wood. It was surrounded by twelve chairs upholstered in red damask. Additional chairs were spaced between twelve enormous freestanding rose alabaster columns.

"Why did they need so many extra chairs?" Allison asked.

"The table could be extended to seat thirty-four."

"If they'd used folding chairs, they could have stored them away in a closet."

"You have a very practical mind," Gabe teased. "Would you have recommended paper napkins, too?"

"You bet, if I had thirty-four people for dinner."

They wandered through the oval music room with its grand piano, the library paneled with gold embossed green Spanish leather, a billiard room that had pale grey-green marble walls and carved yellow alabaster arches.

Each room had its own color and personality. The morning room was furnished with sixteenth-century-style chairs and settees covered in rose silk brocade, and Mrs. Vanderbilt's oval bedroom was a mixture of coral and beige flowered wall covering and cream colored moldings.

After all the opulence and almost overwhelming display of wealth, it was restful to return to the loggia on the lower floor. Through Palladian arches, beyond a lush green lawn was the ocean.

"What a beautiful, peaceful view," Allison commented.

"Do you want to walk down to the water before we push on? I thought we'd go to Kingscote next for a change of pace. It isn't as ostentatiously grand as The Breakers, but it's interesting for its Gothic Revival architecture."

"No more," she groaned. "I'm having trouble remembering everything I just saw."

"It's a lot to take in all at once," Gabe agreed. "Okay, we'll space them out, one historic house a day. How's that?"

"There are eight of them, aren't there? I'm afraid I'll have to skip a couple. I'll only be here a week."

He slanted a glance at her. "You expect to accomplish your purpose by the end of the week?"

"Whether I do or not, I'll have to leave. I can't impose on Mary Louise for any longer than that. Besides, I have to get back to work."

"Surely it's more important to remain here as long as it takes."

"You're implying that I won't have to work if I pull this off?" Allison's blue eyes sparkled angrily.

"That wasn't what I meant, but it *is* true."

"I still have to hedge my bets," she answered mockingly. "If you succeed in proving I'm a fraud, I'll need my job to fall back on."

"I didn't come here with any preconceived ideas," he said quietly.

"That's hard to believe, but I won't argue the point."

Gabe smiled. "You never backed off from an argument before."

"What's the use? I'll never convince you anyway."

"You haven't tried very hard," he said softly.

"There are limits to what even a scam artist will do for money. Let's go back to the car." She stalked off without waiting for an answer.

As he walked alongside her, Gabe remarked, "That's quite a chip you have on your shoulder."

"You'll only have to put up with it for a week. Then you can go home to all the girlfriends who tell you how wonderful you are."

"It will be a nice change." He grinned.

"Well, hang in there. Better times are coming."

"I don't know about that. I'll miss our pitched battles."

"Are *all* of your women compliant?"

"How do you know there are that many?"

"Just an educated guess," she answered dryly.

"You sound like an authority on the male animal."

"I'm not, trust me. I don't know the first thing about men."

"That's hard to believe." Gabe's eyes swept over her admiringly. "You must have made a lot of strong men weak."

"Oh, sure. They can't live without me."

"I can believe it. You could easily become addictive," he said in a silky voice.

His sensuous tone infuriated Allison—because for one crazy minute she couldn't help wishing he meant it. "Is that the kind of line you use to keep Hester happy?" she asked waspishly.

"Somebody has been telling tales out of school."

"It doesn't matter. I knew there would be a Hester."

He didn't deny it. "Is there a Hector in *your* life?"

"Dozens of them," she replied airily. "I play the field, like you do."

"You've never considered getting married?"

"Lots of times. I've also considered moving to a cave, but I decided it was equally impractical." They'd reached the car and Allison ended the conversation by getting in.

Gabe slid into the driver's seat. As they drove out the gates he looked at her inquiringly. "Where would you like to go now?"

"I have an errand to run. You can just drop me off in town."

"It's okay, I'll wait for you."

"That won't be necessary. I don't know how long it will take."

"No problem. I don't have anything else to do."

"I'm sure you can find something more stimulating than following me around day and night. I really hate the feeling of being watched every minute."

"That's the only part of the job I enjoy." He smiled.

"Flattery won't get you anywhere. You can't come with me," she said firmly.

"Now you've piqued my curiosity. What do you plan to do that's so clandestine?"

"Nothing secret, merely personal. I have to buy panty hose, and I don't need a spectator."

"I've been in a lingerie department before. My palms don't turn sweaty with embarrassment."

Allison could believe that. Gabe probably knew more about lingerie than she did—the sexy kind, anyway.

"Pull over to the curb here," she ordered as they drove through the middle of town. When he complied, she got out of the car. "Thanks for the tour. I'll see you later."

"How will you get back to the house? Give me a call when you're finished and I'll come and pick you up."

"You don't have to do that. I'll take a cab."

Traffic started to back up behind him on the narrow street and Gabe had to drive on. She waited until he was out of sight before going into a store to ask directions.

Allison spent a long weary afternoon at the Newport City Hall, going through twenty-five-year-old records. The Van Ruyder name didn't turn up in any of them. None of Monica's three marriages had taken place here.

It was probably too much to hope for, and there was no reason to believe Monica had eventually married the father of her child. She might have told one of the husbands about her youthful affair, though. Since that idea hadn't panned out, Allison's only other option was to question Mary Louise about Monica's boyfriends. The major problem there was the older woman's evasiveness. She didn't really want to talk about her daughter. It seemed strange.

The afternoon had been a waste of time. Allison walked slowly back to the main shopping street, feeling a familiar sense of discouragement. It was difficult enough to trace someone after twenty-five years, but when you didn't know who you were looking for and everyone was conspiring to make sure you didn't find out, the task was almost impossible. Somewhere out there was the man who had fathered her. He could supply the missing pieces of the puzzle, but would she ever find him?

Allison wandered past the shops, reluctant to go back to the house and face more of Gabe's questions. He was upsetting enough without that. As she was passing a beauty shop, Laura emerged, inspecting her right hand.

"Well, hello," Allison said in surprise. "I didn't expect to run into anybody I knew."

"You can hardly avoid it in a town this size," Laura said. "Did you come to shop? The Sporting Life has some nice casual things, although you probably have plenty of clothes."

"It's always fun to look. You don't seem to have bought anything."

"No, I just came to have a nail patched." Laura lifted her hand again. "They're not as good at it as my manicurist in New York, but it will have to do."

"Are you going home from here? I could use a lift."

"Certainly. How did you get downtown?"

"Gabe dropped me off."

"Isn't he a hunk? I suppose that sounds terrible, but what woman wouldn't notice? Like the saying goes—I'm married, not dead." Laura giggled.

Allison didn't want to pursue the subject. "Can I buy you a cup of coffee before we start back?"

Laura consulted her watch. "Why not? We've missed tea, and dinner isn't until eight."

As they walked to a coffeehouse, Allison said, "Maybe I should have gone shopping after all. Do you dress for dinner every night? I'm afraid I didn't bring anything suitable."

"I wouldn't worry about it. We're fairly casual except on the weekends. Tell me frankly," Laura said, once they were seated. "Do you think I'm too old to wear those ultraminiskirts?"

Allison judged her to be quite a bit younger than her husband, maybe only in her early thirties. "I think they'd look great on you. You have an excellent figure."

"I work at it," Laura said matter-of-factly. "I really love short skirts, but Martin is so conservative. He's always afraid of offending his mother."

"Mary Louise seems very open-minded to me."

"Yes, but she's such a perfect lady. You'd never know if she disapproved of something. She always says the right thing and never raises her voice or loses her temper."

"I suppose that's the way she was raised."

"Or else she's a saint. Monica used to use the most outrageous language—words that would impress a marine sergeant. I think she did it to see how far she could go before her mother snapped back. But Mary Louise never did."

Allison held her breath, afraid of saying something that would put Laura on guard. She was so different away from Martin, so much friendlier.

"I'm really surprised," Allison remarked casually. "From the way I've heard Monica described, she was a fantastic person. Everybody loved her."

"The men did—and their feelings were reciprocated. It didn't matter to Monica if they were married or single, either. She liked variety."

"Perhaps she was rebelling against what she felt was a harsh upbringing," Allison said slowly. "I heard her father was quite strict."

"As far as I'm concerned, that psychological jargon is hogwash," Laura said impatiently. "I heard how strict her father was, but that didn't stop her from doing anything she wanted. Did you also hear that he was constantly getting her out of trouble? Monica thought rules were for other people."

"Did you see much of her?"

"More than I wanted to. When she deigned to pay a visit, the whole household was put on alert. We planned our schedules around her. If Monica wanted dinner at ten o'clock, that's when it was served." Laura's eyes sparkled with anger. "It didn't matter what *we* wanted. You wouldn't think Martin was a member of the family. His sister was the only one who mattered."

Laura had obviously resented Monica. The bitterness still remained, making her evaluation of her sister-in-law suspect. Monica was everything Martin wasn't. Maybe she was what Laura wanted to be, too. Nobody was neutral about Monica. She'd evidently had a great impact on people.

Laura gave an embarrassed laugh, suddenly realizing she'd gotten carried away. "I didn't mean to imply that Monica was intentionally malicious, or anything like that. She was really just high-spirited. It's true that she liked to have her own way, but don't we all?"

"How true. It must have been difficult for you, though. A mother always takes her daughter's side over her daughter-in-law."

Laura wasn't about to commit any more indiscretions. "Oh, no, Mary Louise is a perfect mother-in-law." She pushed her coffee cup away. "If you're finished, I'd like to start back."

Allison dressed for dinner that night in a simple blue linen sheath, hoping it would be acceptable. To compensate for her plain outfit she created an elaborate hairstyle, pinning her long hair to her crown, then letting it cascade down in a shining spill of waves and curls.

She took equal pains with her makeup, applying blue eye shadow, tipping her long lashes with mascara and highlighting her mouth with a slick of pink lip gloss.

Her appearance produced mixed results when she joined the others in the den for cocktails. The men's reaction was predictable. Martin scowled at her, while Sergei registered normal admiration for an attractive woman. Gabe's eyes conveyed more than that. They glowed like a predator's sighting a particularly desirable prey.

Mary Louise's expression was the only unexpected one. Her face was wistful as she gazed at Allison. "Monica wore her hair like that to her high school prom," she said softly. "She pinned a single rosebud at her crown. It matched her pink organdy formal."

"Too bad you didn't think to add a rose," Martin said mockingly to Allison.

She ignored him, turning to her hostess. "I took you at your word when you said dinner would be casual."

"You look charming, my dear. We like to be comfortable at home." Mary Louise and Laura wore thin summer dresses.

"I'm glad to hear you admit those charity bashes are uncomfortable," Sergei teased.

"You men look so handsome in your dinner jackets," she said. "I can't imagine why you complain."

"It's a defense mechanism." Gabe smiled. "If we admit we enjoy dressing up occasionally, you ladies will remind us of it when we'd prefer to wear jeans and go to a basketball game."

"Don't you men get enough sports during the daytime?" Laura asked.

"Some of us have to work," Sergei answered.

It was an innocent remark, but Martin took it personally. "I'm sure *you'd* prefer to retire and live off the fat of the land," he said nastily.

"That's an interesting expression." Sergei was unruffled. "I've always wondered where it originated."

"From someone not very bright, obviously," Gabe said. "A fathead?"

After a look at her husband's furious face, Laura said hastily, "Do I have time for another drink before dinner?"

Mary Louise consulted her watch. "It should be ready about now."

Dinner was served in the dining room that night, a formal room with tall, damask-draped windows and Louis VI furnishings. Despite Mary Louise's claim that they dined informally, the table was set exquisitely with a lovely floral centerpiece of garden flowers and tall candles in silver candle holders.

Monogrammed linen place mats held Ainsley china serving plates that were flanked by an array of sterling flatware. At the point of each knife was a water goblet. Next to it were two different size wineglasses, one for red and the other for white. All of the crystal was Waterford.

During the first course, Gabe gazed across the table at Allison. "It's an interesting phenomenon that candlelight can make a beautiful woman look even more enchanting."

Martin's eyes narrowed as he glanced from one to the other. "Your girlfriend Hester doesn't need any help in that department. When are you going to pop the question, Gabe? Or have you already? Let us in on it."

"You'll be the first to know, I assure you," Gabe answered ironically.

"It's funny how weddings seem to be catching." Sergei's voice was bland. "People who have been teetering on the brink, suddenly make up their minds to get married when romance is in the air."

His glance at Mary Louise wasn't lost on Martin. "Are you speaking for yourself? I wouldn't think a man of your age would be interested in marriage—unless he had a powerful incentive, of course."

"Love isn't reserved solely for the young," Sergei answered.

"They think it is." Mary Louise's voice had an unaccustomed edge to it.

"Not all of the young are that shortsighted, if I can be permitted to include myself in that category," Gabe said.

Sergei's eyes twinkled. "I would give a great deal to have your youth and my experience."

"Most people are satisfied to just grow old gracefully," Martin said primly.

"And a lot of people are never satisfied with their lives, no matter what age they are," Gabe commented.

It was not a relaxed dinner, due to Martin's constant sniping and Gabe's refusal to let him get away with it. Allison couldn't enjoy the excellent food and wine, even though she wasn't the object of Martin's malice, for once. She became his target when Mary Louise suggested giving a party to introduce Allison to some of the young people in town. Her purpose may have been merely to change the subject to neutral ground, but Martin reacted furiously.

"Do you want to set off a full-blown scandal? How are you going to explain who she is and what she's doing here?"

"She's our guest," Mary Louise replied. "Well-bred people don't ask questions."

"Get real, Mother! The news is probably all over town by now."

"Then we won't be telling people anything they don't already know."

"We'll be a laughingstock when they find out we were taken in by a—"

"Martin!" Mary Louise interrupted him sharply.

Sergei intervened tactfully. "Will the party be just for young people, or can I come, too?"

"Somebody has to be there to chaperone. Otherwise there's no telling what these kids will be up to." Gabe grinned.

"Who do you think you're kidding with that pious act?" Allison said. "Face it, pal, you're one of us."

"Don't argue, children, there's room for everybody." Mary Louise smiled. "That gives me an idea. We'll make it a multigenerational party. I'll invite my friends and their children and grandchildren. We'll have it this Saturday."

"Isn't that awfully short notice?" Laura asked.

"People aren't booked up every night like they are in New York. There isn't as much to do here. I think we can gather a nice little crowd."

"You're making a mistake," Martin insisted. "Think what Father would say. He'd never permit you to do anything this foolish."

"Unfortunately your father is no longer with us," Mary Louise answered. "If everyone is finished, shall we adjourn to the library for coffee?"

"I don't want any coffee." Martin's mouth was sulky. "Laura and I are going out."

The mood of the evening showed a definite improvement after he left. The others talked and joked easily, with no barbed undertones. Even Allison relaxed and enjoyed the company, including Gabe's. He was so charming that it was easy to forget he was an adversary.

After they finished their coffee, Mary Louise suggested a game of bridge.

"I'm sorry," Allison said regretfully. "I never learned to play."

"You didn't miss anything." Gabe chuckled. "Bridge is responsible for more divorces than infidelity or snoring."

"People do tend to take it too seriously," Mary Louise agreed. "I'll never forget the time my mind wandered and I trumped Peter's ace. He kept me up half the night lecturing me."

"Definitely a man with the wrong priorities," Sergei murmured.

"I saw a game of Trivial Pursuit on the shelf over there," Gabe remarked. "We could play that."

The suggestion met with everyone's approval. Gabe spread the game board on the coffee table and they pulled up chairs around it. Minor squabbling took place over who should ask the questions, but they settled the problem by agreeing to take turns.

Gabe began by asking Allison, "What was the first ready-to-eat cereal?"

"Cornflakes," she answered.

"Wrong, it was shredded wheat. Okay, try this. Where in London are the Crown Jewels located?"

"The Tower of London. Thanks for picking one from the easy category. I'd be mortified if I missed two in a row."

"He's playing favorites," Sergei declared in mock complaint.

"I can't believe Gabriel would take liberties with the rules." Mary Louise smiled.

"To make points with a beautiful woman? He'd be crazy if he didn't." Sergei laughed. "Okay, it's my turn to ask the questions. Who was Howdy Doody's twin brother?"

"It's a trick question," Gabe said. "He didn't have one."

"Wrong. His brother's name was Double Doody."

"You're putting me on!"

"Look for yourself." Sergei brandished the card. "I'll give you another chance. What two U.S. public officials aren't allowed to travel together?"

"A Democrat and a Republican." Gabe grinned. "They'd both want to sit in the driver's seat."

"I believe the correct answer is the president and the vice president," Mary Louise said.

"Correct. See what you get for being a smart aleck?" Sergei said to Gabe. "Mary Louise went ahead of you. Here's one you're bound to know. Who appeared on the first cover of *Playboy* magazine?"

"It was Marilyn Monroe, but I resent your implication."

"You knew the answer, didn't you?" Allison asked dryly.

"My father told me."

"And I'll bet he bought the magazine for the articles."

"This game is getting as controversial as bridge," Gabe complained. "Let's all go into town for a pizza. I'm hungry."

"I can have Florence fix us some sandwiches," Mary Louise offered.

"Don't bother," Sergei said. "I vote with Gabe. It's such a nice night. Let's go out and get some fresh air."

"But it's so late."

"Later than you think. Discover the joy of being spontaneous."

"I never have been," she answered hesitantly.

"All the more reason to start now," Gabe said. "I'll bet you've never even had a pizza. We'll tell them to serve yours with a knife and fork so the culture shock isn't too great," he teased.

After she let herself be persuaded, Mary Louise was enthusiastic. Her eyes sparkled as she glanced around the noisy pizza parlor crowded with young people.

"I can't get over it. A whole world goes on while I've been wasting time sleeping," she commented.

"Stick with us, we'll show you how the other half lives," Gabe joked.

"As if you'd know," Allison scoffed.

Mary Louise covered her hand briefly. "We'll teach each other," she said softly.

They were all hilarious when the pizza arrived and Mary Louise tried to deal with hers. After watching the others covertly, she picked up a slice in her fingers, then looked aghast when long strings of cheese remained attached to the next piece.

An attractive girl about Allison's age stopped by their table. "Mrs. Van Ruyder?" Her voice was incredulous. "I wasn't sure it was you."

"Pinky dear, how nice to see you. I didn't know you were in town. I heard you were working at your father's advertising agency."

"I'm on vacation. It helps to know the boss." She grinned.

Mary Louse introduced her to the others. "I'm so glad we ran into you. I'm having a little party Saturday night and I'd like you and your parents to come. I'll telephone your mother tomorrow. I hope you can make it on such short notice."

"I can't speak for them, but I'd love to."

"Splendid. I want all of you young people to meet Allison. She's visiting us."

"How nice." Pinky glanced mischievously from Allison to Gabe. "Shall I bring a date, or is Gabe up for grabs?"

"He's taken," Allison said. "I believe her name is Hester."

"Bring anyone you like," Mary Louise said, before he could comment. "I hope it's going to be a large gathering."

After Pinky left, Gabe had a chance to deny his relationship with Hester, or at least try to minimize it, but he didn't. That was a good sign, Allison assured herself. Maybe he'd decided to stop coming on to *her.*

Suddenly the high went out of the evening. She was tired and she wanted to go home, but Mary Louise was having such a good time that Allison didn't want to spoil her fun.

"I'm so glad we ran into Pinky," Mary Louise said. "I'd like you to get to know her. She's a dear child. Her mother is Sandra Mayhew—at least that's the way I always think of her, only it's Sandra Gresham now. Anyway, she was Monica's best friend. The two girls were inseparable in high school."

Allison felt a shot of adrenaline. "Will Sandra be at the party Saturday night?"

"I certainly hope so. I'll phone her first thing in the morning. Her parents, too. Curtis and Elinor Mayhew are among my oldest friends."

"Oldest in terms of age, or length of time you've known them?" Sergei asked warily. "Your elderly dowager friends always back me into a corner at parties. The last one wanted to talk about the propriety of putting what she considered risqué oriental prints in the bathroom. They always want me to side with them over their husbands."

"You don't have to worry about the Mayhews. They're more apt to talk sports than erotic art. She's an avid golfer, and he's a fine tennis player."

"That's a relief!"

"They're a very attractive couple. I think Curtis is more handsome now than he was as a young man. He's still tall and trim, and he has the most distinguished looking gray hair."

"Are you trying to make me jealous?" Sergei asked.

"Scarcely. Their marriage is of long duration. Although I must say, Curtis was quite a ladies' man in his youth."

"Don't tell me people of your generation played around?" Gabe teased.

"I wasn't implying anything of the sort!" Mary Louise said indignantly. "Curtis was a bit of a flirt, but he didn't mean anything by it. He and Elinor are a very devoted couple."

"I'm sure they are." Gabe's eyes danced with the amusement he was suppressing. "Behind every happy marriage is a discreet husband."

"I don't consider that funny, Gabriel."

"He wasn't trying to be funny," Allison said. "Gabe simply can't conceive of a man being faithful to one woman."

"I thought you said you weren't an authority on men," he drawled.

Noticing the tension between the two, Sergei intervened smoothly. "You ladies are being too hard on the poor boy. Where is your sense of humor?"

"I'm sorry." Mary Louise smiled ruefully. "Evidently I'm not as 'with it' as I supposed."

"You're doing fine. Would you like anything else to eat?"

"Not another bite. But what is in the tall glasses those youngsters are drinking?" she asked.

"I believe they're called Slurpees or Slushies, or something equally descriptive. Would you like one?"

"I shouldn't. I won't sleep all night."

"I'd like to be the cause of that," Sergei said softly.

Mary Louise's cheeks turned pink and she glanced away. "Oh well, why not? You only live once. Let's all have one of those strangely named drinks."

Allison groaned inwardly. She couldn't put another thing in her stomach; it was already knotted with tension. Would this evening ever end?

Mary Louise chattered on happily about the party and who she planned to invite. Finally Sergei suggested they leave.

"If you can't think of any other concoction you'd like to try, I have a rather early appointment in the morning," he said.

They all said good-night in the downstairs hall, but when Allison started to follow Mary Louise up the stairs, Gabe took her arm.

"I want to talk to you," he said.

"It's late and I'm tired," she answered.

"I won't keep you long. I just want to set the record straight." He held on to her arm, preventing her from following the others. "I didn't appreciate that crack in the restaurant. What makes you think I'm promiscuous?"

"Possibly the way you've been coming on to me when you have a fiancée at home." She tried to pull her arm away, but he wouldn't release her. "Don't bother to deny it! Mary Louise told me about Hester, and Martin confirmed the fact at dinner tonight."

"Did either of them tell you I'm engaged?"

"Well, maybe not in so many words, but I didn't need it spelled out for me."

"You just automatically assumed that when the cat's not around, the rat will play," Gabe said sarcastically.

"Isn't that what you're doing with me? Whether you're engaged or not, you're dating some woman back home on a regular basis. This trip might be business, but that doesn't stop you from trying to have a little fun on the side."

"I'm not succeeding spectacularly," he said grimly.

"I'm sorry for being so uncooperative."

"Has anyone ever told you that you're a very infuriating woman?" he rasped.

"Why? Because I prefer not to be your summer amusement?"

"So far, you're more aggravating than amusing. I've never made love to any woman simply because I was bored and she was available."

"Fortunately I'm not. You don't have to worry about spoiling your perfect record."

"In your case I'll make an exception." He jerked her forward and kissed her hard.

Allison tried to push him away, but he wrapped his arms around her, imprisoning her against his taut body. She struggled, uttering little cries of outrage that did no good. All of Gabe's anger was expressed in his punishing kiss.

Gradually, though, his mouth softened against hers. His arms loosened slightly and one hand curved around her nape in a caress rather than a restraint. Allison held herself rigid, trying to resist his potent attraction. But her struggles ceased as he parted her lips for an arousing kiss that made her legs feel boneless. When he deepened the kiss she clung to him mindlessly, aware only of his lithe body pressed against hers. Their hips and thighs were joined as if they were one person—which she suddenly longed to be.

Gabe finally dragged his mouth away and buried his face in her hair, still holding her close. Allison knew she should move away, but her body didn't agree. This was what she'd known it would be like—only it was even better.

Gabe was the one who ended it. Placing his hands on her shoulders, he put her away firmly. "Go to bed, Allison."

For a moment she stared at him in bewilderment at his harsh tone. Perhaps she *had* provoked him, but after his initial anger faded, didn't that kiss mean anything to him? Was she the only one who entered a magic kingdom?

Allison averted her head and turned toward the stairs. Gabe had really paid her back for her accusation. He showed her how easy it would be for him to score if he felt like it. And then he pushed her away to show he didn't want to.

"Good night, Allison." Gabe's voice was gentle now.

Why not? He'd proved his point. She ran up the stairs without answering.

Chapter Five

Allison had intended to skip breakfast the next day, to avoid meeting Gabe. But when she peeked cautiously into the morning room before slipping past into the garden, Mary Louise was sitting alone at the table.

She glanced up and smiled. "Good morning, dear. Did you have as good a time as I did last night?"

"I...yes, it was a lot of fun." Allision had trouble getting the lie out, considering how the evening had ended.

"I've been on the phone for hours inviting people to the party, and I'm happy to say most of them can come."

"Including Monica's friend, Sandra?" Allison asked casually.

"Yes, and her parents, too, *my* contemporaries. I must say this is a revelation to me. I've always planned these affairs weeks in advance. It took endless conferences with the caterer and the florist, not to mention with my own staff over what china to use and what wine to serve—although Peter always handled that. Everything had to be perfect, especially when he was alive. Suddenly I've discovered that you don't need engraved invitations sent a month ahead, and if there are a few mishaps it won't be a tragedy."

"Welcome to the world of reality." Allison smiled.

"I must seem like a very shallow woman to you."

"Not at all! I didn't mean to imply anything of the kind. You do a lot of good with your money. Why shouldn't you enjoy it, too?"

"You've brought a breath of fresh air into my life. I'm so glad you came," Mary Louise said impulsively.

"I am, too, but time is flying by and we haven't discussed my reason for being here. We really have to talk about Monica."

"I suppose so, but not today. Let's wait until after the party."

"I'll have to leave right afterward," Allison said helplessly.

"Not so soon! You've only been here a few days."

"It will be almost a week on Saturday."

"Can't you ask for more time off from your job?"

"It won't get any less painful to have our talk. I realize you'd rather not believe your daughter had an illegitimate child, but—"

"That would be hurtful, certainly. But what I find difficult to accept is the idea that Monica didn't feel she could confide in me."

"Perhaps she felt you'd be disappointed in her. Teenagers don't always think clearly, especially in circumstances that are traumatic. Maybe she felt she was doing the adult thing by handling it herself."

"We'll never know now." Mary Louise sighed.

"Not what went on in her mind, but we need to find out what happened to her baby. It can have an impact on both our lives. The only person I can think of who might give us the answer is the father of Monica's child."

"You think he'd admit to anything after letting her go through an experience like that all alone?" Mary Louise asked indignantly.

"Somebody must have helped her—with money, if nothing else. The hospital had to be paid."

"Monica had a trust fund from her grandmother. Money wouldn't have been a problem."

Allison refused to let herself become disheartened. "Okay, but she couldn't come and go as she pleased at seventeen. You said she was away at private schools and camps much of the time. She couldn't have left there for a period of months without your knowing, could she?"

"No."

Something in the tone of Mary Louise's voice made Allison look at her sharply. "You don't sound so sure."

"Monica went through a rebellious period when she was seventeen," Mary Louise said slowly. "She broke a number of rules and the school said they couldn't deal with her. I'm sure she was simply influenced by some of the older girls. I wanted to enroll her in another school, but Peter said Monica needed a firmer hand. He sent her to stay with his sister and hired private tutors to come to the house. Poor Monica. It must have seemed like a prison. My sister-in-law was a joyless person. We didn't get along very well." Mary Louise's smile was more of a grimace. "Jane considered me frivolous."

Allison had a premonition. "Where does your sister-in-law live?"

"She died many years ago." After a pause, Mary Louise said, "She lived in Philadelphia."

Allison felt a flash of triumph that she attempted to mask in deference to the older woman's feelings. "All of these things can't be dismissed as coincidence. Do you honestly doubt that somehow or other, Monica had a baby without your knowing about it?"

"No, I suppose I have to agree with you. The possibility occurred to me when Martin said you were born in Philadelphia. He took it as proof that Monica couldn't be your mother, but I began to wonder. That could have been the reason Peter sent her to his sister's for six months and refused to let me contact her. It would have been like him to tidy up the mess without telling me."

"I'm sorry," Allison said in a muted voice.

"I am, too. It's a difficult thing to forgive, but dwelling on it would be futile. My regret now is the years I missed with my grandchild."

"Then help me find out the rest of the story. You don't want to waste any more time." Allison was in the strange position of hedging on her own parentage, something she was almost sure of. But it would be cruel to raise Mary Louise's expectations if there was a chance she was wrong.

The older woman gazed at her silently for a long moment. When she finally answered, it wasn't directly. "Sons are wonderful, but I was so thrilled when I had a daughter, too. I looked forward to sharing all of Monica's little triumphs. I thought we'd go shopping for her prom dress and giggle together about her boyfriends. It didn't happen that way. When I watched my friends with *their* daughters, I realized what a failure I was."

"Oh, no! You're being too hard on yourself."

Mary Louise shook her head. "I was an excellent wife but a terrible mother. I allowed my husband to make all the decisions concerning the children. I don't think Monica ever forgave me for it."

"Your husband was a very strong man," Allison said diffidently.

"And I never challenged him, even when I felt he was wrong. It wasn't until after Peter was gone that I grew into a person in my own right. It's too late to make things up to my children, but I've been given a second chance. I don't intend to make the same mistakes this time."

"I can understand how you feel. That's why it's important to know who the father of Monica's baby was. He's the only one who can tell us what happened to it."

"Perhaps he didn't know."

"I can hardly believe that. It was his child, too, even if it was an inconvenient accident. After the baby was put up for adoption and he was off the hook, he had to be curious about it. If only to be sure it wouldn't turn into his liability. Our problem is tracking him down."

"Sometimes it's best to let sleeping dogs lie." Mary Louise held up her hand as Allison opened her mouth to protest. "Allow me the pleasure of believing I have a grandchild."

"But you *do* have! We just agreed on that. Don't you want to know who she is?"

"You've made a very convincing case for yourself."

"Suppose I'm wrong?"

"I prefer to believe you're not," Mary Louise answered calmly. "All my life I've been sensible and predictable. Just for once I want to indulge myself. And if my dream turns out to be a fantasy, well, I haven't lost anything, have I?" She pushed back her chair. "Excuse me, my dear. I have to invite a few more people to the party. I don't dare phone some of my friends before eleven."

Allison remained lost in thought. In a way she understood Mary Louise's reluctance to face reality, but without the older woman's cooperation, how could she ever arrive at the truth?

Gabe hesitated in the entry for a moment before coming in. "You look as if you're wrestling with a weighty problem," he commented.

"I am."

"Anything I can do to help?"

Allison had been so involved in her thoughts that she'd forgotten about the state of warfare between them. She was suddenly reminded of it. "You don't solve problems, you create them," she answered with a scowl.

"For what it's worth, I'm sorry about last night."

"You should be! I'd made it clear that your advances weren't welcome."

"I'm not sorry about kissing you. It was a revelation." He grinned. "Under that prim exterior, you're a very warm, passionate woman."

She couldn't deny her response, inexplicable as it was. "Then what are you apologizing for?"

"I shouldn't have overreacted when you accused me of being a womanizer."

"So, you're admitting it."

"No, I am not." He bit off each word. "I'm merely saying I should have laughed it off. Anybody who knows me, realizes it isn't true."

"Does that include the women you hit on?"

"Are you *trying* to start another argument?" Gabe came nearer and leaned over her, gripping both arms of the chair. "If you want me to kiss you, just ask. It isn't necessary to provoke me. Unless it makes you feel better to pretend I forced myself on you. Is that it?"

"You did!"

"At first, maybe, then I got enthusiastic cooperation."

"You're a very experienced man," she said defensively. "You know how to make a woman respond to you. That doesn't mean I wanted to."

"Let me get this straight. You enjoyed kissing me, but you're not happy about it?"

"Well, of course I—I mean, I didn't—" She paused and drew a deep breath. "You're just trying to mix me up."

"I don't believe I'm responsible for that." His expression gentled as he traced the curve of her cheek with a long forefinger. "I think you're afraid to show any honest emotion because too many people have let you down in the past."

Mary Louise entered the room scanning some sheets of paper in her hand. Gabe straightened up and Allison rose gratefully from the chair. Her pulse was racing, and she had the uncomfortable feeling that he knew it.

"Good morning, Gabriel," Mary Louise said when she glanced up and noticed him. "We missed you at breakfast."

"I decided to go jogging instead." He patted his flat midsection. "Had to work off that pizza from last night."

"You must be ravenous. I'll have Armand fix you something."

"Don't bother, I'll have an early lunch."

"Have you and Allison made plans?" Mary Louise asked tentatively.

"No." Allison spoke up before Gabe could. "I thought I'd go shopping in the village."

The older woman brightened. "That's just what I was going to suggest! Would you like company?"

"I'd welcome it."

"Splendid. I'll get my purse."

Allison started to follow her out of the room, not wanting to be left alone with Gabe. "I need to get mine, too."

As she walked by him, he murmured, "You can run, but you can't hide."

Allison was disturbed by her instant reaction every time Gabe touched her. The man was awesome! Bruce had never elicited such a response, but that was because she never really loved him. Not that she loved Gabe! That would really be letting herself in for heartbreak.

Allison tried to put the whole thing out of her mind for the afternoon and give Mary Louise her full attention. The older woman was so delighted to be with her. They wandered in and out of shops where Mary Louise urged Allison to buy everything she looked at, however briefly.

"I don't really need any casual clothes," Allison said. "What I'm looking for is a dress to wear to the party."

"They don't carry many dressy clothes. This is strictly a resort area. A lot of these shops close when the season is over."

"I'd better find *something,* or I'll be the only one there in jeans."

"I'm sure it won't come to that. If you don't find anything, you can always wear something of Monica's. I haven't gotten around to giving away the clothes she left here when she visited."

Before Allison could answer, Mary Louise was distracted by an outfit on a mannequin. It was a white handkerchief linen skirt paired with a matching strapless top that had rows of vertical ruffles separated by lines of faggoting. The outfit was pulled together by a gold sash, wrapped and tied in a bow.

"You'd look adorable in that," Mary Louise exclaimed.

"I wouldn't have anyplace to wear it at home."

"But you'd get a lot of use out of it while you're here."

Allison's eyebrows rose when she looked at the price tag. "I'd have to wear it day and night to get my money's worth."

"You must let me buy it for you."

"Oh, no! I wasn't hinting."

"I know you weren't, my dear. I want to."

She was so insistent that Allison had to give in. While the clerk was wrapping the package, an attractive older woman in golf clothes entered the shop. She and Mary Louise greeted each other fondly.

"You're the last person I'd expect to find out shopping," Mary Louise remarked.

"As you can see, I just came from the golf course." The woman laughed.

Mary Louise introduced her to Allison. "You've heard me speak of Elinor. This is Sandra's mother and Pinky's grandmother."

"That makes me feel positively matriarchal," Elinor said.

Was the woman's smile perfunctory, or was she just imagining things, Allison wondered? Elinor was certainly examining her closely. Could Martin be correct, for once?

Had the reason for her visit spread all over town? No doubt. The Van Ruyder servants knew. That's all it would take.

After a few minutes of small talk, the two older women began to discuss a friend's operation. Allison murmured an excuse and went next door to a gift shop she'd noticed. It was a cut above the usual T-shirt and souvenir stores. In a corner was a group of canvases by local artists.

One in particular caught Allison's eye. It was a small oil painting of a woman sitting on a daisy-filled lawn with a group of little girls gathered around her in a semicircle. Allison was charmed by it, and she had a feeling Mary Louise would be, too. She gave it to her when they were seated in a tearoom.

"You didn't have to buy me a present," Mary Louise objected.

"I wanted to. There's no law that says you have to wait till after you go home to send a hostess gift," Allison said lightly.

"I wish you wouldn't talk about going home."

"All right, but open your package. I hope you like it, but the shop owner said it's exchangeable. If you'd prefer something else, my feelings won't be hurt."

Mary Louise's eyes were misty as she gazed at the small canvas. "Oh, my dear, I love it! This is the most thoughtful present I've ever received."

That afternoon together stirred strong feelings in both women. Allison wanted to know what happened to Monica's child as much for Mary Louise's sake now, as her own. The subject wasn't mentioned for the rest of the day, though. They talked and laughed like two old friends—or close relatives.

Martin was less than pleased when he noticed the change in his mother's attitude from that day on. Allison couldn't worry about him, though. She was having too much trouble trying to stay away from Gabe, which was proving to be virtually impossible. Mary Louise, quite innocently, kept throwing them together. She had so many details to take care of for the party that it didn't leave her with much free time.

"I don't want you to get bored," she said, after suggesting that Gabe take Allison to see some of the other Great Houses.

"I'd rather stay here and help you," Allison pleaded.

"There's really nothing you can do, dear. Run along and have fun with Gabe."

"Shall we be on our way, then?" he asked. Only the sardonic expression on his face betrayed his amusement.

"I suppose so." Allison suppressed a sigh, following him outside.

"Your enthusiasm is underwhelming," he remarked as he helped her into the car. "Sydney Carton was more cheerful on the way to the guillotine."

"That's because he knew his punishment would be swift."

"Do you honestly think I want to make you unhappy?" Gabe leaned over her for a moment, examining her flawless features. "You really *don't* know much about men." He walked around to the driver's side before she could answer.

They rode in silence for a while. But when Allison noticed that they seemed to be heading out of town she said, "Where are we going? Aren't most of the houses along Bellevue Avenue?"

"I thought we'd go to Green Animals instead. It's in Portsmouth on the shores of Narragansett Bay. This is the only one of the Preservation properties that isn't actually in Newport."

She was intrigued in spite of herself. "Why would anybody name a house Green Animals?"

"The name refers to a topiary garden begun in the eighteen hundreds by a man named Thomas Brayton. His daughter gave it that name."

"Doesn't topiary mean the practice of clipping bushes into geometric shapes?"

"It started that way with the mazes you still see in Europe. But Brayton took the art a step further. His seven acres of gardens are filled with boxwood shrubs pruned and trained into animal shapes like an ostrich and a unicorn, among others.''

"It sounds fascinating."

"I think you'll find it unique. It's one of the few topiary gardens in this country."

Gabe's description didn't begin to do the place justice. Allison exclaimed over the perfectly sculpted camel and elephant whose smooth shapes were formed by carefully clipped bushes. Across a formal garden bordered by low boxwood hedges, a boar and a bear faced each other, both on raised, circular green platforms made from the same kind of bushes.

"What's that one supposed to be?" Allison seized Gabe's hand and pulled him along. "It looks like a giraffe, but its neck is too short."

"You're right, it's a giraffe. Originally the neck was longer, but it was damaged in the 1950s by a hurricane. In the interest of safety, the neck was shortened. It takes several years for a topiary figure to reach maturity, and pieces damaged by the weather can take many seasons to recover."

"That would make this giraffe over forty years old," she marveled.

Gabe had slipped his arm casually around her shoulders. "That's older than you are."

"I hope I'll be in as good shape when I reach that age. Although, probably not. I don't have as many people taking care of me." She turned a laughing face up to him.

"Poor little Allison. You've never had *anybody* to take care of you."

She was suddenly aware of his arm around her and the deepened quality of his voice. Moving out of his embrace she said lightly, "It builds character. There's something to be said for knowing you can make it on your own."

"But it's a lot nicer to curl up in somebody's arms at the end of a long hard day."

"I'll have to take your word for it."

"I could show you if you'd let me," he murmured.

"Don't you ever give up?" she asked in exasperation. "We were getting along fine for a change. Why do you insist on spoiling things?"

"I'm trying to make them better." He smiled.

"For whom? Certainly not me!"

"That's not true. I have a feeling you've never met a man who appreciated you. I'd like to make love to you the way you deserve, with caring and tenderness." He cupped her chin in his palm and tilted her face up. "I want to undress you slowly and kiss every inch of your beautiful body. And when you hold out your arms to me, I want to gather you close and satisfy you completely."

Allison was powerless to move away, hypnotized by his sensuous voice. She could imagine everything he was describing—and all the things he'd left out. His scorching mouth stringing kisses across her breasts, his seductive hands, searching out every vulnerable part of her.

Mercifully a voice broke the spell. "Excuse me, can I get through?" They were standing in the middle of the path and a gardener wanted to get by with his equipment.

Allison hadn't even heard the man approaching. That was how completely Gabe engrossed her. But it had to stop. She turned to face him squarely.

"I suppose it's too much to appeal to your better nature, but I'm going to try. Could you please knock it off? I'll only be here for a few more days."

He gazed at her speculatively. "I might be open to a deal. Can I see you when we both get back to New York?"

"Why not? The three of us can pal around together."

"I'm not engaged to Hester," Gabe said quietly.

Even if that were true, it didn't make him any more accessible. Allison faced the fact that she could easily fall in love with Gabe. Her attraction to him was more than merely physical. She enjoyed just being with him. He made every minute together special.

But no meaningful relationship could ever develop between them. Gabe came from the same social background as the Van Ruyders. His parents would be just as opposed to her as Bruce's parents had been. Only this time more than her pride would be hurt.

Gabe interrupted her reverie. "It's taking you a long time to make up your mind."

"Why don't we just play it by ear?" she answered evasively.

Gabe was on his good behavior after that and Allison relaxed and enjoyed his company while she could. It wouldn't be for much longer, she thought wistfully.

He took her to Marble House, the result of William Vanderbilt's instructions to build "the very best living accommodations that money can buy." The eleven-million-dollar house was Newport's most ornate and expensive "cottage."

Rosecliff, where *The Great Gatsby* was filmed, rivaled it in opulence. "Just think, I could be walking in the exact spot where Robert Redford walked," Allison said.

"You could be following in the footsteps of a lot of illustrious people," Gabe said. "The house changed hands several times after the original owners died."

She gazed around the eighty-foot-long ballroom with its French marble mantelpiece and crystal and ormolu chandeliers. "How could so many people have so much money?"

"They didn't have to pay taxes. The income tax wasn't introduced until 1913."

"They were still tycoons. Even if I didn't have to pay taxes, all I could afford to build would be a birdhouse."

"They do say money isn't everything." Gabe chuckled.

"Those are the people who already have it."

The remaining days until the party flew by since Allison spent them with Gabe. He was a charming companion and for once, there was no friction between them.

On Friday, the day before the party, Gabe suggested going to the country club for a change of pace, but Allison declined. They were having breakfast with Mary Louise and Sergei.

"I absolutely have to buy a dress today. The party is tomorrow! It's already the last minute."

"I really don't think you're going to find anything," Mary Louise said. "Why don't you look through Monica's things? She had excellent taste in clothes."

"I'm sure she did, but I wouldn't feel right about it."

"It would please me very much, my dear," Mary Louise said quietly.

After her protests proved futile, Allison allowed herself to be persuaded. With mixed emotions, she followed Mary Louise up the stairs and into Monica's room.

The closet in the large bedroom was crammed with clothes. Monica must have had an unbelievable wardrobe if these were the things she left at Rosewood Manor for infrequent visits.

Mary Louise pushed aside a group of long, glamorous gowns. "We don't need to bother with these, since the party will be quite informal."

Allison wasn't convinced. She'd seen the preparations going on all over the house. Florists had turned the ballroom into an indoor garden and banked the entry with masses of blossoms. If that was casual, what would a formal party be like? She decided to let her hostess make the selection.

"Either of these would do." Mary Louise glanced from a short green chemise with billowy organdy sleeves, to a pair of white silk pants with a navy organza tank top. The accompanying jacket was edged in gold braid in a sunburst pattern. "Does either one appeal to you?"

"They're both gorgeous." Allison's attention was riveted on the pantsuit with longing. "I'd be hesitant about wearing the white one, though. I'm afraid I'd spill something on it."

"White silk always has to be cleaned after every wearing. Don't give it another thought."

"Well, if you're really sure." Allison touched the luxurious fabric gently. "I'm just afraid it might bring back memories for you."

Mary Louise's face was expressionless. "Many things remind me of my daughter. This will be one of the happier ones."

On the night of the party Allison took special care with her appearance. Monica's pants and jacket fit Allison perfectly, though the top was a little large. Her high, firm breasts were evidently smaller than the generously endowed Monica.

Other than that, Allison was quite happy with how she looked. The elegant outfit made her look chic and glamorous—as though she actually belonged here. Telling herself not to indulge in foolish fantasies, she sprayed herself with perfume and went downstairs where the family was already gathered.

Gabe's reaction was the one that mattered to Allison and it was most satisfactory. His eyes gleamed as they roamed from her long black hair and finely boned face, to her curved figure. "I won't be able to get near you tonight."

"You have enough girlfriends," Mary Louise chided. "Let the other young men have a chance."

"Thanks a lot," Gabe said wryly.

The guests started arriving soon after, dozens of them. Allison was introduced to so many people that she stopped trying to remember all the names. The one she was most interested in meeting was Sandra Gresham, Monica's best friend.

Allison was chatting with Pinky and a group of her friends when Pinky remarked, "There's my mother and dad." She waved at a couple entering the room.

Sandra was a fashionably thin woman, poised and expensively dressed. Her jewelry was impressive but tasteful, and her hair and nails were perfect. She had everything privilege could confer, yet her expression was faintly dissatisfied.

When Pinky introduced Allison, Sandra's gaze sharpened. "I heard Mary Louise had a houseguest."

"Allison is from New York," Pinky volunteered. "I told her we'd have to get together in the city. She works at Maison Blanc, which isn't far from my office."

Sandra's attention remained riveted on Allison. "How did you happen to come to Newport?"

Allison hesitated for only an instant. "I'd never been here before and I'd heard so much about the area."

"How do you know Mary Louise? I've never heard her mention you before."

"Really, Mother," Pinky protested. "You're giving the poor girl the third degree."

"I'm sure Allison realizes I'm only expressing friendly interest," Sandra answered smoothly. "Besides, people with nothing to hide don't mind answering questions. Isn't that right, my dear?"

"Absolutely." Allison was puzzled by the woman's covert hostility, but she managed a smile.

"So how *do* you know Mary Louise?"

"We met rather unexpectedly and she invited me for a visit." That could have taken place at any time, Allison thought.

"How nice for you. Are you staying all summer?"

"Oh, no, I have to get back to my job."

"Too bad you don't work for your dad." Pinky grinned.

"Who *is* your father?" Sandra asked casually. "Perhaps I know your family."

"I'm an orphan. I'm afraid I never knew who my parents were."

"That's unfortunate, but it can't make any difference at this stage of your life."

Allison was startled by the raw emotion on the older woman's face. It was almost like hatred, although how could that be? "I guess everybody in my situation wonders about their background," she said slowly.

"Maybe you're better off not knowing. Did you ever think of that?"

"I don't agree," Pinky said. "Anybody would be curious, if nothing else."

"That's not reason enough to dwell on something that happened a long time ago. It's pointless to live in the past."

"That's funny coming from you. Mother is the most tradition-bound woman I know," Pinky told Allison. "She still shops in the same stores her mother did—and has the same saleswomen wait on her. She's never changed dry cleaners. She even has the same friends she made in kindergarten!"

That was the opening Allison had been waiting for. "Mary Louise says you were her daughter's best friend," she said to Sandra.

"Is that what she told you? We were friendly for a time, but we drifted apart after high school."

"Have you kept in touch with any of Monica's friends?" Allison asked innocently.

Sandra's smile was unpleasant. "They were mostly male—and usually traumatized after a relationship with her."

"My goodness, that sounds intriguing. Are any of them here tonight?"

"It would be impossible to go anyplace where there aren't. Excuse me, I haven't said hello to my hostess yet."

"I wonder what got into Mother. She's not usually this testy. One of her committee members must have screwed up." Pinky laughed.

Gabe joined them and took Allison's hand. "I believe this is our dance."

She followed him onto the floor, trying to figure out Sandra's behavior. Mary Louise was certainly wrong about the friendship. Sandra detested Monica. Had Monica taken a boyfriend away from her? But surely she wouldn't hold a grudge all these years. And what could she possibly have against *her*, Allison wondered.

"You're very quiet," Gabe commented.

"I just had the strangest meeting with Pinky's mother. She took an instant dislike to me."

"That's hard to believe." Gabe's embrace tightened and his lips brushed her forehead.

She was too distracted to notice. "It's true. I know I didn't imagine it."

"What did she say to you?"

"It was her expression and the tone of her voice as much as anything else. But she asked me a lot of questions about why I was here. I think she knows."

"It wouldn't surprise me. Everybody at the party probably does, too. Servants talk, or Martin might even be responsible. He never knows when to keep his mouth shut. Sandra is probably interested in the gossip, like everybody else."

"It docsn't account for her hostility."

"What you told me doesn't sound too offensive."

"I didn't tell you all of it. She asked about my family, and when I told her I didn't have any she advised me not to go looking for them."

"It could be she's not too fond of *hers*." He grinned.

"I'm serious, Gabe! When I asked if any of Monica's former boyfriends were here tonight, she put me off with a nasty remark. I simply have to find out."

"You think one of them is your father?"

"It's possible. That would explain Sandra's behavior. He could be an old friend from way back. These people don't like anyone to rock the boat. He's undoubtedly married now, and she's afraid I'm going to cause a scandal by making his affair public after all these years."

Gabe's eyes narrowed momentarily. "What *do* you want?"

"Only to talk to him. To find out for sure. I don't want to be a faceless person for the rest of my life."

"A face like yours is a gift from heaven," he said in a husky voice. "But okay, honey, I know what you mean. I'll see what I can find out."

"I'd appreciate it so much. I'm not getting very far on my own."

"This is the first time you've asked for my help."

"It's in your own interest, too. You were sent here to find out the truth about me."

"Does that mean you finally realize I didn't come to do a hatchet job?"

She hesitated. "It doesn't really matter. We have a common goal."

He tipped her chin up and looked deeply into her eyes. "I only wish that were true."

"How can you get romantic when we're finally making progress?" Allison asked impatiently.

"It might have something to do with the perfume you're wearing and the way you fit into my arms," he answered lightly.

"Kindly try to concentrate on what's important."

"That depends on your point of view." He nibbled gently on her ear.

She raised her shoulder to dislodge his mouth. "Be serious, Gabe! We need to circulate and talk to as many people as we can."

"How is that going to help?"

"I don't know. We'll steer the conversation around to Monica and hope they let something slip."

Allison got various reactions, none of them helpful. Mary Louise's friends closed ranks. They were polite, but wary. Did everyone but Monica's mother know what had happened twenty-five years ago? More likely, their reticence was because of her mysterious death. If they knew how it happened, they weren't talking publicly about that, either.

Some of the guests reserved judgment about Allison, but Pinky's grandparents were charming to her. Curtis Mayhew, Elinor's husband, was as dashing as Mary Louise had said. He was still a very handsome man. His tanned face was surprisingly young looking, despite his silvery hair, and his lean physique was a tribute to the amount of tennis he played.

"It's always a pleasure to see a pretty new face," he told Allison jovially. "I hope you plan to be around for a while."

"I'm afraid not," she answered. "This is certainly a wonderful place for a vacation, though."

"I'm trying to persuade her to stay on," Mary Louise said.

"There's a great deal to see," Elinor remarked.

"I know," Allison agreed. "Gabe took me through a lot of the historic houses."

"It was Mary Louise's idea." Gabe chuckled. "I could have been much more creative."

"It's something tourists are required to do before enjoying the things they came for," Curtis said. "Are you a tennis player, my dear?" he asked Allison. "You're welcome to be my guest at the club anytime."

Sandra joined their group. "Up to your old tricks, Father?" she drawled. "I knew I'd find you with the prettiest new face. He worships youth," she told Allison.

"I wouldn't put it that strongly," Curtis protested mildly. "I don't see anything wrong with enjoying the company of young people, though. You can be certain they won't talk about their arthritis or latest gastric upset."

His wife smiled. "You're so intolerant, darling. Some of us get old and achy. We don't all have your secret of eternal youth."

"Father's secret is the right kind of exercise." Sandra's nasty smile made the innocent remark sound snide.

In just a few moments she'd destroyed the festive mood of the group. Sandra's parents were too well-bred to tell her to knock off whatever was eating her, but Elinor looked pained and Curtis's face was carefully expressionless.

Allison knew she wasn't going to find out anything with Sandra there, and she preferred not to put up with her bad temper. "Will you excuse us?" she asked. "I want to sample some of those great looking hors d'oeuvres."

When they were out of hearing, she said to Gabe, "If that woman were *my* daughter, I'd disown her!"

"She's certainly not a barrel of laughs, is she?" he asked.

"*Now* do you believe she disliked me from the moment we met?"

"I wouldn't take it personally. She obviously has a chip on her shoulder. Maybe she had a fight with her husband before she got here."

"In which case, she should have stayed home."

The evening was great fun, even though Allison didn't find out anything new about Monica. There were long periods when she forgot that was her goal. The times she danced with Gabe, for instance. It felt so right in his arms. When he molded her body to his and rested his lips on her temple she was filled with an aching kind of happiness.

Pinky and her friends weren't a source of information, but Allison enjoyed being with them. They were amusing, and they accepted her without question.

"If you're not doing anything on Monday, why don't you and Gabe come over to my house for lunch and swimming?" Pinky suggested.

"I'd love to, but I have to go home no later than Monday. I'm due back on the job Tuesday."

"You only work a four-day week? I'll have to speak to my father about that," Pinky joked.

"When I put in for vacation time I planned on an extra day at home to do the laundry and take my clothes to the cleaners—all those things you have to do after a trip."

"Too bad. Well, how about tomorrow? A bunch of us are going to the yacht club for some sailing and windsurfing."

"It sounds great, but I have to wait and find out if Mary Louise has anything planned. Can I let you know?"

"Sure, but not too early." Pinky grinned.

The party didn't break up until late, but Allison wasn't a bit tired. She didn't want the night to end.

After the last guest had left, Gabe loosened his tie and said, "Let's get some air. It was hot in there with all those people."

Allison followed him into the garden, inhaling the rose-scented air. "But wasn't it a glorious evening? I've never been to a party like that. I thought they only existed in the movies."

"So you think you could get used to this way of life," he remarked casually.

"Who couldn't?" She laughed. "I've almost forgotten about the world of the subway and the supermarket. It's a good thing I'm going home Monday."

"Without getting what you came for?" Gabe's face was enigmatic in the filtered moonlight.

"I'm not happy about it, but I don't know what more I can do. Mary Louise won't tell me anything, and I struck out with her friends. I finally convinced her that Monica did have a baby, but maybe it's just too soon for her to want to know all the circumstances. I can only hope that in time she'll want to find out."

"That kind of leaves you in limbo, doesn't it? Or do you plan to follow up on the other possibilities?"

"No. I don't want to disrupt any more lives. I'm afraid I was only thinking of myself. I didn't realize the kind of heartache I could cause." She lowered her head and touched a rosebud gently. "If I never find out who my parents were, people will just have to accept me for what I am."

"I can't imagine anyone rejecting you for any reason." Gabe framed her face in his palms and looked deeply into her eyes. "You're as near perfection as a mortal woman can get."

"Isn't that a little extravagant?" She smiled tentatively, aware of his sudden change of mood.

"It doesn't begin to do you justice," he answered huskily.

Putting his arms around her waist, he drew her close. Allison didn't put up even a token struggle. This might be the last time she was alone with Gabe. She wanted to feel his firm mouth on hers, his urgent body promising more joy than she'd ever known.

"Sweet Allison, you're driving me crazy," he groaned, stringing hungry kisses over her face. "I want to make love to you."

"It's late," she murmured. "We should go to bed."

"You're right." He urged her hips closer to his. "It's inevitable. You know that, don't you?"

"No." Her answer was a faint whisper. The warmth of Gabe's body was lighting a fire deep inside Allison, seducing her will to resist.

"Don't fight it, angel. There's something very powerful between us. I felt it the first day we met." His warm mouth slid down her neck. "Don't tell me you didn't feel it, too?"

"I..." She drew a sharp breath as Gabe's hand curved around her breast. A bolt of electricity jolted through her as his thumb gently circled the sensitive tip, turning her liquid with desire. She clung to him, unable to stand alone.

"You do want me," he said exultantly.

His deep kiss raised the level of excitement almost unbearably. Allison moved against him, uttering tiny sounds of pleasure. As his hand slipped under the hem of her tank top and she reached up to unbutton his shirt, Mary Louise called to them from the house.

"Gabriel, will you lock up when you and Allison come inside? I'm going to bed."

Her voice brought Allison back to reality with a jolt. She averted her face and moved out of Gabe's arms. How could she have gotten so carried away? In another moment she would have made love to him right there in the garden!

"Allison? Are you two still out there?" Mary Louise called again.

"Yes, we...we're coming right in," Allison answered hastily.

Gabe put his hand on her arm. "Don't go. We can't leave it like this."

She took a deep breath to steady herself. "What almost happened would have been a mistake. I'm very attracted to you, but I don't do this sort of thing."

"This sort of thing?" He gripped her shoulders hard. "I want to make love to you, not just have sex!"

She gazed up at him uncertainly. "I wish I could believe that."

"Who made you too afraid to believe somebody could care about you? All men aren't like him."

"Good night, children," Mary Louise called. "I'm going upstairs."

"Wait! I'll go with you." Allison practically ran toward the house.

For just a moment she'd teetered on the brink—until Gabe reminded her of Bruce. She'd believed him, too. When would she ever learn?

Gabe didn't try to stop her. When she looked back she saw that he remained motionless, staring after her. In the moonlight his features looked carved out of stone.

Chapter Six

Gabe's attitude changed drastically after the emotionally charged incident in the garden. When Allison joined him and the others at breakfast on Sunday morning, he glanced up and smiled sardonically.

"There she is, last night's winner," he said with veiled sarcasm.

"Everybody did find her adorable. I got so many nice comments," Mary Louise said happily, unaware of his true meaning.

Sergei was more astute. He glanced covertly at the young pair. "It was a nice party, but I think we were all a little tired at the end."

"Not me. I could have partied all night if I'd had somebody to keep me company," Gabe said. "I almost had Allison convinced, but she chickened out on me."

"You young people never know when to go to bed," Mary Louise commented.

"Don't include Allison," Gabe drawled. "She was a good girl."

Fortunately Mary Louise rang the bell to summon the maid. "What would you like for breakfast?" she asked Allison. "On Sundays we dispense with the buffet."

"Just coffee will be fine," Allison said.

"You have to eat something. Try one of Armand's mushroom omelets. They're delicious."

"All right, that sounds good."

Allison would have agreed to anything. She just wanted to finish breakfast and get out of there. Gabe was only warming up with those hidden barbs and mocking amusement. Things were bound to get worse. He had the upper hand because he knew she couldn't snap back at him.

Sergei tried to lighten the tension by talking about last night's party. Mary Louise joined in and for a short, blessed time, Gabe behaved himself.

Allison was trying to force down some of her omelet when Anita came to tell her she had a telephone call.

"Bring her the cordless phone," Mary Louise instructed. "Her eggs will get cold if she takes it in the other room."

The call was from Pinky. "I'm going to leave for the club in fifteen minutes, so I thought I'd better call you. Are you coming?"

"I haven't talked to Mary Louise yet," Allison said.

"About what, dear?" the older woman asked.

"I wondered if you had any plans for today—some that included me, I mean."

"Sergei and I plan to spend a relaxing day by the pool. You're welcome to join us of course, if you have nothing else to do."

"Pinky and her friends are going to the Yacht Club," Allison said tentatively.

"Then by all means go with them. You'll have a lovely time."

After Allison had accepted, Pinky said, "The invitation includes Gabe, too."

Allison gave him a quick glance before lowering her voice and turning away slightly. "He might have something else to do."

"You won't know until you ask him."

"I'd rather not. He might think he has to accept."

Allison's furtive behavior automatically drew Gabe's attention, leaving no doubt that she was discussing him. "If you're talking about me, don't worry. I'm willing to take a chance on anything. Unlike some people." Raising his voice he said, "Tell Pinky I'd be delighted to come."

His voice carried, as he expected it to. "That's great!" Pinky said. "Don't hurry. I'll see you when you get there."

Allison's mood was stormy as she changed into her bathing suit and pulled on jeans and a T-shirt over it. By the time she went downstairs where Gabe was already waiting, she was spoiling for a fight. It was hard to contain herself until they were in the car driving away.

"This is a good day for surfing," he remarked. "Just enough wind."

"How can you sit there and make small talk after the way you acted?" she demanded.

"Which time? I seem to have committed a lot of indiscretions with you."

"You certainly have, but I was referring to breakfast this morning. Why didn't you come right out and tell Mary Louise and Sergei what happened last night?"

"Because nothing did. It would have made a very dull story."

"Aren't you a little old to sulk?" Allison asked caustically. "You must have been a real brat when someone tried to take away your teddy bear."

"Actually I was very generous with my toys. But I did get a little cranky when somebody raised my expectations with no intention of gratifying them."

"Are you implying that I'm a tease?" she asked indignantly. "*You're* the one who wouldn't stop coming on to *me!* I told you I wasn't interested."

"That wasn't the message I got in the garden last night."

She turned her head away and stared out of the window, unable to deny it. "Last night was a mistake," she said in a low voice.

"What's the matter, Allison, did I almost make you lose sight of your goal?"

"I don't know what you're talking about."

"It's always nice to have a contingency plan in case your first one doesn't work out. In one of your few moments of honesty, you admitted to a hankering for the good life. If you can't make your claim to be Monica's daughter stick, you can always marry a wealthy man. There were plenty of them there last night. You're missing a bet by not putting me on the list, though. I'm not exactly poor."

"You are absolutely loathsome!"

"I have to agree. A gentleman doesn't try to force a lady to admit the truth."

"Is that why you insisted on coming today? To make sure I don't get my hooks into some poor unsuspecting millionaire's son?"

"Why else would I be here?" Gabe's face was impassive.

"You could have saved yourself the trouble. Even *I'm* not tricky enough to snare my victim in one day. That's all I have, since I'm going home tomorrow."

"I'll believe *that* when I see it, too. I don't think this week will ever end," he said grimly.

"I'm sorry you're not enjoying yourself," she said sarcastically. "*I* am. You've no idea how much fun it is to have someone harass you constantly."

"You haven't exactly made *my* life a garden of earthly delights, either."

Allison had an instant flashback to a moonlit garden and Gabe's hands caressing her body. His mouth wasn't compressed into a thin line then. It had been warm and seductive against hers. How completely she'd been fooled. This was how he really felt about her.

Gabe's expression softened as he glanced over at her averted face. "May I make a suggestion? How about a truce for today? We can resume hostilities tomorrow on the way to the airport."

"I'd like that—I mean, the part about the truce."

He reached over and took her hand. "Okay, it's a deal. No more recriminations."

Allison was relieved as they drove into the entrance to the yacht club, even if it was only a temporary respite. Gabe's opinion of her shouldn't matter, but it did—and there was nothing she could do to change it. She stole a look at his handsome profile. At least this last day with him wouldn't be marred by bitterness.

Pinky and her friends were milling around the big lounge deciding who wanted to go sailing and who preferred windsurfing. She and the people who had been at the previous night's party welcomed the newcomers exuberantly. They were all vocal about how much they'd enjoyed themselves.

"You see what you missed by frolicking out in Hollywood with all those starlets?" Pinky said to a handsome blond young man. "Stu just flew in this morning," she explained to Allison. "Meet Stuart Harrison the Third."

"Stop trying to make me sound stuffy." He took Allison's hand and held onto it. "I'm really a fun guy. Please call me Stu."

"Is that a name, or a perpetual condition?" Gabe asked.

"Gabe, old man!" Stuart clapped him on the shoulder. "I haven't seen you in a dog's age. How the heck are you?"

"Still working for a living. We can't all live on our trust funds."

Gabe's voice had a slight edge. It wasn't difficult to deduce that he didn't care much for Stuart. Allison found him amusing, though. The fuss Stuart made over her was flattering, too.

"Hey, I'm doing a service to the economy." Stuart laughed. "Why should I take a job from somebody who really needs it?"

"That's very noble, but how much call is there for a guy whose greatest talent is mixing a perfect martini?" Pinky joked.

"Do you want the art to die out?" Stuart chuckled.

"Are we going sailing, or are we going to stick around here all day?" one of the young men demanded.

"I vote for sailing." Candace Weatherby linked her arm with Gabe's. She was a curvy blonde with big brown eyes and a sensuous mouth. "How would you like to crew for me?"

"You make it sound very tempting." He gazed down at her and smiled.

"Okay, that takes care of Gabe," Pinky said. "How about you, Allison? Do you want to crew or windsurf?"

"I'm afraid I've never done either one. Couldn't I just go along for the ride?"

"Sure, I guess so," Pinky answered after a moment's hesitation.

"That puts an extra person on somebody's boat," Candace objected. "If we're going to race, we have to give that boat some kind of advantage."

"I didn't realize it would be a problem," Allison said. "Go ahead with your race. I'll just watch and cheer everybody on."

"That wouldn't be much fun for you," Pinky said.

"I'll take Allison on my boat, and you don't have to give me a handicap," Stuart said.

Allison grew increasingly embarrassed at the fuss she was causing as everyone joined in the discussion, offering various solutions.

Gabe settled the matter decisively. "I'll give Allison a windsurfing lesson while the rest of you race."

"You're supposed to crew for me." Candace pouted.

"I'll make it up to you," he promised with a melting smile.

Allison's gratitude toward him evaporated. After they left the others and were walking toward the beach she said, "You didn't have to baby-sit me. I would have been okay on my own."

"That wouldn't have been polite. None of us would have been comfortable about leaving you out."

Allison was annoyed to discover she was an obligation. "You didn't have to be a martyr and volunteer," she said stiffly.

"What makes you think it was a duty?"

"What else could it be? You had the chance to go sailing with a buxom blonde."

Gabe grinned. "She *is* rather well endowed."

"I certainly can't compete in *that* department—even if I wanted to." Allison pulled her T-shirt over her head and flung it on the sand. Underneath she was wearing a relatively modest blue tank suit, the color of her stormy eyes.

His gaze was appraising as she unzipped her jeans and cast those aside, too. "Quality is as important as quantity."

"You don't have to be polite," she said curtly. "I know my own shortcomings."

"I can't see that you have any—except for a very short fuse."

Allison was suddenly ashamed of herself. Gabe had put his own pleasure aside for her, and she was behaving like a shrew. All because she was jealous of Candace. Why not admit it? To herself, at least.

"I'm sorry," she murmured. "I don't know why I'm always so defensive. I guess old habits die hard."

Gabe's expression was gentle as he gazed at her bowed head. "You can relax, honey, you're among friends."

That was the best he had to offer her, Allison thought poignantly. But it was better than nothing.

She didn't have time to dwell on it after Gabe started to teach her to windsurf. It was a lot harder than it looked. He was very patient, but after half an hour she hadn't made much progress. The board was slippery and she had trouble keeping her balance.

"Hold onto the mast and shift your weight when the board tilts." He was positioned behind her with one arm around her waist.

"Easy for *you* to say," she panted. "This thing is as unpredictable as the stock market."

"Don't worry, I won't let you fall off." His arm tightened as a swell lifted the board.

Allison was suddenly conscious of their closely contoured bodies, locked together spoon fashion. The intimate feeling of Gabe's bare chest against her equally bare back brought visions of a different kind of coupling. The clean, salty smell of his skin worked as a kind of added aphrodisiac. She rested her head on his solid shoulder and tilted her head to look up at his strong features.

"Hey, pay attention or we—" The laughing complaint broke off sharply. His breath caught as he gazed at her lambent face.

Almost in slow motion, his head descended, blotting out the sunshine. But his mouth supplied all the warmth Allison would ever need. She parted her lips, welcoming the sensuous invasion of his tongue. Gabe shifted her in his arms, wrapping her so closely to his taut frame that she was unmistakably aware of his desire. Her own desire rose joyously to meet it.

For one exquisite moment they were oblivious to everything except each other. Then a gust of air filled the sail, causing the board to heel sharply. They were pitched off, still clasped in a heated embrace.

The cool water brought Allison to her senses. She bobbed to the surface, coughing and sputtering.

Gabe surfaced beside her. "Are you all right?"

"Yes, I . . . I guess I lost my grip on the mast."

"Windsurfing takes concentration," he said softly, reaching out to brush the wet hair off her forehead. "What distracted you?"

"Nothing, I . . . my arms got tired."

"Why is it so difficult for you to admit your feelings?"

"I just did. I told you. I got tired." She started to swim for shore. "I've had enough instruction for today."

Gabe stared after her for a moment. "I've almost given up hope of ever teaching you anything," he muttered under his breath.

When they got back to the clubhouse, Allison was relieved to find the others had returned also. During the general milling around it was easy to distance herself from Gabe.

He didn't seem to mind. Possibly because Candace made a beeline for him. That made up for any disappointment he might have suffered, Allison thought waspishly. He was giving the curvy blonde the same seductive smile he'd used on *her.*

Allison turned abruptly to the man standing next to her. "Who won the race?" she asked.

"*I* did, naturally." Stuart's teasing smile took the arrogance out of his statement.

"Then it's lucky Gabe took me off your hands."

"I would gladly have settled for last place if I'd had *you* aboard."

"You don't really mean that. I'll bet you hate to lose."

"Everybody does, but I give it my best effort when the prize is a beautiful woman. How involved are you and Gabe?"

"Not at all."

Stuart looked skeptical. "He brought you here today. You're both staying at Rosewood Manor."

"That's why we drove over together. Does it look like we're involved?" Allison waved negligently at the couple across the room. They were engaged in what looked like an intimate conversation.

"I guess I jumped to conclusions."

"Obviously. Gabe and I don't even get along very well."

"The man's a fool if he doesn't appreciate you."

"You can't win 'em all," she answered lightly.

"Since Gabe is out of the picture, how about a date tonight? There's a dance at the country club every Sunday."

"Well . . ." She glanced over again at the other couple. This was her last night in Newport and she'd counted on spending it with Gabe—frustrating though it might be.

"I see." Stuart raised an eyebrow. "You two are a little more involved than you're admitting."

"You're wrong." Her jaw set as she watched Candace hook an arm around Gabe's neck and whisper something in his ear. Allison turned back to Stuart with a forced smile. "I'd love to go to the dance with you. The only reason I hesitated was because I didn't know if my hostess had anything planned for tonight."

"I'm sure she'd let you out of it."

"I'll have to check with her."

Allison was already regretting the momentary annoyance with Gabe that prompted her to accept a date with Stuart. This was her last night with Mary Louise, too. She really should make a final stab at convincing her to face reality.

"No second thoughts. You said you'd go to the dance with me and I intend to hold you to it," Stuart said playfully.

Pinky came over to join them. "How did the windsurfing go?" she asked Allison.

"Not great. I couldn't seem to get the hang of it."

"This was only your first lesson. You'll catch on. It's easier than waterskiing."

"I wouldn't even attempt *that.*"

Stuart gave her a surprised look. "You don't water-ski? I can see I have a lot to teach you." He gave her an intimate smile.

"Lots of luck," Gabe said dryly. He had strolled over to their group, with Candace clinging to his hand. "I tried, but I didn't get anywhere."

"Maybe there's something wrong with your technique." Stuart put his arm around Allison's shoulders.

"Nothing that *I* can see." Candace laughed.

A young man named Jason came over to talk to Pinky. "I have a couple of errands to do after I drop you off. Are you ready to leave, or do you want to catch a ride with somebody else?"

"No, I have to go home, too." Pinky turned to include Allison and Gabe. "If you two aren't doing anything tonight, we're all going to the country club."

"I already invited Allison," Stuart said. "She's going with *me.*"

Candace gazed through her lashes at Gabe. "Poor Gabe. Does that leave you at loose ends?"

"Not if you'll go to the dance with me," he answered.

"I thought you'd never ask." She laughed.

"That's all settled then," Pinky said. "I'll see you both tonight."

They all began to leave at once and everyone regrouped in the parking lot, discussing plans for the evening. Allison and Gabe didn't have anything to say to each other, which suited her fine. She had no interest in fencing with him.

After they'd driven in silence for a few blocks, he slanted a glance at her set profile and remarked, "You did all right for yourself today."

"You know I didn't," she answered coolly. "Windsurfing isn't my sport."

"I guess you'll just have to stick to hunting."

She whipped her head around to look at him indignantly. "I never shot anything in my life!"

"I was referring to a different kind of hunting. You have an unerring gift for setting your sights on big money. Did you know Stu was loaded, or did I give it away when I mentioned his trust fund?"

Allison felt a stab of pain that she didn't allow to show. "That gave me my first clue, and then I confirmed it by talking to him."

"A girl can't be too careful," Gabe said mockingly. "You know how many phonies there are in the world."

"I'm not in any danger of being taken in by them. That's for amateurs like you people."

He frowned when she didn't flare up at him. "Your act isn't very convincing, Allison. You're not as tough as you sound."

"I don't let very many people see this side of me, but I don't have to keep up a front with you," she taunted. "You knew I was a fortune hunter from the very beginning."

"Not from personal experience. What's the matter, don't I have enough money for you?"

"You're not a good prospect," she answered carelessly. "Too much competition."

"A woman with your charms doesn't have to worry about that." The glance he raked over her body was insolent.

Allison struggled to hang on to her temper. "There's always someone with more bountiful charms. You didn't have any trouble switching your attention today."

Something flared in Gabe's eyes and was masked instantly. "A man likes to hear a few words of appreciation every now and then."

"I'm sure you'll find Candace very accommodating," she replied stiffly.

"It does look like a promising evening."

"For both of us," she snapped as he braked to a stop in front of the Van Ruyder mansion.

Allison was out of the car instantly. She went into the house without a backward glance at Gabe, who followed with a thoughtful look on his face.

Mary Louise was coming down the staircase. "Did you and Gabriel have a nice day?" she asked.

"*He* did, anyway." When the older woman looked at her with a slight frown, Allison managed a smile. "I'm afraid I disgraced myself. I fell off the surfboard."

Mary Louise's brow cleared. "I'll have to speak to Gabriel about that. He should have taken better care of you."

"He was too busy making out with a blonde named Candace."

Gabe came into the house in time to hear Allison's statement. "That's not what happened at all," he told Mary Louise. "I was completely at the mercy of a predatory female."

Her laughing eyes appraised his tall, broad-shouldered frame. "You look as if you can defend yourself."

"*If* he wanted to," Allison said.

"Gabriel does have a lot of women running after him. Let's give him the benefit of a doubt."

"That's something Allison has never done," he said. "I was merely making a date with the young lady so I'd have somebody to take to the dance, as long as she accepted a date with Stu Harrison."

"You're both going out? I must tell Anita to serve dinner in the morning room, since there will just be Sergei and myself," Mary Louise said. "Martin and Laura have an engagement, too."

"I don't really want to go to the dance," Allison said truthfully. It wouldn't be any great joy to watch Candace wind herself around Gabe all night. "I'll stay home with you."

"Nonsense, child. I'm delighted that you're enjoying yourself."

"We haven't spent much time together," Allison persisted.

"We will tomorrow," Mary Louise promised.

"I have a noon flight, which means I'll have to leave here no later than eleven. That doesn't give us any time to speak of."

"Won't you reconsider and stay longer?" Mary Louise pleaded.

Allison hesitated. "I guess I could reschedule and take an evening flight." She was conscious of Gabe's enigmatic gaze. He was sure this was only a show of reluctance before letting herself be persuaded to stay. "It's such a lot of bother for just a few hours, though. Besides, Gabe would never forgive me," she said mockingly.

Mary Louise looked puzzled. "What does Gabriel have to do with it?"

"We planned to keep each other company on the plane," he cut in smoothly. "Don't give it another thought," he told Allison. "I could force myself to stay another week."

"I thought you might." She turned to the older woman. "If you're sure you don't mind my going out tonight, I'd better go wash my hair."

Allison's temper simmered all the time she was blow-drying her hair and putting on makeup. Her blue eyes smoldered as she applied eye shadow and mascara. She let her long hair hang loose around her shoulders, but her face got the full treatment—blush on her high cheekbones, pink gloss over deep pink lipstick, the works. Gabe was about to see what he was missing, she thought grimly.

The dress Mary Louise had bought her was perfect for an informal summer dance. The ruffled top was softly feminine, and the gauzy fabric was subtly sexy. Allison went downstairs complacently anticipating Gabe's reaction.

She had to settle for Stuart's. Gabe had already left.

Stuart was properly impressed, however. "You look fantastic!" He held her arms out from her sides, gazing at her slender body with avid eyes. "What did you do to yourself?"

"Took a shower and washed my hair," she answered briefly. His admiration wasn't as satisfying as Gabe's, somehow. "I'll say goodnight to Mary Louise and be with you in a minute."

The older couple were having cocktails in the library. They both checked her out with approval. "You look lovely, dear," Mary Louise said. "You'd better take a sweater, though. It might get cool later. Do you have your key?"

"It's in my purse." Allison laughed. "What time do I have to be home?"

"I know you're joking, but you do need your rest. You were up until all hours last night."

"You'd better run along before she reminds you to buckle your seat belt and phone if you're going to be late." Sergei chuckled.

Mary Louise's smile was misty. "You'll have to excuse me. It's been a long time since I've seen one of my children off on a date. I was always a worrier and old habits die hard."

"She'll be perfectly safe at the country club," Sergei teased, taking her hand. "And I'll be here to watch the clock with you."

Allison felt misty-eyed herself as she waved goodbye. Nobody had ever cared when—or even if—she came home.

The country club was crowded and very festive. Pinky and her crowd were already there, seated at a long table. She beckoned to them.

"Where have you been?" Pinky indicated the chairs next to her. "I saved you a place."

Allison wasn't thrilled to find herself sitting next to Gabe. Candace was on the other side of him, looking very sexy in a halter-neck dress that plunged deeply to show a lot of cleavage. She was monopolizing his attention, which didn't bother him in the least. He was smiling at her with amused tolerance.

Gabe did glance around after Allison was seated. "I see you finally made it," he remarked. "We thought maybe you stopped off someplace."

"Stu was a little late picking me up."

"That's not very promising." Gabe smiled mockingly. "He wasn't exactly counting the minutes till he saw you again."

She forced herself to match his tone instead of lashing back. "The night's young yet. He'll be putty in my hands by the time it's over."

"Stu has a reputation as a smooth operator. Make sure it's not the other way around."

"I can take care of myself."

"You haven't shown very good judgment so far."

"Because I wasn't taken in by *your* line? That only proves my point."

"I must be losing my touch," he said lightly.

"At least you're finally admitting it was all an act," she said, hiding her hurt.

"Not the part about wanting to make love to you." His voice deepened. "I still do."

Stuart put his arm around Allison's shoulder. "Stop hitting on my girl, Gabe. You have your own date."

"I couldn't cut you out if I tried." Gabe's smile was humorless. "Allison knows what she wants."

"That makes two of us." Stuart's embrace tightened. "What can I get you to drink, angel eyes?"

"Just a glass of white wine. No, wait." She looked directly at Gabe. "Make that champagne. I'm going for the gold tonight."

"Whatever your little heart desires." Stuart signaled to a waiter.

"Good hunting," Gabe murmured as Candace poutingly reclaimed his attention.

Allison tried to ignore him and enjoy herself, but it was difficult. She was conscious of his eyes following her, misinterpreting her every move.

Stuart was another problem. After Gabe's assurance that he had the inside track, Stuart was determined to pursue it. He held her in a tight embrace on the dance floor, and slid kisses over her cheek. She tried to put distance between them, with little success.

"You'll never get away from me, baby doll," he murmured. "We were made for each other."

"How can you tell on such short acquaintance?"

"I knew it the minute I laid eyes on you." He massaged the back of her neck. "You're the girl I've been looking for all my life."

"You must be very hard to satisfy," she said lightly. "I was told you've dated scores of them."

"Don't believe everything you hear about me. Rumors spring up because I don't lead a conventional life, holding down a regular job like most people. They think all I do is chase girls."

"But it isn't true?"

"Certainly not." He grinned. "I play tennis and golf, too. They're very time-consuming."

Gabe appeared next to them with Candace in his arms. He took note of Stuart's close embrace. "I see you're making progress," he commented sardonically.

"I'm trying to." Stuart chuckled.

He thought Gabe's remark was directed at him, but Allison knew better.

She found Stuart pleasant enough company when he didn't come on too strongly. He was amusing, and his admiration was a welcome antidote to Gabe's barbed comments. The only thing that bothered her slightly was the amount of Scotch he put away over the course of the evening. But it didn't seem to affect him, and it wasn't up to her to deliver a lecture.

All of the group were close friends. They changed partners and cut in on each other frequently. Allison danced with everyone except Gabe, which was a pure plus. They always got into an argument, so what was the use? Gabe evidently shared her view, since he didn't come near her.

It was almost midnight before he finally did ask her to dance. Maybe because he thought it would look strange, otherwise. He'd danced with all the other girls. Allison had kept track.

She rejected the belated invitation coolly. "You don't have to be polite. The evening is almost over, anyway."

"The orchestra is still playing," he answered mildly.

She shrugged. "Oh, all right."

"I *could* say, if it's such a chore, forget it," he remarked mockingly. "But I won't."

Allison walked stiffly beside Gabe to the dance floor, very conscious of his hand on her waist.

She was even more tense when he put his arms around her. It brought back memories of another time he'd held her close—for a different reason. His body had been urgent with desire then, and his mouth was a flame that ignited her own passion. The disturbing vision was dissipated by his derisive question.

"How are you making out with Stu?"

"Just dandy. I don't have to ask how you're doing with Candace. She's been clinging to you like ivy."

"It looks like we both struck gold. Do you plan to continue your romance with Stu in New York?"

"I haven't told him yet that I'm leaving tomorrow."

"It shouldn't be any problem. He spends a lot of time in the city. I'll call you for a progress report," Gabe said casually.

"I can't imagine why that would be of any interest to you. Your only concern was protecting the Van Ruyder fortune, and you've done that. Mary Louise didn't fall prey to my evil scheme. You won. We don't need to have any further contact."

"She's become very fond of you."

"And you think I'll use that to keep the pressure on?" Allison gave a harsh laugh. "That really presents you with a problem, doesn't it? You can't keep an eye on me every minute. Maybe you can tap my phone and hire a private detective to tail me."

"I was going to suggest that you accept Mary Louise's invitation to stay on until we resolve this matter. It would make things easier all around."

"I have no desire to make things easier for you," she replied hotly.

"Tell me something I *don't* know."

She stared at him suspiciously. "Why are you urging me to stay all of a sudden? On the way to the yacht club today, you said you couldn't wait to get out of here."

He smiled smugly. "That was before I met Candace."

Allison's flash of anger almost surpassed her feeling of rejection. "You'll just have to conduct your own long-distance romance," she said curtly. "Unlike the rest of you, I have to work for a living."

Stuart tapped Gabe on the shoulder. "I said you could *borrow* my girl. That means you're supposed to bring her back within a reasonable time."

"Nothing about Allison is reasonable." Gabe's smile was derisive, even though he added urbanely, "Every encounter with her is an unforgettable experience."

The evening ended soon after that. As a group of them stood under the outdoor canopy waiting for their cars to be brought around, Allison thanked Pinky for her hospitality.

"I'm glad we got to spend the day together, anyway. I wish you weren't going home tomorrow," Pinky said.

"What's all this?" Stuart demanded. "It's the first I've heard of it. You can't leave now," he told Allison. "We just met."

"I know. It's too bad," she said with simulated regret.

"Where are you going? Maybe I'll come, too."

"I'm returning to the working world. You wouldn't want to expose yourself to that," she joked.

"Not if I can help it." He grinned. "Life is too short to spend it with your nose to the grindstone. Stay here and play with me."

"Sorry, I used up all my playtime."

Stuart's car was brought around. It was a low, racy sports car, customized with all sorts of extras. Allison thought the discussion was over, but he brought it up again as they drove away.

"I really don't want you to go, Allie."

"That's very flattering, but I have to."

"Let's go have a drink and discuss it."

"It's after closing time. Nothing will be open."

"I know of an after-hours joint."

"I don't want any more to drink, Stu, and it's getting late. I really have to go home."

Allison had difficulty persuading him, but he finally took her back to Rosewood Manor. Instead of parking in front of the entrance, however, he stopped the car on a curve in the driveway under a large tree that cast a deep shadow. Even moonlight didn't filter through the thick branches.

When Stuart cut the engine she said lightly, "Is this my punishment? You're making me walk the rest of the way?"

"I don't play rough. I'm a lover, not a fighter." He snaked an arm around her waist and cupped her chin in his hand, urging her face toward his.

The liquor on his breath was unpleasant. Allison turned her head away. "I really have to go in, Stu."

"Not yet." He jerked her toward him and mashed his mouth against hers.

She struggled, but he had a grip like steel. When she finally managed to pull away slightly, his rasping breath told her he was aroused and potentially dangerous.

She tried to defuse the situation. "Come on, Stu, we're too old to make out in a car like teenagers. This car isn't built for it, anyway."

"You're right, gorgeous." He slid his hand under the hem of her skirt and caressed her thigh. "Let's take a stroll around to the pool and find one of those nice padded chaises."

She pushed his hand away. "Are you crazy? The whole family is at home!"

"Yeah, I guess it would be a little public." He gave a lewd laugh. "How about under this big tree? It's sort of kinky, but why not?"

She shoved him away and reached for the door handle. "You're disgusting!"

"Okay, so we'll go back to my place." He grabbed her arm and yanked her back, catching her off balance. As she sprawled at an angle across the seat, he curved a hand around her breast and strung wet kisses down her neck. "Anyplace you say, baby."

"Take your hands off me! Don't you understand the meaning of the word no?"

"Not when you've been sending me signals all night." His expression turned ugly. "There's a word for women like you."

"And there's one for men like *you*, but I don't use that kind of language."

Allison struggled upright and reached for the door again, but Stuart grabbed her roughly. "You've been asking for it and you're going to get it. No woman makes a fool out of Stu Harrison."

"That's because God got there ahead of us." She gritted the words through clenched teeth.

He swore pungently and gripped the front of her dress. With a swift movement he ripped her bodice to the waist. Allison gasped at the realization that he was out of control.

She fought him furiously. Stuart was stronger than she, but the sports car was an unlikely ally. A wide console separated the bucket seats, hindering his attempt to drag her onto his lap. By scratching and clawing until one arm was free, Allison finally managed to grab the door handle and turn it. She hung on as the heavy door swung open, tumbling her onto the ground.

She was on her feet in an instant, running for the house, but Stuart was right behind her. With a sinking feeling, Allison realized she'd never be able to get inside before he caught her. It seemed like a miracle when the front door opened and Gabe was silhouetted by the light.

She ran into his arms, clasping him tightly around the waist and burying her face in his shoulder. Gabe's arms closed around her as Stuart came pounding up.

"What the hell is going on?" Gabe demanded.

"Stay out of it," Stuart rasped. "This is between Allison and me. It's none of your business."

Gabe's face was flinty. "I'm making it my business. What did you do to her?"

Allison reluctantly withdrew from his comforting embrace. This was her mess to clean up. "It's all right. We just had a misunderstanding."

Gabe's expression darkened even more when he noticed her torn dress. She hastily pulled the two sides together, her cheeks warming.

"Leave us alone, Gabe," Stuart ordered. "I have a few things to say to Allison."

"I hope you can talk without any teeth," Gabe answered. "Because I'm going to knock yours out if you're not off the property in ten seconds."

Stuart blustered, but he wasn't reckless enough to ignore the rage in Gabe's eyes. With exaggerated nonchalance he returned to his car and revved the engine loudly as an act of defiance before driving away.

Allison went into the house silently, with Gabe following. She didn't want to discuss what had happened, but she was sure he did. Well, he was entitled.

"Are you all right?" He lifted her chin to look at her searchingly. "Did he hurt you?"

"No, I'm okay. I'm just glad you were here."

"I am, too." He smoothed her ruffled hair gently.

"What were you doing downstairs at this hour? Not that I'm complaining, but why weren't you in bed?"

"I was waiting to lock up. I thought you might forget."

There was something evasive about his answer. "You were waiting for me to come home, weren't you?" she asked quietly. "You expected something like this to happen."

"I know Stu better than you do."

"You might have warned me."

"Would it have done any good?"

"Of course it would! I'd have been able to discourage him ahead of time without hurting his feelings."

"That's very important, isn't it?" Gabe asked mockingly. "It wouldn't do for Stuart Harrison the Third to get his feelings hurt."

"I simply meant the situation wouldn't have gotten out of hand if I'd set him straight tactfully."

"What you really mean is, you're afraid I've scared him off permanently." Gabe's taut body radiated fury. "Maybe you didn't welcome my intervention after all."

The emotional scene she'd been through with Stuart had left Allison defenseless. She couldn't snap back at Gabe as she normally would have. Let him think whatever he wanted about her. He would anyway.

Gabe's anger drained away as he gazed at her tear-bright eyes and drooping shoulders. He reached out a hand to her face, then dropped it abruptly. "Go to bed, Allison, before I do something I'll regret," he said harshly.

Chapter Seven

Allison got out of bed reluctantly the next morning. She groaned at the prospect of all she had to do—pack, stand in line at the airport, go through the hassle of getting a cab in New York City. What she tried to avoid thinking about was Gabe and last night's fiasco.

Why did he misinterpret everything she said or did? It was so frustrating. First he showed concern over the horrendous incident with Stu, then he practically accused her of inviting it! She couldn't seem to do anything to please him.

Mary Louise and Sergei greeted Allison pleasantly when she went in to breakfast. Gabe merely nodded.

"How was the dance last night?" Mary Louise asked. "Did you enjoy yourself?"

"Yes, it was very nice," Allison answered politely. "The coffee smells heavenly," she remarked, hoping to divert her hostess.

"Armand made eggs Benedict this morning. Try some," Mary Louise urged, only momentarily distracted. "What time did you get home?"

Sergei smiled. "Are you going to ground her for breaking curfew?"

"Don't be absurd. I thought I heard voices during the night. I simply wondered what time it was."

Gabe spoke up for the first time. "That must have been the three of us saying good-night. Stu and Allison came home right after I did. I'm sorry we were so noisy."

"I wasn't complaining," Mary Louise said with a smile. "It feels good to have young people around again, coming and going at all hours."

"Speaking of going—I'd better phone the airport and see if I can change my ticket to a later flight," Allison said.

"Won't you please stay longer?" Mary Louise pleaded. "At least for another week."

Allison shook her head. "I wish I could, but I have to go back to work."

"You can telephone your place of business and tell them you're going to be unavoidably detained."

Allison smiled wryly. "They might tell me I'm unavoidably fired."

"I'm sure they wouldn't be that unreasonable. You could at least ask," Mary Louise coaxed.

"What do you have to lose?" Gabe surprised her by asking.

Allison couldn't imagine what he was up to. Maybe disagreeing with her had just gotten to be a habit, but she couldn't hold out against all of them. Sergei sided with the others. Finally she agreed to make the call, just to end the argument.

Carla Fenton was Allison's friend, as well as her boss. She knew Allison's whole story, including why she'd gone to Newport.

"I'm so glad to hear from you!" Carla exclaimed. "I've been dying of curiosity. What happened? Was your mission accomplished?"

"No, the woman I came to see died a month ago."

"Oh, I'm so sorry! Is this the end of the line, or were you able to find out if she really was your mother? I guess you could hardly question her relatives, under the circumstances."

"It was a little sticky at first. Monica's brother was ready to call the police, but his mother listened to my story. She's a wonderful woman. She actually invited me to stay here at the Van Ruyder estate. That's where I'm calling from."

"Wonderful! That must mean she believes you're her granddaughter."

"Not necessarily." Allison sighed. "She's so desperate for a grandchild that she's willing to accept me, no questions asked."

"Don't fight it." Carla laughed. "You're an heiress. They are *the* Van Ruyder family, aren't they? The Park Avenue ones?"

"Yes, but that part isn't important. All I want from them is the truth."

"You have something against being rich?" Carla asked skeptically.

"I can't even conceive of it—at least, not this rich. You have no idea how these people live. The house is a mansion, and there are servants to do everything but cut up your meat."

"That's bad? I'll bet you could get used to it."

"You don't understand. It wouldn't answer my questions. I came here to find out who my parents were, so I don't always have to write down 'unknown.' That might not sound like a big deal, but I found out the hard way that it is to some people."

"Bruce is a jerk and so are his parents," Carla said succinctly. "You're well rid of him, but I understand what you're saying."

"Unfortunately Mary Louise doesn't want to dig any deeper. I believe she's afraid to find out anything that will prove I'm wrong."

"Do you think you are?"

"I honestly don't, but I'm up against a wall of silence. She's wonderful to me in every other way. That's the reason I'm calling. Mary Louise wants me to stay longer. I told her it was impossible, but she insisted on my asking."

"No problem. Business is always slow during the summer months. Our kind of customers are all vacationing at one resort or another. Some of the salespeople have been asked to take voluntary time off."

Allison had mixed emotions, thinking of Gabe. "It would really be all right if I took another week?"

"Absolutely. You'd be crazy to pass up an opportunity like this. Take lots of snapshots so I can see how the other half lives." Carla laughed. "That's probably as close as I'll ever get."

Allison met Gabe when she came out of the library where she'd gone to use the phone. She braced herself for another confrontation, but he surprised her.

"I want to apologize for my behavior last night," he said quietly. "I shouldn't have hassled you about Stu."

"It's all right," she murmured. "You were there when I needed you. That's what counts."

"You've very forgiving." After a moment's hesitation he said, "Did you change to a later flight?"

"No, my boss said I could stay." She gave him a lopsided smile. "It looks like we're stuck with each other for another week. Unless you're willing to leave me here without supervision."

Gabe's smile suffused his entire face. "Who would ride to your rescue if I wasn't around?"

"You don't have to worry. I intend to stay far away from Stuart Harrison the Third."

His expression changed. "Do you *want* me to leave, Allison?"

She glanced down to pick an invisible piece of lint off her blouse so he wouldn't read the truth in her eyes. Another week with Gabe wouldn't change their relationship, but it was like a gift from heaven.

His jaw set as he stared at her bowed head. "I guess I got my answer."

She looked up quickly. "You can't leave me now. I have terrible judgment about men. What if I meet up with another Stu?"

Gabe's taut body relaxed and he frowned at her with mock severity. "Okay, but I don't intend to lose any more sleep over you. You'll just have to hang out with *me* this week."

Mary Louise joined them in time to hear his joking remark. Her face lit up. "Does this mean you're going to stay?" she asked Allison.

"For another week. That will give us lots of time to talk," Allison added deliberately.

"That's wonderful, dear! I'm so pleased."

"I am, too. Why don't we sit down now over another cup of coffee?"

"I wish I could, but I have a committee meeting this morning and I must make a few phone calls first. We'll get together later this afternoon."

As Mary Louise bustled off, Allison said to Gabe, "I don't know what to do with her. Why did she insist that I stay if she doesn't plan to spend any time with me?"

"You have a whole week to wear her down."

One of the maids came into the hall to tell Allison she had a telephone call. Stuart phoning to apologize? She couldn't think who else it could be.

Gabe's face was grim as the same thought occurred to him. "You don't have to talk to him—unless you want to."

She didn't. "Tell the gentleman I've gone out."

"That's giving him the benefit of the doubt," Gabe muttered.

"It's Miss Gresham on the phone," Florence informed her.

"It was so hectic last night that I forgot to give you my phone number in the city," Pinky said after Allison picked up the receiver. "I'm glad I caught you before you left."

"I'm not leaving after all. I managed to get another week's vacation."

"That's super! Will I see you today? The gang was going to drop over here for a pool party, but we decided to go to the club for a few sets of tennis instead. I can have Stu pick you up."

"No, thanks, that didn't work out."

"Did he get out of line last night? What a geek!" Pinky said disgustedly. "Well, no problem. I can stop by and pick you up, or maybe Gabe could give you a lift. If he doesn't have a date with Candace. They got really chummy last night."

"*She* did, anyway," Allison said coolly. "The poor man couldn't get away from her."

"He didn't seem to be trying too hard." Pinky laughed. "Candace knows all the right moves."

"She and Stu would make a good pair."

"They've already been that route. She's out for fresh game. Listen, I have to run. Shall I pick you up?"

"No, thanks, I'll get there on my own if I can make it," Allison said.

"Get where?" Gabe had come into the library looking for her.

"Pinky and her crowd are going to the tennis club."

"It sounds like fun. Do you want to go?"

"No, but don't let that stop *you*. Candace will undoubtedly be there," Allison couldn't help adding.

"Then you have to come, too." He grinned. "It's your turn to protect *me*."

"Are you sure you want protection?"

"I'm not crazy about predatory females. I'm just perverse enough to want the ones I can't have."

Allison felt immensely better. "That certainly rules out Candace."

"So, why don't you want to go to the tennis club?"

"It certainly doesn't have anything to do with *her.*"

"Okay, then I repeat, why don't you want to go?"

"I have some things to do," she answered vaguely.

"Like what?"

"Do you have to know every move I make?" she demanded.

"I do when you're acting strangely. What do you plan to do today?"

"Nothing special." Allison knew Gabe wouldn't give up until she gave him a valid reason. Since she couldn't think of one he'd accept, she had to tell the truth. "I don't know how to play tennis," she muttered.

"Is that all? What's the big deal?"

"It's just one more reminder that I don't belong here." Allison's frustration boiled over. "I don't play tennis, I can't windsurf or sail. I don't even know why I agreed to stay another week. Mary Louise won't sit down and talk openly to me. If I had any sense I'd get on a plane and go home tonight."

Gabe folded his arms and gazed at her calmly. "Are you through feeling sorry for yourself?"

"As usual, you're totally wrong about me! I have a very positive attitude about myself. Maybe I don't excel at a lot of the sports you people are proficient in, but that's only because I never had an opportunity to learn."

"I couldn't have said it better myself." His hand closed around her wrist. "Come with me."

"Where are you taking me?" She had to trot to keep up with his long strides as they left the house and began walking across the green lawn.

"I'm going to make a tennis player out of you, since you seem to regard it as some sort of Holy Grail."

"That was only an example. It won't work, Gabe. You tried to teach me how to windsurf, and look what happened."

His pace slowed as he gazed down at her. "What happened had nothing to do with your ability. I won't try to teach you contact sports from now on."

"Windsurfing isn't a contact sport," she murmured.

"It isn't supposed to be. That's how we got into trouble," he said wryly. They had reached the tennis court where he took two rackets and a can of balls out of an equipment box. "Okay, first we'll work on your forehand."

Gabe lobbed easy balls across the net in the beginning, so Allison could return them and build her confidence. He taught her how to serve and how to stroke fluidly.

She was panting by the end of the lesson and her muscles ached, but she was exhilarated.

"You did great." Gabe put his arm around her shoulders as they walked off the court. "You could be an excellent tennis player if you kept at it."

"You're just saying that."

"Why would I?"

Allison gazed up at his handsome face. "Because you're a very nice man," she said softly.

His arm tightened, drawing her against his lithe body. After a brief moment he released her, saying lightly, "Too bad good guys finish last."

The next couple of days were a pure delight. Allison and Gabe hung out with Pinky and her crowd at private clubs, eating, drinking and being waited on. It was a once-in-a-lifetime vacation. That's the way Allison resigned herself to thinking of her visit.

On the occasions when she and Gabe had dinner with Mary Louise and Sergei, Martin was mercifully absent so the evenings were very pleasant. Mary Louise couldn't do enough for Allison, but she resisted every effort to turn the conversation to Monica.

"I'm ready to give up," Allison remarked to Gabe as they returned to the house on Wednesday afternoon. "I'll never be able to pin Mary Louise down."

"You still have time left." He stopped the car in front of the door. "She might be out in the garden. See if you can corner her there. I have some phone calls to make. I'll see you later."

Allison wandered into the garden without much hope. There was no sign of Mary Louise, but she lingered to enjoy the beautiful surroundings. After strolling along a brick path for a while Allison sat on a wrought-iron bench under a flowering tree, gazing at a bed of purple and white petunias.

Footsteps on the path turned out to be Sergei's. "You're looking very pensive," he said. "Is anything wrong?"

"Nothing is allowed to go wrong at Rosewood Manor." She smiled ruefully. "Mary Louise doesn't permit it."

"Can you blame her for not wanting to face reality? None of us would if we didn't have to. Let her have her fantasies," Sergei said gently. "She hasn't had a lot to make her happy, in spite of what you might think."

"You love her very much, don't you?"

"More than anyone will ever know," he answered quietly.

"Then why on earth don't you ask her to marry you?"

"I'm sure you know why."

"She's in love with you," Allison said bluntly. "Isn't that more important than the opinion of a few mean-spirited people?"

Sergei looked startled. "You're wrong about Mary Louise. She likes having me around, but only as a friend. I provide her with companionship and make her laugh when she gets discouraged. If she knew how I felt, she'd be uncomfortable. I wouldn't even have her friendship anymore."

"She does know how you feel—or at least she guesses."

"How do you know that?" he asked intently. "She's never given me any indication."

"If she were my age, Mary Louise would probably propose to *you*. Women go after what they want in today's world. But you have to realize that Mary Louise was raised with all kinds of silly inhibitions. She'll wait for you to tell her you love her—and you'll blow it because you're afraid of public opinion."

"Do you think that would stop me if I really thought she loved me?" he demanded.

Allison smiled. "Take my advice and go for it, pal."

Sergei's eyes gleamed with excitement. "Thanks, I might just do that! How about you?"

"I don't know what you mean."

"In spite of my advanced years, my eyesight is still excellent. I've watched you and Gabe together. You light up a room."

"Your eyesight might be good, but you jumped to the wrong conclusion. It's different with Gabe and me. The only thing involved is sex."

"Are you admitting the feeling is mutual?" Gabe had approached so silently that neither of them heard him.

After a glance at their faces, Sergei rose from the bench. "This seems to be the day for letting it all hang out. I'm going back to the house to do some serious thinking."

There was a moment of silence after he left. Gabe broke it. "You haven't answered my question."

"We've been getting along so well. Why rock the boat?"

As she started to walk by him, back to the house, he put his hands on her arms. "It's time we were up-front with each other about our feelings."

"I'm not sure that's a good idea," Allison answered carefully. "It will only lead to an argument."

"Maybe not, if we both feel the same way," he said softly.

"I already know how you feel, but it hasn't changed your opinion of me. You still think I came here under false pretenses. You're just willing to overlook it for a few passion-filled hours." Bitterness colored her voice.

Gabe cupped her cheek gently in his palm. "An entire week with you wouldn't be enough. I don't care anymore why you came here. I'm just glad you did."

Allison stared at him, feeling a dawning happiness that warmed her like sunshine. Was it possible that Gabe really cared about her?

As they gazed at each other wordlessly, Anita came down the path. "There's a gentleman to see you, Miss Riley."

Gabe's bemused expression changed to a scowl. "Stu again? What does it take to discourage the jerk?"

"It's a Mr. Bruce Dunham," the maid said. "Shall I bring him out here, or show him into the drawing room?"

A chill raced up Allison's spine. How had Bruce found her—and why? Gabe mustn't be allowed to meet him! She couldn't bear to have him find out about her humiliating rejection.

"Tell the gentleman I'll be right with him," she said hastily.

Gabe's hand closed around her wrist, preventing her from leaving. "No, bring him out here."

The maid couldn't fail to notice the sudden tension between the two, but she was too well trained to question a direct order. Especially since Gabe's was delivered with greater authority. After a moment's hesitation, Anita returned to the house.

"You had no right to do that," Allison said in a low voice. "This has nothing to do with you."

All the former tenderness was gone from his face, leaving it cynical. "Everything you do concerns me. I'm the Van Ruyder watchdog, remember? I'd like to meet your confederate."

"It's typical of you to jump to conclusions, but you happen to be wrong. Bruce is . . . he's just someone I used to know."

"He evidently prizes the relationship more than you do," Gabe drawled. "He couldn't wait another week to see you. Or did he come for a progress report?"

"I have no idea why he came," Allison answered truthfully.

"A glitch in plans?" Gabe asked sardonically. "From the look on your face, this is obviously a departure from your original strategy. It will be interesting to hear his explanation for this unexpected appearance."

"My hostess might require one, but I don't have to answer to you." Allison jerked her wrist away and turned toward the house.

It was too late. Bruce was hurrying along the path toward them.

He looked a little surprised to see Gabe, but his face lit up at the sight of Allison. "It's great to see you, Allie! I've missed you like the very devil."

"What are you doing here, Bruce?" she asked tautly.

He looked slightly taken aback, but not for long. "I've been phoning you for days. I was getting worried when I couldn't get you, so I called Carla at the store. She told me where you were and I decided to hop over and pay you a surprise visit."

Knowing Carla's opinion of him, Allison could figure out what happened. Carla couldn't resist the opportunity to rub it in. She wanted Bruce to know what he'd missed out on— the chance to marry an heiress. She probably told him it was an accepted fact.

"It's been too long, Allie," Bruce said in a deepened voice.

"We can't talk now," she said. "Tell me where you're staying and I'll phone you."

"Why don't you ask Mary Louise to put him up here?" Gabe asked mockingly. "There's plenty of room and she'd do anything you asked. Allison has made a lot of progress in a short time," he told Bruce.

"That would be fantastic!" Bruce's eyes shone with excitement. "I'd love to meet the Van Ruyders."

"Gabe was only joking," she said sharply. "I couldn't possibly ask Mary Louise to let you stay here."

"Let her work on it. Allison prefers the subtler approach." Gabe looked appraisingly at the other man. "Since she won't introduce us, we'll have to do it ourselves. I'm Gabe Rockford." He didn't extend his hand.

"Nice to meet you, Rockford. I'm Bruce Dunham, Allison's fiancé."

Gabe's jaw tightened. "I see. Well, it's nice to keep your little scheme in the family."

"He is not my fiancé," Allison stated grimly. "How could you tell him a thing like that?" she asked Bruce.

"Don't be angry at me, darling." He gave Gabe a humorous wink. "We had a little falling out. You know how it is."

"No, I'm afraid I don't," Gabe replied. "Why don't you tell me? What did you and Allison argue about?"

"It isn't important." She cut in swiftly, before saying to Bruce in a determined voice, "We have nothing further to discuss—and certainly not here."

"I know you were hurt, sweetheart. I handled things badly and I'm sorry. But everything's going to be all right now."

Allison stared at him, wondering how she'd ever considered herself in love with Bruce. He was handsome enough, blond and athletic, the perennial college boy even in his thirties. It was strange that she'd never noticed how weak his chin and mouth were. Or how superficial he was. Bruce was practically salivating at the prospect of being part of the Van Ruyder family.

"Why didn't you tell me you were related to the Van Ruyders?" he asked.

"Allison is full of little secrets," Gabe drawled. "You never know for sure what she's up to."

"You can say *that* again! I was knocked for a loop when Carla told me the news. This solves everything!"

"That's the nice thing about money," Gabe remarked satirically.

"This is about more than money. The Van Ruyders are the cream of society. There won't be any opposition to our wedding now," Bruce told Allison.

Gabe's eyes narrowed. "Somebody objected?"

Bruce barely heard him. He was glancing toward the imposing mansion. "Maybe we could have the wedding right here. Wouldn't that be spectacular?"

Allison was so furious that she no longer cared who knew the shameful story of her broken engagement. Did Bruce honestly think she'd excuse his parents' unforgivable behavior and his own spineless failure to stand by her?

"I wouldn't get your hopes too high," she said bitingly.

"You could at least mention it. You never know if you don't ask."

"I'm sure your mother would love to get her toe in the door, but I can't help her climb the social ladder."

"Don't be bitter, darling. Mother really likes you. She's just a little old-fashioned about some things. I know you'll get to be great friends after we're married."

"There isn't going to be any marriage," Allison said bluntly. "Monica Van Ruyder was not my mother."

"But Carla said—"

"Carla was just pulling your chain."

"I don't understand. You're a guest here. How can that be if you're not related to them? They wouldn't invite a perfect stranger into the house. You didn't know them before, did you?"

"It's a long, involved story." Allison just wanted to get rid of him. Bruce had already done his damage. "Take my word for it, I'm as unacceptable now as I was before."

He looked distressed, yet unwilling to give up. "Maybe not. The Van Ruyders must like you," he said thoughtfully. "That should count for something."

"Go away, Bruce," she said tautly. "It's over."

"I don't intend to give up this easily."

"Why not? You did last time."

"I never saw this side of you," he complained. "You've changed."

"*You* haven't."

"Don't be that way. We can work this out, Allie." He reached for her hand.

Gabe stepped between them. "I think the lady asked you to leave."

Bruce's weak mouth curled. "Now I'm beginning to get it. You found a better prospect," he said to Allison.

Gabe answered for her. "*Any* man would fit the description."

"I don't have to take that from you!" Bruce flared.

"You do if you don't get out of here." Gabe's eyes glittered dangerously, although his voice remained calm. "The choice is up to you. Either leave of your own free will, or I'll take great pleasure in throwing you out."

"Is that what you want?" Bruce demanded of Allison.

"Just leave," she said wearily.

"Okay, but this time I won't be back," he blustered.

The only sound in the silence that fell was Bruce's footsteps receding down the path. Allison wished Gabe would leave her alone, too, but he stayed.

"Why didn't you tell me?" he said finally.

Her mouth twisted in self-mockery. "If you were once engaged to someone like Bruce, would you brag about it?"

"How long ago did all this happen?" Gabe asked quietly.

"A couple of months ago. He called me a few times afterward, but I haven't seen him until today."

"He let his parents break you up? That seems incredible."

She shrugged. "I told you I was a lousy judge of men."

"What objection could they possibly find with you?"

"That should be fairly obvious. I'm a nobody of uncertain parentage—although I'm sure they spoke more graphically among themselves." She smiled sardonically.

A look of pain crossed Gabe's face. He made an imperceptible movement toward her, but something about her stiff posture warned him off.

"I didn't want you to know," she continued in an unemotional voice. "It isn't something I'm proud of. That's why I was so upset when Bruce turned up here, not because he was a conspirator in some nefarious scheme."

"I'm sorry. I was way out of line."

"It doesn't matter. You've always been suspicious of me. Why should today be any different?"

"Seeing Bruce again upset you. I can understand that. But you're not being fair. I came here with an open mind."

"Why do men find it impossible to tell the truth?" she asked angrily. "You had doubts then, and you still do."

"Certainly things bothered me in the beginning," he admitted. "Like your timing. It seemed a little questionable that you only decided to look into your background after Monica was gone and couldn't confirm or deny your claim. Now I understand why your visit came when it did, and what motivated it."

"How did she die?" Allison asked abruptly. "No one would ever tell me that, either."

"Her death was enough of a tragedy for the family," he said evasively. "Talking about it is painful."

"You see? You still don't trust me!"

"She died of alcohol and enough pills to stock a pharmacy," Gabe answered reluctantly. "How she accomplished it is a mystery, because she was in a rehab center at the time. Monica was a master at manipulating people, no doubt about it. She talked somebody into supplying her needs."

"How did you manage to keep a thing like that a secret?"

"I suppose most of Mary Louise's friends had their suspicions, but a lot of them have skeletons in their own closets. They banded together in a code of silence, and some influential people were successful in keeping the cause of death out of the newspapers. You can see why the family doesn't want the circumstances to become known."

"Was it suicide?"

"Who knows? Although I doubt it. In my personal opinion, Monica was too fond of life to exit willingly. She might just have been rebelling against the rules of the sanatorium, the way she broke rules all her life. To show she could do it. Unfortunately this time she didn't get away with it."

"What a terrible waste."

"Yes, she was living proof that money can't buy happiness."

Allison stiffened. "Is that directed at me? You never quit, do you?"

"Aren't you overreacting rather drastically? It was just a general statement, and not a very original one at that."

"You'd be sensitive, too, in my position," she answered heatedly. "Ask Sergei what it's like to have people suspect your every motive. If Mary Louise would only cooperate with me, I'd be out of here like a shot. All I want is to know who I am. Why can't anyone understand that?"

"I do, honey," he answered gently. "I didn't before, but after finding out what that clown Bruce put you through, I do now."

He moved toward her, but she backed away. "I don't need pity."

Gabe's face darkened as he grabbed her by the shoulders and jerked her toward him. "Has anybody ever told you that you're a very aggravating woman?"

"Add that to the list of all the other things you don't like about me."

His jaw set. "You sure don't make it easy for somebody to be on your side."

"When were you ever?" she scoffed.

"If you weren't so busy fighting the whole world, you might have noticed that I care about you."

"I'll bet you also brought home stray dogs and cats when you were a little boy. Well, thanks, but I don't need anybody's help. I can fight my own battles."

Gabe swore under his breath. "I can't seem to make a dent in that stubborn little mind of yours, so maybe I can get through to you this way."

He jerked her into an almost bruising embrace and kissed her so hard she was breathless. Allison made indignant little sounds of protest, which he ignored. His arms were wrapped around her, welding her body to his taut frame. Struggling was useless. She was completely helpless in his arms.

Gradually Gabe's fury lessened and the pressure of his mouth was no longer punishing. His kiss became sensually provocative, sparking a response from Allison. She stopped struggling when his tongue teased her lips apart for a stirring exploration of the moist interior.

Gabe's tight grip had loosened, becoming an embrace instead of a restraint. His hands caressed her back, wandering down to cup her buttocks and urge her even closer to his hardened loins.

Allison's response was immediate. She curled her arms around his neck and returned his kiss with the same urgency. She wanted to get even closer than this, to feel his nude body against hers, filling her with joy.

Gabe finally dragged his mouth away and buried his face in her hair. "Why do we always argue, when all I want to do is make love to you?" He kissed her temple, her closed eyelids, each corner of her mouth. "I never thought I could love anyone this much. You have me bewitched."

Allison tensed, sure that she'd heard what she *wanted* to hear. "What did you say?"

He lifted his head to smile at her. "I said you're bewitching."

"No, before that."

"I can't remember. You see how befuddled you've made me?"

Allison knew it was too good to be true. He'd gotten carried away in the heat of passion, but he wasn't about to repeat the error.

Gabe stroked her hair tenderly. "All I can think about is how much I love you."

She stared at him incredulously. "Do you really mean it?"

"Don't tell me you didn't know. Haven't I made a complete idiot of myself, getting jealous and making a scene over every man who comes near you?"

"They're both such jerks," she said uncertainly. "I didn't think it was anything personal."

"How about my unremitting suggestions that we make love?" he teased. "Didn't that give you a clue?"

"Not really. That doesn't necessarily involve love."

"It does with me. I want more than your body, sweetheart, I want all of you." His kiss this time held great tenderness. After a satisfying few moments he tilted her chin up. "I haven't heard a similar commitment from you. Am I just kidding myself?"

"Is this answer enough?" She pulled his head down for a passionate kiss.

When he could speak, Gabe said huskily, "We're going to have a marriage made in heaven."

Allison could only stare at him. "You're asking me to marry you?"

"Of course I am. Haven't you been listening?"

"Yes, but I thought you only wanted..."

"I do." He chuckled wickedly. "Constantly. Our life together will be one long honeymoon."

Allison came down to earth with a thud. "We can't get married, Gabe."

"Give me one good reason."

"The same one that broke off my engagement to Bruce. I have no background, no family, even my name doesn't belong to me. I know you'll say it doesn't matter, but it will to your parents. Trust me."

"You're right about it not mattering to me, and it won't to my parents, either. They aren't the kind of narrow-minded bigots that spawned a wimp like Bruce."

"I'm sure they're kinder and more intelligent, but they still won't approve."

"I think they will, but that's really beside the point. I'm a grown man. The choice is up to me."

Allison turned away. "You're very close to your parents. I've heard the affection in your voice when you talk about them. It must be wonderful to have a relationship like that," she said wistfully. "I would never want to spoil it for you."

"You couldn't be anything but a blessing." Gabe smoothed her hair gently. "I wish I could give you what you've missed, darling. It isn't possible to change the past, but from now on you'll have a family that cares about you. My parents will love you as much as I do."

"I wish I could believe that," she said somberly.

"Wait and see." He took her hand. "We'll phone them right now with the good news."

"No." She pulled her hand away. "Let's wait until we get back to New York."

"You have nothing to be afraid of, angel. They're wonderful people."

"I'm sure of that, but I'd just rather meet them in person first."

Gabe wasn't satisfied, but after a lot of coaxing he finally agreed. "Okay, you win. I guess I'll have to settle for Mary Louise and Sergei. I have to tell *somebody* we're engaged."

"I'd rather you didn't, Gabe."

"Listen to me, Allison. I don't intend to let you get away," he said firmly. "We are going to get married."

"I want to so much that I'm afraid to believe it will actually come true. Let's just keep this our secret for a little while. If nobody knows, nothing can happen to spoil things."

"My dearest love, what can I do to assure you that my feelings will never change?"

"Just keep on loving me," she whispered yearningly.

"That's the easy part." He sighed. "I can see you need more assurance than mere words, so I'll have to give it to you."

"What do you mean?"

"I'm going to find out who your parents were."

"I'm beginning to think that's impossible. Mary Louise is the only person who might have a clue, but she refuses to tell me anything. Her friends clam up when Monica's name is mentioned, and the father of the baby has kept the secret all these years. He isn't about to admit it now. What more can I do?"

"You can leave it to me. Cross-examining witnesses is my field of expertise. I don't let them off the hook—as you've noticed." He grinned.

Allison gazed at him with pure love in her eyes. "I'll bet you've never had a witness so willing to cooperate."

"I'll remind you of that later tonight," Gabe murmured.

Chapter Eight

Gabe took Allison out to dinner that night to celebrate their engagement, although they didn't tell anybody that was the reason.

"I think Sergei guesses," Gabe remarked as they were having champagne to toast the occasion.

"I hope it gives him ideas," Allison said. "We had a talk this afternoon and I advised him to propose to Mary Louise."

"What did he say to that?"

"He said he'd consider it, but I'm not so sure. I understand how he feels."

"*I* don't," Gabe said impatiently. "When two people love each other, that's all that matters. Even more so in their case. They aren't getting any younger."

"Is that why you asked me to marry you?" Allison teased. "Because you're afraid of advancing old age?"

The candle's flame was reflected in his eyes as he gazed across the table at her. "Would you like proof of my virility?"

"I wasn't questioning that," she answered softly.

His hand tightened on hers. "It's going to be so good with us, sweetheart."

Allison didn't have to be told that. She couldn't wait to lie naked and uninhibited in Gabe's arms. Her whole body throbbed in anticipation of his torrid caresses.

Drawing a shaky breath, she said, "We'd better talk about something else."

"You're right, what I have in mind for us is very private. This is not the place."

"So...what would you like to do after dinner?" she asked brightly.

He chuckled. "I wouldn't call that changing the subject."

"You're not cooperating," she complained.

"Okay, angel, let's talk about our wedding. Do you want a big one with all the trimmings? The only trouble is, those things take time to organize. If it was solely up to me we'd get married right away, but I realize a bride wants the full treatment."

"I'll have to think about it," she replied.

"I don't like the sound of that. We're getting married if I have to drag you to the altar," he warned.

Allison decided she was being foolish. Even if history repeated itself and their marriage never took place, why deny herself the joy of planning for it? Who knows? Maybe her luck would change.

"Where will we live afterward?" she asked. "Do you have an apartment? I know so little about your everyday life. We always seem to talk about me."

"Ask me anything you like. I have an apartment we can use for now, but we'll undoubtedly want more space. Until we find something, you can redecorate my place any way you please."

"I wouldn't know how to go about it."

"My mother will be glad to help. She's good at that sort of thing. At one time they had an apartment in London, their town house in New York and the home here. She finally decided it was a lot easier to stay in a hotel when they traveled. They have a standing invitation to stay with Dad's brother when they come to Newport, though. I do, too. There's plenty of room."

"Do you feel sad about going back to your old home? Is that why you stayed with Mary Louise instead of your uncle?"

"He happens to be out of town, but I stayed at Rosewood Manor so I could keep an eye on *you*." He laughed. "I didn't know you'd turn into a commitment for life."

"That sounds like a sentence," she complained.

"I couldn't ask for a more perfect cellmate."

"Would you have come if you'd known?" she asked softly.

"Like a shot. You're the woman I've been searching for all my life."

They were gazing wordlessly into each other's eyes when the waiter arrived with their first course.

During dinner, Gabe told Allison about the summers he spent in Newport as a boy, and later a teenager.

"Was Monica here when you were?" Allison asked.

He nodded. "I used to see her racing around town in a red convertible. My friends and I all thought she was really cool, although we were too young to understand the whispered gossip about her." Gabe laughed. "I'll never forget the look on my mother's face when I asked her what skinny-dipping meant."

"Did she tell you?" Allison smiled.

"No, she sent me out to pick strawberries for dinner, figuring I'd forget about it by the time I got through. We had a kitchen garden in those days. You don't know what a tomato tastes like until you've eaten one right from the vine."

"I wish I could have seen your summer home."

"Would you like to stop by after dinner?"

"I thought you said your uncle is out of town."

"He is, but I have a key. I'm welcome to use it anytime."

Gabe's former home wasn't as opulent as Rosewood Manor, but it was by no means average. A tall iron fence enclosed the extensive grounds that surrounded the three-story, rough-cut granite home. On one side, an open porch stretched the length of the house, with a line of spaced pillars supporting the sheltering roof.

"I didn't expect anything this grand," Allison gasped.

"It's modest compared to the Van Ruyder place. Come inside, I'll show you around."

Her eyes widened at the polished parquet floors covered with oriental rugs in the double drawing room, the expanse of Tiffany glass bricks and tiles that formed one wall of the dining room.

The bedrooms upstairs were equally spacious and luxuriously furnished. Most of them served as guest rooms now, Gabe explained, since his cousins were grown and had left home.

"Which room was yours?" Allison asked.

He led her to a bedroom at the back of the house, overlooking a rectangular swimming pool that was an opalescent glimmer in the moonlight. The pool lights had been turned off, since nobody was in residence. Allison stood by the window, entranced.

"It looks so mysterious in the dark," she remarked. "Like an enchanted lake in a fairy tale."

"I can turn on the pool lights. Would you like to go swimming?"

"We don't have our bathing suits with us."

"All the better. I'll leave the lights off and we'll go skinny-dipping. Since I've grown up, I found out what that meant."

Excitement fizzed through her as Gabe put his arm around her waist and slowly slid her zipper down. "I've never gone skinny-dipping," she murmured.

"It's easy." He slipped the dress off her shoulders and unhooked her bra. "First you take off all your clothes."

"You're doing it for me," she said faintly.

"I'll let you return the favor in a minute." He lowered his head to string a line of kisses across her breasts.

Allison uttered a delighted cry as his tongue circled one of her sensitive nipples. He heightened the pleasure by capturing one little bud between his lips while her dress slithered to the floor.

Molten desire filled her as his fingers slipped inside the waistband of her panty hose. She could barely stand while he rolled them down her hips, sinking to his knees in front of her. When she was completely nude, he caressed her thighs lingeringly.

"You're so exquisite." He stared at her with glittering eyes. "This is the way I've dreamed of seeing you."

"I dreamed about you, too," she murmured.

"Did you, darling? Was I doing this?" He kissed the soft skin of her stomach, then moved lower for an intimate kiss that destroyed all of her inhibitions.

Allison sank to the floor beside him and unfastened his tie. Her fingers were shaking as she impatiently tore open his shirt while Gabe fueled the flames by caressing her breasts.

"My wonderful, passionate Allison," he said huskily. "Tell me you're mine."

"Now and forever," she promised fervently. "There will never be anyone else for me."

"I intend to make sure of that." He kicked free of the slacks she'd unzipped and gathered her in his arms.

The sensation of their bare bodies joined together was so arousing that she moved against him restlessly, asking wordlessly for the ultimate embrace. Gabe's passion equaled hers. He parted her legs and plunged deeply, sheathing himself inside her.

They were consumed by their need for each other, almost wild in their desire to give and receive pleasure. Their bodies were taut with the rapture brought by every driving stroke. The flame that devoured them burned brighter and brighter until it was finally extinguished in a gush of satisfaction. Their tense bodies relaxed and they clung together, utterly at peace.

"You are the love of my life," Gabe murmured, when his breathing slowed.

"And you are mine," she whispered.

They were quiet in each other's arms for long moments. Then Gabe began to chuckle. "I had a lot of fantasies in this bedroom when I was a little boy, but I never dreamed one like this would come true."

"You must have been a very precocious little boy." She smiled.

"About average. All little boys think about sex—big ones, too. What did you fantasize about?"

"Not sex. I was a late bloomer."

"What *did* you dream about?" he persisted.

"Oh, the usual girl things," she answered evasively.

"They must be really wicked if you don't want to talk about them," he teased. "You might as well tell me, because I don't intend to let you off the hook."

Allison knew he meant it. "I used to dream that my parents would come to get me one day," she said reluctantly. "They'd hug me and explain that I was kidnapped when I was a baby, and they'd been searching for me ever since."

Gabe's face sobered. "I'm sorry," he said in a muted voice.

"I knew you would be. That's why I didn't want to tell you. You're feeling guilty because you grew up in a mansion, but it's okay. You have to play the cards fate deals you, and look what happened. We both wound up in the same place. That's kind of ironic."

"It just proves we were meant to be. Although I would have found you no matter where you were."

"Maybe, but you must admit I made it easier for you." She tried to jolly him out of his subdued mood. "Didn't I hear you mention something about skinny-dipping?"

"Right. You took my mind off it temporarily."

"Well, I should hope so." She laughed, reaching for her clothes.

"What are you doing? I thought we were going for a moonlight swim."

"We are, but I have to put on something to wear out to the pool."

"Why? You're only going to get undressed again." He took her hand and led her out of the bedroom.

"This feels totally decadent," Allison protested as she and Gabe walked naked down the stairs.

"We merely shed our inhibitions." He stroked her bare bottom. "What's wrong with that?"

"What if your uncle should come home unexpectedly?"

"In the middle of the night?"

"It could happen. How would you explain what we're doing here completely nude?"

"Very simply. I'd just tell him a band of roving Gypsies stole our clothes."

"Gypsies in Newport, Rhode Island?"

"That's as likely as Uncle Herb turning up at two in the morning." Gabe opened the door to the outside patio. "Come on, let's go swimming."

The water felt unbelievably sensuous on Allison's bare body. While he swam the length of the pool, she floated languidly, letting the buoyant water hold her in its embrace. The ripples Gabe churned up lapped over her, like fleeting caresses.

He surfaced beside her, sprinkling her playfully with drops of water. "Are you just going to lie there and look gorgeous?"

She smiled enticingly. "What would you like me to do?"

"A leading question if ever I heard one." He leaned forward and touched his tongue to a drop of water on her shoulder, then to the one on the slope of her breast.

"You haven't answered it," she murmured.

"Does this give you a clue?"

His mouth glided over her breasts while his fingers traced an erotic pattern on her inner thighs. Allison's body sprang to instant life in response to his intimate caresses.

"I never get tired of touching you," he said huskily. "I want to know every secret inch of you."

She responded by searching out the hard male proof of his passion, wanting to know him in the same way. Gabe uttered a hoarse cry and gathered her in his arms, capturing her mouth for a deep kiss that she returned just as urgently.

When the water caused their bodies to sway apart, Allison wound her legs around his waist. She couldn't bear to be parted from him, even for an instant. For long moments they clung together, kissing almost frantically and murmuring unintelligible words of love.

Then Gabe gripped her hips and completed their union. It was like nothing she could have imagined. The heat from their joined bodies was so intense that it warmed the water that streamed over them, heightening the molten pleasure. Their ecstasy built like the tidal wave that finally engulfed them.

When it was over, Gabe carried Allison out of the pool and lowered her gently to a padded chaise. He dried her tenderly with some large towels he took from a wooden chest, then lay down beside her and took her in his arms again. No words were needed. They were content to lie quietly and savor the aftermath of their love.

Finally Allison stirred. "This has been so wonderful. I wish we could stay all night."

"We can, if you like. I suggest we go upstairs to bed, though." He chuckled. "That's the only place we haven't made love, but the night isn't over yet."

She stroked his face lovingly. "It's very tempting, but we have to go back to Rosewood Manor."

"Why?"

"Because we do. You know how it would look if they knew we'd stayed out all night."

"Everyone would guess we made love, which we did. I don't care who knows it. I'd like to tell the whole world how much I love you."

"That's so sweet, darling, but Mary Louise wouldn't understand. She lives by a very rigid code of ethics."

"I'm not so sure. After being exposed to us and Sergei, I think she's becoming liberated." Gabe grinned. "Besides, she'll make allowances when we tell her we're engaged."

"You promised you wouldn't!"

"After tonight, do you honestly think I'd let anyone or anything come between us?" When she looked at him with large, reproachful eyes, Gabe groaned. "Okay, angel, whatever you say. I don't know why I even bother. I've yet to win an argument with you."

"You can't have any complaints about tonight. We were both winners," she said softly.

He answered by kissing her with exquisite tenderness.

Gabe was up early the next morning, in spite of the fact that he'd had only a few hours sleep. On his way down to breakfast he stopped at Allison's door. When she didn't answer his light tap, he went inside.

She was curled up in the big bed sound asleep. He stood over her for a moment with a face softened by love. She opened her eyes when he leaned down to kiss her.

"I didn't mean to wake you, darling." He stroked her cheek. "Go back to sleep."

She gazed up at him with shining eyes. "Just tell me one thing. Was last night a dream?"

He reached under the covers to stroke her sleep-warm body. "I couldn't have imagined such perfection."

She made a soft sound of contentment. "When is your uncle Herb coming home? I could be persuaded to go back there."

"I'll take you up on your offer later. First I have something to do." He tucked the covers around her and kissed her tenderly. "Go back to sleep, angel."

Mary Louise and Sergei were having breakfast when Gabe joined them in the morning room.

She greeted him with a smile. "Good morning, Gabriel. Did you and Allison have a pleasant evening together?"

"It was very nice," he answered with admirable restraint.

"Where did you go for dinner?"

"To the Mariner's Roost for seafood."

"You should have told me that's what you wanted. Armand makes a divine lobster thermidor."

"Perhaps they felt like going out," Sergei remarked.

"They're certainly free to do whatever they like. Where did you go afterward?" she asked Gabe.

Sergei groaned. "Mary Louise, sweetheart, you're going to drive them away if you keep checking up on them."

"I'm only expressing interest," she answered defensively. "I want to be sure they're enjoying themselves."

"You're a perfect hostess. Nobody could question that. But maybe you should concentrate your energies on Sergei," Gabe said smoothly. "There are a lot of ladies around who would appreciate all he has to offer."

She gave the older man a special smile. "Sergei knows how much his friendship means to me."

"That's my claim to fame—good old Sergei, everybody's best friend." He rose, suppressing a sigh. "If you'll excuse me, I have an appointment this morning. I'll see you later."

Gabe slanted a covert look at her as she watched Sergei walk out the door. "One day he'll leave and he won't come back. Have you thought about that?"

"I've gotten used to people leaving me." Her wistful expression turned ironic. "Only Martin remains a constant in my life."

"This is presumptuous of me, but perhaps you'd be better off if you nudged him out of the nest."

"He's all I have left," Mary Louise said simply.

Gabe tried to suppress his impatience. "Children shouldn't be your whole life after they're grown. You could have a great deal more if you wanted."

"Nobody has offered me anything."

"You know Sergei is in love with you."

"Not enough to brave public opinion," she said sadly. "So I guess it isn't really love. He enjoys my company, but he doesn't want the headaches that go with marrying a Van Ruyder. And who can blame him?"

"I've heard him mention the possibility—and he didn't cringe at the thought."

"He was only joking. I was supposed to understand that."

"Answer me this. If Sergei asked you, would you marry him?"

"We used to play the what-if game when we were children. It always concerned things that were never going to happen. Like, what if you were the Queen of England?"

"That's a defeatist attitude. Anything is possible if you want it badly enough."

"Perhaps at your age."

"At any age. You just have to seize the opportunity when it comes along. I hate to see you and Sergei pass up a chance at happiness because neither of you is willing to be candid about your feelings."

"The man has to express himself first."

"Not anymore. The world has changed, Mary Louise."

"Not my world, I'm afraid." She sighed. "Or Sergei's, either. We still live by the old rules. You young people are lucky. You don't have a lot of silly hang-ups. My generation put too much emphasis on unimportant things—everything from money and family, to the correct attire for each occasion. It's different today, I'm happy to say. People aren't bound by tradition as we were."

Gabe was reminded of Allison's humiliation with Bruce, and her reluctance to chance another rejection. "We're more liberated, but certain things still matter. Like family. Allison has a burning need to know who her parents were."

Mary Louise's expression brightened. "She's such a darling girl. I felt an instant rapport with her."

"Then why won't you talk to her?"

"I don't know what you mean. We've had some lovely conversations together."

"You do know what I mean, Mary Louise," Gabe said quietly. "I realize it's painful to talk about Monica, but Allison needs to find out the truth, and you're the only hope she has. You should want to know, too."

After a long pause, the older woman said, "All my life I've been shielded from the truth. Perhaps Peter was right. It's better not to know."

"Forgive me for saying this, but that's a very selfish attitude. You're condemning Allison to limbo."

"Try to understand, Gabriel. If I had conjured up the perfect granddaughter, it would be Allison. She's warm and caring and open with me, everything my daughter wasn't. I already love her like my own. I hope she'll let me treat her like a granddaughter. I want to do so much for her."

"As hard as it is to believe, Allison doesn't want a penny from you."

"I do believe it, which makes her all the more special."

"Then give her the greatest gift possible, her own identity."

Mary Louise's face was expressionless. "What happens if we pursue this and discover that Monica was not her mother?"

"I guess it's back to square one. Allison said there were two other possibilities."

"Exactly. Then she disappears from my life and some other woman gains a grandchild. Perhaps somebody who isn't even happy about the news." She looked at him squarely. "Allison deserves more than she's ever gotten out of life. I intend to make up to her for all the unhappy things that happened to her in the past."

"It isn't that simple. Suppose she wants to get married? What if objections were raised because of her lack of background?"

"Any man who would let that bother him isn't worthy of her," Mary Louise said scornfully.

"I agree with you. But other people might voice objections—like maybe his parents." Gabe walked a fine line, hampered by his promise not to reveal their engagement.

She looked at him with a frown. "Are you telling me it happened to the poor girl?"

"I didn't say that," he answered quickly. "I was just pointing out what *could* happen."

"It seems remarkably unlikely to me." She looked at him consideringly. "There's something you're not telling me."

He laughed ruefully. "Mothers are all alike. You always think we're keeping something from you."

"And we're usually right. What did Allison tell you last night? *Is* she engaged?"

"She expressed her frustration at having to go home without finding what she came for," Gabe answered evasively. "I told her I'd speak to you."

"If that hypothetical story you told me is true, I *have* been selfish," Mary Louise said slowly. "Poor little thing. It breaks my heart to think of her being treated like a second-class citizen because of something she wasn't even responsible for."

His jaw set grimly. "It will never happen again." When Mary Louise looked at him with dawning interest, Gabe said swiftly, "You're the one who can make sure of that."

"How?"

"Tell me everything you know. Is there any doubt in your mind that Monica had a baby when she was eighteen?"

"I guess I have to accept the fact. Your father phoned yesterday with at least partial confirmation of Allison's story. The birth record she described does exist. He said you were to phone him when you came in, but I'm afraid I forgot to deliver the message."

"I'll give him a call," Gabe said absently. "That seems to be pretty conclusive evidence."

"I have to agree. There could hardly have been two teenage Monica Van Ruyders. It isn't exactly a common name."

"You never suspected anything? Even if she was away at school and camp a lot, surely you didn't go for months at a time without seeing her."

"I've thought about it a great deal. The summer she must have gotten pregnant was not a happy time. Monica was always rebellious, but that summer she and her father were constantly at sword points. I tried to smooth things over, but Peter simply got angrier and Monica became more defiant. Finally he announced that she was out of control and he was sending her to his sister's to complete her final year of high school."

"Do you think Peter knew she was pregnant?"

"Looking back, I'm sure of it. That would account for his frustration, which translated into anger. Peter wasn't used to situations he couldn't control."

"Would he keep something that serious from you?"

"Without a doubt. Peter knew I would never allow him to give up the baby for adoption. In most ways I was a perfect wife. I never challenged his authority, but he must have known there were limits. So he didn't take a chance. I don't think I can ever forgive him for robbing me of my grandchild," Mary Louise said somberly.

"I'm sure he thought he was protecting you." Gabe hesitated for a moment. "One thing I don't understand. If the baby was such an embarrassment, why didn't he arrange an abortion? It would have been a lot easier all-around."

"Peter didn't believe in abortion. His tidy solution was to send Monica to his sister's. That way nobody would find out, and the inconvenient incident—as I'm sure he thought of it—would be resolved." Bitterness colored Mary Louise's voice.

"Your sister-in-law was willing to go along with this deception?" Gabe asked incredulously. "What was he blackmailing her with?"

"That wouldn't have been necessary. Jane always thought I was too permissive with my children. It's easy to criticize when you don't have any of your own. She undoubtedly welcomed a chance to apply some discipline. Poor Monica. The punishment for her indiscretion seems unduly harsh—house arrest with her aunt as warden."

"How about Monica's schooling? Did they just pull her out for five or six months?"

"There wouldn't have been any other way to hush it up. She undoubtedly had private tutors."

"After she returned home, did Monica ever give you a hint about what happened?"

"No, she was just more outrageous. Peter began to avoid her—whether out of guilt, or the realization that he couldn't handle her. I don't know. It was easier for everyone that way."

Gabe was thinking deeply. "Monica's baby was born at the end of May, so it must have been conceived the latter part of August. Was she here in Newport?"

"Yes, we always opened the house on the first of July and stayed until the beginning of September. When the children were younger they went to camp for part of the summer, but Monica was seventeen that year. She'd outgrown camp."

"So the father of her child was somebody she met here that summer."

Mary Louise looked doubtful. "The same families came with their children every year. You know what Newport is like. We all know each other."

"Could she have had a romance with one of the town boys? Or maybe a college kid who came here to work for the summer?"

"Anything is possible, as I'm finding out. But if it was one of those, she never brought him home. I wouldn't have a clue as to who he could be."

Gabe refused to be discouraged, although the odds were getting longer. He could only hope Monica's affair wasn't just a brief encounter. "Did she have a crush on any of the boys you knew? Sometimes kids who couldn't stand each other one summer, fall madly in love the next."

"You didn't know Monica very well. She played the field. I believe that's the way you young people put it. There were always swarms of youths buzzing around her, but she didn't seem partial to any special one. I think what she enjoyed most was the attention."

"There must have been some boys she dated more than others," Gabe persisted.

"It's so long ago. I only remember hordes of eager young men showing up every night to take her out. She was never without a date."

"Think hard, Mary Louise. You knew the families of all these boys. Surely you remember some being here more than others."

"Well, I do recall two of them. One was Daniel Wallace. We were quite friendly with his parents in the city, as well as here in Newport. He was a very polite young man. Very well brought up."

That depends on your definition, Gabe thought cynically. "Did he and Monica continue to see each other all summer? He didn't suddenly stop coming around?"

"I know what you're implying," she said quietly. "You think he might have become scared off if Monica told him she was pregnant."

"It's happened before."

"You're wrong about Daniel. I'm sure he would have stood by her if that had been the case. But it's a moot point because there was never any rift between them. To my recollection, he was part of the group all summer."

"It's possible that Monica didn't tell him she was pregnant."

"In which case, he doesn't know to this day." Mary Louise looked troubled. "Daniel is married now. He has a lovely family. What good would it do to rake up the past?"

"I don't intend to jeopardize his marriage," Gabe assured her.

"You can't guarantee that. We're a small community. Gossip spreads like wildfire."

"All I want to do is talk to him. There's no reason for anyone to get suspicious. You said there were two boys who seemed to have an edge," he continued, to deflect her objections. "Who was the other one?"

"It was Pembroke Clay." Mary Louise's expression changed to disapproval. "I'd say he was a lot more likely candidate than Daniel. He has a lovely mother and father, but I must say I never cared much for Pembroke."

Gabe looked interested. "I saw him at the country club dance the other night, but we didn't get a chance to talk. What didn't you like about Cokey?"

"I always detested that ridiculous nickname," she sniffed.

"You must have had other objections beside that."

"It's a terrible thing to say, but I never trusted that boy. Oh, he was always on his good behavior around Peter and me, but it was clearly an act. In my opinion, Pembroke was the instigator of those wild escapades Monica was involved in."

"That's very possible," Gabe murmured diplomatically.

"I'm not saying Monica was blameless. Perhaps they egged each other on. Who knows? He made as much of a mess out of his life as she did."

"In what way?"

"For one thing, he's been married and divorced twice."

"Unfortunately that's not unusual in today's society."

"The circumstances were," Mary Louise said with distaste. "Both divorces were messy. In one of them he was accused of having an affair with an actress. It was well publicized, so he could scarcely deny it. The other divorce was equally sordid. I'd rather not go into the details."

"Is he still a stockbroker?"

"I presume so, since his father owns the brokerage house. I see his mother now and then, but we seldom mention Pembroke."

"He sounds like a good prospect," Gabe said thoughtfully. "I'll look him up."

"Does that mean you don't have to speak to Daniel? I'd really feel very badly if any of this got back to his wife. Especially since I'm sure he and Monica weren't involved in that way."

"You can trust me to be discreet."

"You haven't left me much choice." She sighed.

"What is it you want, Mary Louise?" Gabe asked quietly. "To pretend nothing ever happened? After all, it was more than twenty-five years ago. We could just let the entire matter drop. Danny's marriage would be safe. Cokey wouldn't have any more complications in his life. That's the way Peter would handle it. The only loser would be Allison, but her expectations from other people have never been high."

Mary Louise was silent for long moments. "You make me very ashamed of myself, Gabriel. I thought I'd grown as a person since my husband died, but I'm just as much a slave to convention as he was. Peter did a cruel thing to Monica, and now I'm proposing to do the same thing to Allison."

"The circumstances are quite different, and you're acting out of love, not a misplaced sense of propriety. But I'm glad you see that the truth has to come out."

"Yes. Allison deserves that much."

"I'll talk to both men. Do you happen to know if Danny is here in Newport?"

"He and his family are staying with his parents for a couple of weeks. I ran into his mother, Marjorie, in town the other day."

"Luck is on our side for once. It won't be easy getting either one to admit responsibility, however, so I'd like to chase down any other leads you can think of."

"I really haven't a clue," Mary Louise said helplessly. "Monica never confided in me, not even little things after she reached her teens."

"How about a close girlfriend?"

"She was much more interested in boys than girls."

"She must have had at least *one* girlfriend."

"For a few years, Monica and Sandra Gresham were good friends. They went to the same schools and knew all the same people. I was very happy about it because Monica had so few girlfriends."

"Did they grow apart after the summer ended? You seem to indicate they didn't keep in touch as they grew older."

"It was more than a gradual parting of the ways. They must have had an argument sometime during the last month we were here. Sandra stopped coming over to the house and Monica never mentioned her anymore. When I questioned her about it, she said Sandra was a bore and a killjoy. I felt badly that they stopped seeing each other completely, but you can't patch up your children's squabbles for them. I'm sure Sandra's mother tried, too. Our families were close friends. It was useless, though. The girls never made up."

"Monica didn't tell you what the argument was about?"

"No, she just said it wasn't important."

"It obviously was to Sandra," Gabe mused. "Suppose the falling out was over a boy they both liked. Perhaps Monica took him away from Sandra. That could break up a teenage friendship."

"You think he could be the boy Monica had an affair with?" Mary Louise asked dubiously. "Why is he any more of a candidate than the dozens of others she dated?"

"I don't know. It might be a long shot, but at this point I'm stumped enough to grasp at any straw. It's worth talking to Sandra about, anyway."

"She's changed a lot since she was a girl," Mary Louise said slowly. "Sandra was always so happy-go-lucky in those days. Nothing ever bothered her."

"She certainly *has* changed," Gabe agreed. "At your party Saturday night she was spoiling for a fight with *someone.*"

"I wonder if her marriage is happy."

"I don't know, but it isn't our problem. I'll try to tackle her when she's in a good mood."

Mary Louise's face was troubled. "You'll tell me what you find out, won't you?"

"I'll give you a full report," Gabe promised.

After leaving Mary Louise, Gabe returned to Allison's room. He found her still in bed, fast asleep. Resisting the urge to kiss her awake, he started to leave quietly. But Allison sensed his presence.

She opened her eyes and smiled at him drowsily. "I must have gone back to sleep. Why were you up so early?"

He went over to sit on the edge of the bed. "I wanted to talk to Mary Louise before she went off to one of her meetings or luncheons."

Allison sat up in bed. "Did you tell her about us?"

"I promised I wouldn't." His smile faded. "Don't you trust me?"

"Of course I do! I don't know why I asked that." She sighed. "Why do you put up with me?"

He eased the strap of her nightgown down her arm and kissed her shoulder. "That's fairly obvious. You have the most beautiful body of any woman I've ever known."

"Is that my only attraction?"

Gabe was quick to catch the wistfulness in her voice. He raised his head to gaze at her tenderly. "I never thought I'd meet anyone as wonderful as you are in every way. I want to get married as soon as possible and live with you for the rest of my life."

"Darling Gabe." She threw her arms around his neck.

He held her closely for a minute, then began to explore her ear with the tip of his tongue. "I also want to fool around."

She gave a shaky laugh. "Well at least you're honest about it."

"Absolutely." His hand cupped around her breast. "How about it?"

"I don't feel right about making love in Mary Louise's house." Allison drew back reluctantly. "She wouldn't approve."

"She would if you'd let me announce our engagement."

"Not really. It would still make her uncomfortable—and me, too."

"All right, angel. I don't agree with you, but it has to be right for you, too." He tousled her hair playfully. "If I can't make love to you, put on something less revealing. You look much too sexy."

"I'm sorry." She smiled. "I didn't bring any granny gowns."

"You won't need them, or anything else to sleep in after we're married. I'll keep you warm."

"Married." She savored the word, gazing at him dreamily. "That sounds so wonderful."

"Stop looking at me like that, or I won't be responsible," he warned. "Get out of bed, woman. We have work to do."

"Like what?"

Gabe told her the results of his conversation with Mary Louise.

Allison's blue eyes sparkled. "Do you really think you're onto something?"

"I don't want to get your hopes too high, but it's a distinct possibility. We'll start with Danny Wallace."

"Because he's the most likely candidate?"

"No, I think Cokey Clay is a hotter prospect, but I want to check Danny out first. Mary Louise is worried that his marriage might suffer if any of this got out. I don't want her to stew about it any longer than necessary if he wasn't involved."

Allison looked troubled. "I wouldn't want to jeopardize anyone's marriage."

"Don't worry about it." Gabe's face hardened. "There's no free lunch. Monica paid the price for their indiscretion. Now it's his turn—if Danny is the right man."

"Even so, I wouldn't want to hurt his wife. She didn't have anything to do with it. I don't want to hurt *anybody*. I just want to find out the truth."

"She won't know anything unless Danny tells her, I promise. Now, hurry up and get dressed. I'm hoping we can track him down at the yacht club. He was always an avid sailor."

She hopped out of bed. "Just give me a few minutes to shower and dress, and I'll be right with you. Oh, Gabe, I'm so excited!"

He chuckled. "I'd prefer to excite you in a more rewarding fashion, but I understand. See you downstairs in half an hour."

Chapter Nine

It was almost noon when Allison and Gabe arrived at the yacht club. There weren't many people in the dining room yet, so they went into the cocktail lounge, which was busier.

The bartender finished serving a group at the end of the long polished bar, then came over to take their order. His face lit up when he saw Gabe.

"Well, if it isn't Mr. Rockford. We haven't seen you around these parts in quite a while. Where have you been keeping yourself?"

"My dad decided I'd been living the good life long enough, so he sent me out to make a living," Gabe joked before turning to Allison. "I'd like you to meet Mike, the indispensable man," he told her. "The club couldn't run without him."

"That's what I try to fool them into believing." Mike laughed.

"It's true. Your job takes a lot more know-how than just pouring drinks. Remember the time those young kids got rowdy and how you straightened them out?"

The two men chuckled as they reminisced about past summers. Gabe mentioned several people before asking about the one he was really interested in.

"I understand Danny Wallace is here with his family," he remarked casually. "Does he come around very often?"

"He's here today, working on his boat. Been out there all morning. It seems to me those yachting types get more fun out of working on their boats than sailing them." Mike grinned.

"They're a special breed," Gabe agreed. "I think we'll stroll down and say hello."

"Be careful he doesn't hand you a paintbrush," Mike advised.

As they walked down to the dock Gabe said, "I wasn't just buttering Mike up. He does know everything that goes on around here. He could have told me where to find Cokey, too, but I didn't want to arouse his suspicions unnecessarily. I can probably find out from somebody else."

"Too bad Mike wasn't around when Monica was a teenager. He wasn't, was he?"

"No, he's only been here about fifteen or sixteen years. I was just out of prep school when he started, and Monica was getting her first divorce. Any gossip he might have heard was about her more recent affairs."

They were walking along the marina past moored boats of every size, from modest to impressive. Music and laughter wafted from several where people were partying in the brilliant sunshine. Several of the groups called to Gabe and invited him aboard, but he put them off with a vague excuse.

"There's Danny up ahead," he told Allison.

Daniel Wallace's boat was a sleek racing sloop named the *Carefree*. It was deserted except for a man in cutoff dungarees sanding a section of railing.

Allison stared at him avidly as they covered the short distance. It gave her a funny feeling to think that this stranger might be her father. He was nice looking in a forgettable sort of way. About medium height and well built except for being slightly overweight. Could the flamboyant Monica have been attracted to this ordinary man? Possibly, when she was a teenager.

He didn't look up until they were standing a few feet away. "What's doing, Danny?" Gabe called.

"Gabe?" The other man looked surprised and pleased. "I haven't seen you around these parts in ages. What are you doing in Newport?"

"Just hanging out."

"I hear your parents sold their house here."

"Yes, they got tired of the yearly hassle."

"My folks are starting to feel the same way. I'd hate to see them sell, though. We've all had a lot of good summers here. You must miss your old place. I'll bet it holds a lot of memories for you."

"Priceless ones." Gabe squeezed Allison's hand. "It's okay, though. My uncle bought the house and I can use it anytime."

"Is that where you're staying?"

"No, Allison and I are staying at Rosewood Manor." Gabe introduced them.

"Come on board for a drink," Danny said.

He fixed Bloody Marys and they sat in canvas chairs on the deck. Allison mostly listened as the men talked.

"How is Eloise?" Gabe asked politely about Danny's wife.

"She's fine. We have three children now."

"That's great."

"I never thought I'd say this, but it really is." Danny laughed. "How about you?" He included Allison in his smile. "When are you going to settle down?"

"That's what my parents keep asking me." Gabe grinned. "So?"

"There's nothing like a reformed stud," Gabe joked. "When *you* give up la dolce vita, you want the rest of us to suffer along with you."

"You can't be talking about *me*. I wasn't a party animal."

"Don't hand me that. You ran around with Monica Van Ruyder, didn't you?"

Danny slanted an uncomfortable glance at Allison. "I took her out a couple of times, that's all."

"That's not what Mary Louise said. She remembers you being underfoot constantly."

Danny tried to change the subject. "How's Mary Louise doing? I'm surprised she's still living in that big house. Everyone thought she'd sell it after Peter died."

"I guess it's like you said, it holds a lot of memories. For you, too, undoubtedly."

Danny stood abruptly. "Let me freshen your drinks. Unless you have a lunch date," he added hopefully.

Gabe stretched out his long legs. "No, we don't have any plans," he said blandly.

When Danny had gone to mix the drinks, Allison whispered, "He doesn't want to talk about Monica. That's a good sign, isn't it?"

"Not necessarily. He might just feel constrained with you here."

"Why would he, if his conscience is clear?"

"Memories of Monica are apt to be X-rated, and he's a family man now."

"Maybe," she answered skeptically. "But you won't know unless you get him to talk about her."

"I'd have a better chance if we were alone." Gabe's expression turned innocent as Danny reappeared with their drinks. "This is really nice. I don't get to unwind much in the city."

"It's a real rat race, isn't it?" Danny agreed. "How long are you staying?"

"Only this week, which is a good thing. I think I've put on five pounds already. Armand is one great chef." Gabe snapped his fingers as if remembering something. "I forgot to tell Mary Louise we wouldn't be in for dinner tonight. Did you remember to mention it to her?" he asked Allison.

"No, I forgot, too," she said, following his lead.

"We'd better let her know. Would you phone and leave a message?" As Allison rose he said, "I'll meet you back at the clubhouse."

After she left, Danny said, "That one's a real knockout."

"Does she remind you of anyone?" Gabe asked idly.

"A movie star, you mean?"

"No, I was thinking of Monica."

Danny looked startled. "There's a certain resemblance I suppose, but Allison isn't anything like her."

"I thought you didn't know Monica that well."

Danny's eyes narrowed. "What the hell is going on, Gabe? Why all this talk about Monica after all these years?"

"Why does it bother you?" Gabe countered. "What I find even more curious is your claim that you barely knew her. Mary Louise says you dated Monica regularly."

"Maybe I did. It was a long time ago. Who can remember back that far?"

"Men don't forget a woman like Monica."

"She wasn't a woman then, for God's sake! She was a teenager."

"A remarkably precocious one."

"How would you know? You were just a little kid then."

"I heard the gossip about her. Children understand more than people give them credit for."

"Okay, so she was no goody-two-shoes. What difference does it make now? Show a little decency, man! Monica is dead. Let the past die with her."

"I'd be happy to, but she left some unfinished business behind."

"What do you mean?" Danny asked warily.

"Monica had a baby when she was eighteen. It was hushed up, and nobody ever knew about it. The infant was given up for adoption."

Danny stared at him. "Are you saying that girl Allison is Monica's daughter? Is that why you asked if she reminded me of anyone?"

"The child was conceived when Monica was seventeen," Gabe continued without answering the question. "The summer she spent here in Newport."

"You don't think that *I*... that's the most outrageous..." Danny was practically stuttering in his furious denial. "What is this, a shakedown? She'll never get away with it!"

"Relax, Allison doesn't want anything from you. She just wants to know who her father was."

"Well, it wasn't me!"

"Convince me," Gabe gazed at the other man impassively, trying to judge whether he was telling the truth or not. "It's a simple matter of deduction. You had the inside track with Monica, she got pregnant. Who else could it be?" Gabe knew it *wasn't* that simple, but he hoped to shake some facts out of the other man while he was too rattled to lie.

"You're way off base! I didn't have the inside track with her, Cokey Clay did. Although you could never be certain where you stood with Monica—she went after every boy in town. But if what you're telling me is true, you should be talking to Cokey. He's your man, not me."

"Possibly, but only if you weren't sleeping with her, too."

Danny's eyes shifted. "That's a hell of a thing to say."

"I could phrase it more delicately, but it wouldn't change the facts. One of Monica's boyfriends fathered her child, and I intend to find out which one."

"*Why?*" Danny's voice was filled with anguish. "What good will it do to disrupt a lot of lives? Whatever happened back then is over and done with."

"Not for the child, it isn't."

"What month was Monica's baby born?" Danny asked unexpectedly.

"May 27."

A look of relief flooded Danny's face. "Then I couldn't be the father!"

"How can you be so sure?"

"First I need your word that none of this will go any further."

"You have it," Gabe assured him.

"I don't know how much you actually know about Monica." Danny was silent for a long moment, remembering. "To say she was sexually active doesn't begin to describe it. Anything and everything went with her. She taught the *guys* things!"

"You're saying she was a nymphomaniac."

"She enjoyed sex, no doubt about it, but it was also an ego trip for her. Or maybe a lot of it was about power and control. Every boy in town had to be in love with her— whether he was going with another girl or not. The rewards were great," Danny said reminiscently. "For a while, at least. Then as soon as she was sure of you, you were yesterday's news."

"That's kind of a switch on what men have been doing to women for years," Gabe remarked.

"It still hurts. But that's how I can be sure I'm not the father of Monica's baby. She set her sights on me in June, right after we both got here. Not that I'm complaining. It was fantastic while it lasted. And then, just like that it was over. Cokey arrived, and she tossed me aside like a used towel. I couldn't believe it, so I hung around, hoping she'd change her mind.''

"That would explain why Mary Louise said you were always over there," Gabe mused.

"You were supposed to remain faithful even after the queen bee moved on to your successor," Danny said dryly. "After a while I got discouraged and started dating Cheryl Sturtevant. That didn't set well with Monica, so she whistled me back. We went out together a few times, even did some heavy necking, but she never slept with me again."

"It's hard to believe she could keep you dangling like that without coming across."

"Can you remember what it was like to be a seventeen-year-old boy with raging hormones? Monica was unbelievable in bed. Hell, she was better than women twice her age. God only knows where she learned it all. I would have done anything to get her to take me back."

"Can you remember the last time you slept with her?"

Danny's mouth twisted wryly. "I can remember *every* time. It was the Fourth of July, how's that for irony? The high point of the summer, climaxed by rockets going off. I wonder if she planned it that way. Anyhow, I took her home early in the morning, feeling like the king of the barnyard. Then she told me it was over."

"Did she give you a reason?"

"Monica wasn't into explaining, but I knew there was somebody else."

"Cokey Clay?"

"He moved in, so I suppose so. Although I think she was fooling around on both of us. One man wasn't enough for Monica."

Gabe shook his head in disbelief. "It's just a wonder she didn't get pregnant sooner."

"At least I wasn't responsible. If the baby was born in May, it must have been conceived in August. That puts me in the clear. I wasn't even here then. My grandfather had a stroke, and we closed up the house and went back to New York."

"I guess that's pretty conclusive," Gabe said. He set his glass down and stood.

"Do you intend to talk to Cokey?"

"He's next on my list."

"I'm sure he had the same experience with Monica that I did." Danny's face was troubled. "I didn't enjoy telling you all those things about her. It's rotten to speak ill of the dead."

"Somehow, I don't think she would have minded," Gabe said thoughtfully. "Monica's whole life seemed to be a quest for attention."

"I've often wondered if she ever really cared about *anybody,*" Danny said somberly.

Gabe puzzled over the question as he walked back to the clubhouse. Was Monica's rebelliousness due to her father's overly stringent upbringing, or was she just basically selfish and self-centered? Maybe it was just as well that Allison never met her mother.

She was waiting impatiently for him on the veranda overlooking the marina. "What did you find out?" she asked before Gabe even reached her. "Did he admit anything?"

"I told you not to get your hopes too high, honey."

Her face fell. "He must have told you *something*. You were gone for ages!"

"We had a long talk. I had to lead up to it gradually."

"Okay, but what did he finally say?"

"That he dated Monica that summer, but they didn't have a physical relationship." Gabe gave Allison a highly expurgated version of what he'd learned—as much for her sake as Danny's. "It was one of those innocent high school romances."

"How do you know he was telling the truth?"

"I'm sure he was, but even if their relationship wasn't completely pure, Danny couldn't be our man. He wasn't here that August." When her mouth drooped, Gabe said, "Don't be discouraged, this is just the opening gun. I always thought Cokey fit the profile better than Danny. I'll phone around to locate him, and we'll tackle him next."

Gabe had no trouble finding out that Cokey was part of a house party at the home of one of the regular summer residents. He also learned that they would all be having dinner that night at the country club.

Before leaving for the club that evening, Gabe and Allison stopped by the library where Mary Louise and Sergei were having cocktails.

"Armand is going to think you don't like his cooking," Mary Louise joked.

"I'm sorry to keep running out on you every night, but with any luck, this will be the last time," Allison said.

Mary Louise's smile faded. Gabe had told her they were going to the country club expressly to talk to Cokey. "Let me know what you find out."

"Tomorrow," Gabe promised, taking Allison's hand. "Don't wait up. We might be late tonight."

After they left, Sergei commented, "They make a nice couple."

"I think they're falling in love," Mary Louise said softly.

"I think they already have." He chuckled.

"Wouldn't it be wonderful if they decided to get married? I'm so fond of both of them. We could have the wedding right here."

"Don't start calling the caterer. Every love affair doesn't end in marriage."

"It should. If two people are in love it's a logical conclusion."

Sergei had leaned forward to pick up his drink, so he didn't see the glance she slanted at him. "In an ideal world perhaps. But in their situation, I'm not sure they could make a go of it. Allison hasn't had the privileges Gabe has. I don't know if she'd be happy in his world."

"That's utterly ridiculous! She's a lovely, intelligent girl. The man who gets her will be very lucky."

"I agree, but people can be remarkably cruel to somebody who doesn't belong."

"Not while Gabriel is around. He'd make short work of anyone foolhardy enough to slight his wife."

"Is that the basis for a good marriage, though?" Sergei's expression turned grim. "Partners should be equal. How would a woman—or a man—feel if his spouse always had to protect him from slights?"

They both knew they were no longer discussing Allison and Gabe. "He should consider the source," Mary Louise said impatiently. "Not everybody would feel that way."

"Just one would be enough," Sergei replied harshly.

She suppressed a sigh. "Then he doesn't really love her."

"Or maybe his expectations are too high. None of it would matter if he thought she really loved *him.*"

Mary Louise gazed at him in dawning delight. Before she could answer, Martin and Laura came into the library. They were dressed to go out.

Martin glanced around the room. "Where are your houseguests?"

"Gabriel took Allison to the country club for dinner," Mary Louise answered.

"They use this place like a hotel," he complained.

"I didn't realize you missed their company," she said ironically. "I'll try to arrange a little family dinner for tomorrow night."

"Don't bother on my account. I was only thinking of you. *You're* the one who wants her around. I just hate to see her take advantage of you like this."

"I appreciate your concern, but it's misplaced. Sergei and I are looking forward to being alone tonight." She gave the older man a special smile.

Martin's eyes narrowed. "You're staying home again? It's rather unusual for you to be so reclusive. What's the matter, are you afraid to be seen in public with him?" he drawled.

Mary Louise's smile was erased by a flash of intense anger. Her voice shook with the effort to control it. "You will apologize to Sergei this instant!"

Martin was startled by the extent of his mother's fury. "I was only joking," he said placatingly.

"It is never funny to insult someone."

"Sergei knew I was only kidding around."

"That's not a suitable explanation. I am deeply ashamed of you, Martin. May I remind you that this is my house and Sergei is my guest. If you find the living conditions here intolerable, I suggest you make other arrangements."

He looked shocked. "I said I was sorry."

"Don't tell me, tell him," she said adamantly.

Martin was so chastened that his apology almost rang true. Laura was equally nervous. After making an ineffectual attempt to smooth things over, she hurried her husband out of the room.

When Mary Louise and Sergei were alone, she said, "Martin's behavior was inexcusable. There is nothing I can say except to assure you it will not happen again."

Sergei hadn't reacted to Martin's snide attack, or Mary Louise's impassioned rebuke. His face was equally impassive now. "Don't worry, it isn't that important."

"Yes, it is! I won't put up with intolerance, and certainly not in my own son."

"He's just being a little overly protective. It's understandable."

"You're far too generous. I can't tell you how embarrassed I am."

"You're making a great deal out of nothing. Martin was right about one thing. We have been staying home too much. Would Armand's feelings be mortally wounded if we went out to dinner tonight?"

"I don't suppose so, but we were going to stay home and...discuss things." She looked at him searchingly. "Wouldn't you rather do that?"

"We can settle the world's problems over dinner in a restaurant." He stood, smiling pleasantly. "You're too far away at that big table in the dining room. I'll get my jacket and be right down."

Mary Louise's expression was forlorn as she watched him go.

The country club was crowded with regulars, representing three generations. Pinky was there with a group, and some of Mary Louise's friends were dining with their children. They all greeted Allison warmly, giving her a nice feeling of acceptance.

She was distracted, however, by the more pressing need to find Cokey Clay. Gabe finally located him at the bar.

Allison disliked the man on sight, although he obviously approved of *her*. After a brief inspection of her lovely face, his gaze lingered on her curved figure.

"How do you young fellows wind up with all the beautiful girls, when we're the ones with experience?"

"Maybe we just know how to treat a lady," Gabe drawled.

"Is that the line he's been feeding you?" Cokey asked Allison. "Don't you believe it. I could make you very happy, given the chance."

"Come off it," Gabe said. "She's young enough to be your daughter."

"Not unless I was a very early bloomer."

"Which you were, as I remember. You used to hang out with Monica Van Ruyder. She wouldn't have won any merit badges in the Girl Scouts."

"Ah, Monica. She was quite a gal." Cokey's mouth curved in a reminiscent smile. "Terrible thing about her death. I heard it was some kind of accident. I must say I'm not surprised. She used to drive like a crazy woman."

"She did a lot of crazy things."

"You don't know the half of it. I could tell you stories." Cokey slanted a glance at Allison. "But that's all in the past. The poor woman is dead, and buried now."

"She was a legend in her time all right. I've always wanted to ask—" Gabe broke off and turned to Allison, "This can't be very interesting to you. Why don't you join Pinky and her crowd? I'll be with you in a few minutes."

She took her cue gratefully this time. Much as she wanted to find her father, Allison couldn't help hoping Cokey wasn't the man. Everything about him repelled her, but from all she'd heard, he was just the sort that would appeal to Monica.

Cokey watched her go. "That's one beautiful babe. Is she as good as she looks?"

Gabe's jaw set, but he kept his voice pleasant. "Not as good as Monica, from all reports."

"Oh, hell, you're talking about the solid gold Cadillac of women. I never had anybody before or since like Monica."

"She was only a kid when you dated her."

"In years maybe, but not in experience. She liked to try everything. I remember one night..."

Gabe tried to conceal his distaste as Cokey related incidents better left untold. "Did this go on all summer?" he asked.

"You better believe it! She was dating Danny Wallace, but she dumped him as soon as I came to town."

"Then you went with her until the beginning of September when it was time to close up the houses and go home?" Gabe persisted.

"You bet. It was the best summer of my life."

"Did Monica date any other boys while you two were seeing each other?"

"No way! I was quite capable of taking care of her needs," Cokey said smugly.

Gabe's eyes were cold as he dropped his act. "Where were you when her baby was born?"

"What?" Cokey's mouth dropped open. "What the hell are you talking about?"

"If you were as close as you say, you must have known she got pregnant that August."

"This is the first I've heard of it, I swear to God! Are you putting me on? I never heard anything about Monica having a baby."

"It was put up for adoption at birth."

Cokey continued to look dazed. "They sure kept it a secret. I wonder who the father was."

"Come off it! How can there be any doubt? You just told me she didn't see anybody else all summer."

Cokey squirmed uncomfortably. "I'm afraid I exaggerated a little."

"Am I supposed to believe you made up all those lurid stories? I didn't know you were that inventive," Gabe said mockingly.

"They were all true. What I stretched the truth about was the length of our affair. It lasted less than a month, not all summer like I said."

"But you only decided to change your story when it turns out your summer of love might have some far-reaching consequences. How convenient."

Cokey's face reddened. "I don't give a damn if you believe me or not. What business is it of yours, anyway?"

"I happen to represent Monica's daughter. You don't have to worry, though. It isn't going to cost you anything. She just wants to establish her parentage."

"You'll have to look someplace else." Cokey's lascivious manner had vanished. He was now eager to convince Gabe, even at the expense of his macho image. "What I told you about Danny is true. I did take Monica away from him, and for a few weeks it was sex city. We made love in places you wouldn't believe! I figured I was the luckiest kid on the block. Then I began to suspect she was cheating on me, like she cheated on Danny when I came on the scene. Finally she dumped me the same way. It isn't something a man likes to admit, so I pretended we kept on heating the sheets until we both had to go home. You can understand that, can't you?"

Gabe didn't bother to answer. "Who was the new favorite?"

"I never knew, and that was kind of strange. Monica always liked to talk about her new conquests—like the guys do. But that time she clammed up. All I could find out was that he was older, probably a college man."

"You'd think she'd brag about that," Gabe said thoughtfully.

"Maybe her parents wouldn't have let her go out with him if it got back to them. She was only seventeen, and he could have been twenty or more."

"That might account for it. You think she sneaked out to meet him?"

"If that's what it took. Her parents' opposition would only have made him more attractive. Anyway, he had the inside track for the rest of the summer. I couldn't get another date with her. If Danny said he did, he was lying."

"When did you and Monica break up?" Gabe asked intently.

"Early in August."

"Could you be more specific?"

"Hell, you're talking about twenty-five years ago!"

"I know, but think hard, it's important."

"You want the exact date? How can I—wait a minute! It was the third of August. I remember because my father's birthday was the next day. Some relatives were coming in for a big party my parents were throwing, and I had to pick them up at the airport. It made me late for my date with Monica, and she was gone by the time I got to her house. I told myself that was the reason for our breakup, but it only speeded things up."

"So you didn't sleep with her after roughly the second of August?"

"She wouldn't even go out with me again. I assume the next guy lasted till summer was over. That was about Monica's attention span—three weeks to a month. If she got pregnant, it was by him."

"Are you sure you don't know who he was? The same people came back every year. A newcomer would be noticed. Did somebody have a houseguest or a visiting relative?"

"They undoubtedly did, but it isn't something I'd remember. People had guests all the time. Her new love interest could just as easily have been one of the college kids who come for the summer to work in the restaurants and hotels. Monica could have met him in town. That might be the reason she was so secretive about the guy. Her father would have thrown a fit."

Gabe sighed. "If he was a transient I'll never track him down."

Cokey's relief was evident. "That means you believe I'm telling the truth."

"I suppose so. No decent man would make up the kind of sexual exploits you bragged about."

"It's easy to be judgmental now," Cokey whined. "But you have to remember, I was only seventeen at the time."

"And you haven't grown up since then." Gabe slid off the bar stool and walked away.

Allison searched Gabe's face for some clue as he approached the table. She wasn't reassured by his brooding expression, although he managed a smile when he saw her.

"You don't look like you're bringing good news," she said tentatively.

"That depends on your viewpoint. Cokey isn't your father, either."

"Why do I feel like celebrating? We're back where we started, but I'm really glad I'm not related to him."

"You have good judgment."

"Where do we go from here?" Allison's face was troubled. "Mary Louise only gave you those two names."

Gabe hesitated. "I'm afraid you might have to face the possibility that we'll never find the man we're looking for."

"You're giving up?" she asked hopelessly.

"Not by choice, honey. But we're up against almost insurmountable odds. Monica dated a lot of boys that summer." He only hoped Allison never discovered the extent of her activities.

"The one she became pregnant by couldn't have been just a casual date. Didn't Danny or Cokey give you any clue as to who it could be? You said all the summer people knew each other."

"That doesn't narrow the field. Cokey suggested it might have been one of the transients who worked here briefly that summer."

"Oh, no! That *would* make finding him impossible."

"It doesn't matter, darling." Gabe squeezed her hand tightly. "I love *you*. I don't give a damn who your parents were, and neither will my mother and father."

"You might be right," she said unemotionally.

Gabe sighed. "I could prove it if you'd just let me tell them we're engaged. They'll welcome you with open arms, I promise."

The abrupt end of her dreams left Allison numb. She wanted to believe Gabe, but bitter experience had taught her otherwise. Gabe would never walk out on her like Bruce had, but he enjoyed a close relationship with his family. Could their love survive if she caused a rift with his parents? She honestly didn't know.

"How could anyone not love you?" he asked in a husky voice.

"You can tell them if you like," she answered tonelessly.

After looking at her expressionless face he sighed again. "I can tell I haven't convinced you of a thing. Okay, honey, I'll just have to keep digging."

"There aren't any more leads."

"Then I'll just have to turn up some. Let me think about it overnight."

"What are you two discussing so seriously?" Pinky asked. "You've had your heads together for half an hour."

"I've been telling Allison we were meant for each other." Gabe smiled.

"Don't take him seriously," Pinky advised her. "He's one of those guys you can catch, but you can't keep."

"Just what I need right now," Gabe muttered under his breath. "Are you ready to leave?" he asked Allison.

"You haven't had dinner yet," Pinky protested.

"We just stopped in for a drink," he answered.

As they were driving away, Gabe said to Allison, "Perhaps you wanted to stay. I should have asked you."

"No, I don't feel much like partying right now."

"That's what I thought. We'll find a nice, quiet restaurant instead."

"I'm really not hungry, but I'll have a cup of coffee with you while you have dinner."

"I have a better idea." He pulled into the curb in front of a small deli. "Wait here, I'll be right back."

He returned a short time later, carrying a large grocery bag.

"What did you buy?" Allison asked curiously. "If you have any thoughts about whipping up a snack in Armand's kitchen, forget it! He'd be terminally insulted."

"Especially if he knew we preferred a hero sandwich to paté à la maison."

Her spirts started to rise as they drove through the gates to his uncle's house. "I won't tell if you don't."

"I'm not allowed to tell *anything,*" Gabe complained, but he put his arm around her shoulders and kissed her temple as they entered the house. "You can sit out by the pool while I make some sandwiches. I'll bring you a drink."

"No, I'd rather be with you."

"That's what I like to hear."

He kissed her lightly, then more purposefully as the flame that was always present between them ignited. When she turned to face him and put her arms around his waist, Gabe dropped the bag of groceries and took her in both arms.

Their bodies were molded together as they kissed and moved against each other in sheer delight. While his tongue probed deeply, he caressed her back down to the curved slope of her bottom.

Allison's hands wandered over him in the same way, tracing the width of his broad shoulders, the bunched muscles in his arms. She could never get over the wonder of his perfect physique. When she dug her fingers into his taut buttocks, Gabe uttered a hoarse cry and urged her against his hardened loins.

"There's never been anyone like you," he muttered. "I think about you night and day. Don't ever leave me, darling."

"Not if you really want me."

"Can you have any doubt? I couldn't live without you."

Swinging her into his arms, he carried her up the stairs to his bedroom. After setting her on her feet, he slid her zipper down and gently urged the dress off her shoulders. It slithered to the floor, leaving her in just a pair of brief panties. The night was warm, so she hadn't worn a bra or stockings.

Gabe drew in his breath audibly at the sight of her slender, nearly nude body. "God, you're beautiful," he said huskily. "You're almost too perfect to be real."

She gave a throaty laugh, feeling a heady sense of power over this magnificent man. "You should know how real I am." She pushed the jacket off his shoulders and loosened the knot in his tie.

"You seem different every time," he said, drawing her into his arms and sliding his lips over her bare shoulder.

"There haven't been that many times," she murmured.

"We're going to have a whole lifetime together, my love, and I'm going to know every inch of your exquisite body."

He began an inflaming exploration right then, lowering his head to string a line of scorching kisses from her breast to her navel. Allison anchored her fingers in his thick hair as his mouth continued its erotic path downward.

He removed her panties with tantalizing deliberation, pausing to kiss the smooth skin of her stomach. She quivered as his kisses grew more intimate, feeding her mounting passion.

Sinking to her knees, she flung herself into his arms. The impact caught Gabe off balance and he landed on his back, carrying her with him. Allison rained kisses over his face and neck, pressing her hips into his.

Gabe's arms tightened and he rolled over, taking her with him. His deep, sensuous kiss was a prelude of what was to come. After a few smoldering moments he released her.

"Don't leave me," she pleaded as he got to his feet.

"I couldn't if I wanted to," he answered tenderly.

Gabe threw off his clothes and returned to lift her into his arms and carry her to the bed. Without loosening his embrace, he positioned himself between her legs.

Allison raised her hips, inviting him into her depths. His entry was exquisitely satisfying. She clamped her arms and legs around him, rising to meet his thrusts as molten sensation flowed like a blazing stream through their bodies. The final eruption left them limp, but totally satisfied.

Much later, Gabe said softly, "Do you know how much I love you?"

"You just showed me." She smoothed his hair, gazing at him adoringly.

"Do you think you can stand a lifetime of this?"

"I'm counting on it." She smiled. Allison put aside her trepidation for the moment. No matter what the future held, nothing could take away what they had just shared.

They talked softly for a while, then Gabe swung his long legs out of bed.

"Do we have to leave already?" she asked wistfully.

"Not for hours. I just thought you might have worked up an appetite." He grinned, leaning down to kiss the tip of her nose. "Stay here. I'll make some sandwiches and bring them up to you."

"No, I'll come with you."

"Just can't let me out of your sight, can you?" he teased.

"Don't push your luck." She pretended to frown.

He cupped her chin in his palm and looked deeply into her eyes. "I don't know how I ever got this lucky, but you're mine now and I'll never let you go."

I hope not, Allison answered silently.

Gabe refused to let her help, so Allison sat on a kitchen stool and watched while he sliced a loaf of French bread in half horizontally. He piled cold meat and cheese on one half, and lettuce and tomatoes on the other. The finished product was tremendous.

"It looks delicious, but we can't eat all that," she remarked.

"Speak for yourself. I used up a lot of energy." He grinned.

"They just don't make men like they used to," Allison commented mischievously.

"Maybe not, but you're stuck with me. Till death do us part. So don't think I'll let you get away with changing your mind."

She was jolted back to reality. None of her problems had been solved. "What are we going to do now, Gabe?"

His laughing face sobered as he noted her dejected expression. "Can't you give it up, honey?"

"I guess I don't have any choice."

"All right." He sighed. "Let's figure out where to go from here."

"That's the whole problem. We're at a dead end."

"Not necessarily. We bombed out with Monica's boyfriends, but somebody must know who she was having an affair with. We just have to find out who that person is."

"Maybe she didn't tell a soul. Mary Louise said Monica was very secretive."

"It isn't normal for a teenage girl not to confide in *some-body*. Like a best friend, for instance."

"From all appearances, she didn't have any girlfriends. Except for Sandra Gresham. They were good friends for a while, but something happened and they broke up."

"That sounds promising. I think we'll have a talk with Sandra tomorrow."

Allison's face lit up with hope. "Do you think that might lead somewhere?"

"It's a definite possibility." Gabe smoothed her hair lovingly. "Now do you think I could have your full attention for the rest of the night?"

"You can have a lot more than that," she answered softly.

Chapter Ten

On the way back to Rosewood Manor that night, Allison's misgivings returned.

As they walked up the staircase she said, "If Sandra Gresham holds the only clue to Monica's past, I'm afraid we're in big trouble. You saw how strangely she acted around me. I doubt if she'd tell us anything even if she knew it."

"She was just out of sorts the night of the party," Gabe said reassuringly. "What could she have against you? She'd never seen you before."

"That's what's so puzzling. But if I'm right, how will we get her to talk to us?"

"Mary Louise can give us some pointers on how to handle Sandra. I'll speak to her in the morning." Gabe put his arms around Allison at her bedroom door. "You don't have to get up, I'll take care of it."

"No, I wouldn't be able to sleep anyway. Time is running out, and I'm getting really tense."

"I thought I relaxed you," he teased. "I guess I'll just have to spend the rest of the night taking your mind off the problem."

"I wish you could." She sighed.

"Are you doubting my ability?" he parted her lips for a sensuous kiss.

Allison allowed herself the luxury of relaxing in his arms for a long moment before drawing away reluctantly. "You'd better go to bed. We don't want to wake the family."

"Okay, angel, if you insist. But I won't accept any excuses after we get back to New York. I want to see your beautiful face on the pillow next to me every morning when I wake up."

"It's late, Gabe. We'll talk about it some other time."

"There's nothing to talk about. We're getting married." He tipped her chin up and kissed her briefly. "Get some sleep, darling, and stop looking for things to worry about."

Allison tried to shake off her apprehension as she got undressed. If only she had Gabe's confidence that their marriage would work. She didn't doubt his love, but could it survive the pressures that would be put on him?

The cold distaste directed at her by Bruce's parents was a memory that wouldn't go away. If it happened again she could live with it for Gabe's sake. He was worth putting up with almost anything. What she couldn't endure was to watch their relationship change as he was forced to make repeated excuses for her.

Allison's expression was bleak when she considered her alternative.

The atmosphere at breakfast the next morning wasn't as sunny as usual. Mary Louise and Sergei both seemed distracted and Allison was subdued.

Only Gabe was charged with energy as he explained their problem. "Sandra is just about our last hope. As far as I can tell, she's the only person Monica would have confided in. The difficulty is getting her to talk. She's not the most approachable person in the world.''

"No, she's a difficult girl," Mary Louise agreed. "Sandra hasn't given her parents much pleasure. Not that Elinor has ever said a word to me, but I know they don't have a good relationship. It's hard to understand. Curtis and Elinor are both such charming people. Everybody loves being with them."

Gabe gently guided her back to the subject. "I might not get anywhere, but I'd like a chance to talk to Sandra. It has to be a casual meeting so she won't have her guard up automatically. I thought you could tell me what her interests are. If she plays golf or tennis, for instance, I could bump into her accidentally in the clubhouse and ask her to have a drink."

"You needn't go through all that. Sandra is coming for tea this afternoon. The garden club is meeting here."

"Fantastic! Mary Louise, you're a lifesaver."

Allison frowned slightly. "How can you make Sandra believe it's just a casual meeting? What would a man be doing at a ladies garden club meeting?"

"We have a few male attendees," Mary Louise said. "Old Mr. Pennington is one of the charter members. He's hard-of-hearing now and he falls asleep if the reading of the minutes takes too long, but we don't wake him unless he snores." She smiled.

"I promise to be attentive and stay awake," Gabe said. "I'll wait until—" He paused as Florence approached.

"You have a long-distance telephone call, Mr. Rockford," the maid said.

He groaned. "That must be Dad. I forgot to call him."

"Give him my best," Mary Louise said. "Your mother, too."

Gabe's surmise was correct. His father's voice came over the line, slightly testy.

"I told you to take a short vacation, Gabriel, not an extended sabbatical. May I remind you that you still have a job here in New York?"

"I left a message saying I needed another week. Didn't you get it?"

"I received the message, not the meaning. Why haven't you phoned to give me a progress report? You *are* still working on the case, I presume."

"I've been giving it my full attention," Gabe assured him.

"Then I don't understand why it's taking so long. You must have made up your mind by now. Either the girl is a fraud or she isn't."

"There was never any fraud involved," Gabe said sharply. "Allison always believed she was Monica's daughter."

"And what do *you* think?"

"I don't believe there can be any doubt that Monica had a baby when she was eighteen. The evidence is pretty conclusive. Mary Louise said you checked the hospital records and found out Allison is telling the truth."

"We sent an investigator to Philadelphia to verify the allegation, which proved to be correct. That part isn't subject to argument, the girl's credibility is. You were supposed to ascertain that."

"You can drop the legalese, Dad. You're not arguing a case in court, and Allison isn't a suspected criminal."

Burton Rockford's eyebrows rose at his son's harsh tone of voice. "I wasn't accusing the young woman of anything," he said mildly. "I'm merely trying to find out what progress you've made in resolving the matter. Mary Louise is a friend as well as a client. I need to be sure her interests are being protected."

"You don't have to worry about that. Allison doesn't want a penny from her."

"Aren't you being a little naive? There are millions at stake here."

"I know it's hard to believe. You'd have to meet Allison to understand. She doesn't care about the money. All she wants is to find out who her parents were."

"And then what? If she succeeds in convincing Mary Louise that Monica was her mother, you think Allison will just leave it at that? Nice to have met you, let's have lunch sometime?" Burton's voice was derisive. "If she didn't already know what a grandchild would mean to Mary Louise, I'm sure she does now."

"You're as bad as Martin!" Gabe said heatedly. "You think everybody has some personal ax to grind. Okay, so maybe a lot of people are greedy, but that doesn't mean everyone is. I know Allison. She's the most honest, trustworthy person I've ever met."

After a long pause, Burton said, "Then you're telling me she really is Monica's daughter?"

"It certainly looks that way. The problem after all these years is getting absolute proof. The only way to do that is to find Allison's father. That's the reason it's taken me so long. I talked to two possibilities, but they didn't pan out. Now I'm going to talk to Monica's best friend, in the hope that Monica confided in her."

"And if she didn't?"

"Then I have to convince Allison that it doesn't matter."

"I don't understand."

"She had a bad experience with some bigoted people who rejected her because she's an orphan. I tried to tell her people like that aren't worth losing sleep over, but the poor kid is afraid it will happen again. She won't let me tell you—" Gabe stopped abruptly. "It was evidently a very traumatic experience. That's why she needs to find out about herself."

"I see," Burton said without inflection.

"You'd really like her. Mary Louise is crazy about her."

"Are you saying she believes Allison is her granddaughter?"

"She doesn't give a damn whether she is or not. Allison is everything she ever wished for in a grandchild."

"This is exactly the sort of thing I sent you there to prevent!" Burton exclaimed sharply. "The girl is undoubtedly clever. She's succeeded in charming both you and Mary Louise. I can understand Mary Louise's vulnerability, but not yours. I thought you were too mature to be taken in by a woman, no matter how beautiful and innocent appearing. That was evidently my mistake."

Gabe's anger rose to meet his father's. "You have no right to talk about Allison that way. The fact that she made something of herself with no help from anybody means nothing to you. All you can see is a nameless nobody looking for a handout. I thought you, of all people, would keep an open mind, but obviously I was wrong. She said you'd react like this, but I couldn't believe it. I still can't."

Burton took a deep breath. "I suggest we both calm down and discuss this reasonably. I get the impression that you're strongly attracted to her. Can you blame me for wondering if she's clouded your judgment?"

Gabe made an effort to rein in his temper. "I suppose it appears that way, but I haven't found a single indication that she's lying about her past, or her reason for coming here. I'm convinced that she isn't trying to exploit the Van Ruyders. If I can't prove she's Monica's daughter, Allison will bow out of their lives, even though Mary Louise would give her every inducement to stay. It's *because* of my feelings for Allison that I've done everything humanly possible to prove her story, one way or the other. I hope you believe me."

"I've never had any reason to doubt you, son," Burton answered more quietly. "I'm sorry if I seemed to judge Allison prematurely. She sounds like a very unusual young woman."

"That's not an unqualified vote of confidence," Gabe said slowly. "Are you bothered by her lack of background?"

"I can think of a lot of reasons for disapproving of someone, but that isn't one of them," Burton replied crisply. "When are you coming home? I can't justify this trip as work-related for much longer."

"You talked me into it." Gabe laughed. "Now you'll just have to live with the consequences."

Burton's face was impassive as he cradled the receiver. After a moment he picked it up again and tapped out a number.

"How would you like to go to Newport for a few days?" he asked when his wife answered.

"That might be nice," Lily Rockford said. "What date did you have in mind?"

"Tomorrow morning."

"You must be joking! I couldn't possibly get away that soon."

"Of course you can. How long does it take to throw a few clothes in a suitcase?"

"Men never understand all the things women have to take just for a weekend. But there's more involved than that. We have all sorts of commitments. The Willoughby's anniversary party is Sunday night, and we promised to show up at Midge Forsythe's gallery show on Saturday. I have a million other things to do besides."

"Are any of them as important as meeting your future daughter-in-law?"

"*What?*"

"I have reason to believe that Gabriel has finally met his match. I don't think we have anything to say about it, but I'd like to take a look at the young woman."

"When did this happen? What's her name? Do we know her?"

"I'll tell you all about it when I get home. In the meantime, start packing. Hebert and Jean are still in Europe, but we can stay at their house."

"Does Gabriel know we're coming?"

"No." Burton's smile was on the grim side. "I decided one surprise deserves another."

Gabe sat through the garden club meeting with more patience than Allison did. She fidgeted in her chair, wondering how they were going to get Sandra alone. The woman was avoiding her. Allison was sure it wasn't her imagination. Every time she approached, Sandra moved away.

After the meeting was over, the ladies broke up into little groups as they waited for tea to be served. Mary Louise moved among them graciously, pausing when she came to Sandra.

"Would you do me a favor, my dear?" she asked the younger woman.

"Anything at all." Like most people, Sandra was fond of Mary Louise.

"Will you take Allison into the garden and show her which roses we discussed today. I don't think she knows a Peace from a Tropicana." Mary Louise laughed merrily.

Sandra's smile vanished. "I'm not that knowledgeable myself. Get Crystal to do it."

"Nonsense, my dear. You're too modest."

"Mind if I tag along?" Gabe took Sandra's arm and steered her toward the door to the terrace. "I might learn something. The only thing I know about roses is that they're delivered in long white boxes."

Allison followed wordlessly as he led the way down a path away form the house. Sandra was equally silent, resentment evident in every line of her stiffly held body.

She stopped by a bush covered with clusters of sweetly scented pink blossoms. "This is one of the antique roses they were talking about. It's called Ballerina, although I know you couldn't care less."

"That's not true," Gabe protested. "I'll admit I'm no gardener. Unfortunately I have a black thumb. I've killed off so many houseplants there's a wanted poster of me in all the nurseries."

"Then what are you doing at a garden club meeting?" Sandra demanded.

He smiled engagingly. "Nostalgia for the garden my mother used to have when we owned a house here. She was very involved in horticulture. I remember there was a rose festival every year. It was a big event," Gabe told Allison. "Lots of parties naturally, and even our very own rose queen." He turned back to Sandra. "Wasn't Monica elected queen one year?"

"She could have been. I don't remember."

"Really? I can recall every detail of those summers. I was just a kid then and I thought you teenagers were really neat. That's when I discovered it was all right for boys to like girls." Gabe laughed. "You and Monica were always surrounded by guys I admired, like Cokey Clay and Danny Wallace. Who were some of the others you ran around with?"

"That's ancient history," Sandra said curtly.

"It's fun to look back after all these years, though. I'll bet you two dated every boy in town."

"*She* did, anyway."

"She was really one of a kind, wasn't she? Did Monica tell you ahead of time about all those crazy escapades she cooked up?" He chuckled indulgently. "You were the only person who knew all her secrets."

"I don't know where you got the impression that Monica and I were close friends. We weren't. I hadn't spoken to her since we were seventeen."

"Why was that?"

Sandra's eyes smoldered with suppressed emotion. "It really isn't any of your business."

"I was just curious. You *were* good friends at one time— probably Monica's only girlfriend. What happened that was so terrible it broke up your friendship?" Gabe asked softly.

"I was fooled into believing we ever had one." Sandra's inner fury erupted. "She was the friend from hell! Monica didn't care who she hurt, as long as she got what she wanted.

She was a monster! I didn't see it at first, and when I did it was too late.''

"Teenagers can be cruel," he said gently. "But it isn't healthy to bury your resentment and let it fester over the years. Wouldn't you feel better if you talked about it?''

Sandra was breathing rapidly, almost oblivious to their presence as she relived the past. Then her eyes focused and she stared at Gabe with active dislike. "Leave me alone. I have nothing more to say to you.''

When she turned to go back to the house, Allison blocked the path. She couldn't let her get away. Sandra obviously knew who Monica's lover was, and she'd been so close to revealing the information.

"Please don't go yet," Allison begged. "I don't want to probe any sore spots, but we need to find out some things about Monica.''

"What makes you think I'm interested?''

Sandra tried to brush by her, but Allison held her ground. "Did you know Monica became pregnant when she was seventeen?'' There was no time for subtlety.

Sandra laughed harshly. "She did *everything* when she was seventeen—and before.''

"You did know, didn't you?'' Gabe asked quietly.

"What difference does it make now? She's dead.''

"I'm not asking out of idle curiosity. Anything you tell us will be kept in strictest confidence. I just want to know who fathered her child.'' Allison took a deep breath. "I think Monica was my mother.''

"Big surprise! Am I supposed to gasp in amazement?'' Sandra's mouth twisted sardonically. "I noticed the resemblance immediately.''

"Then you must understand why it's important to me to find out who my father was.''

"Pick any of a dozen men.'' Sandra shrugged contemptuously. "It could be any one of them.''

Gabe stared at her with narrowed eyes. "If you really believed that, you wouldn't be so bitter after all these years.

You know precisely who the man is. Why won't you tell Allison?''

"It's over and done with—or at least it should be. Why do you want to ruin his life? That's what Monica was good at." Sandra spat out the words. "She wasn't happy unless she was destroying somebody."

"I didn't come here to make trouble," Allison said earnestly. "I promise not to contact him or let a word of this conversation go any farther. All I want to know is who I am. You can understand that, can't you?"

"If you're really sincere you'll go away and leave us alone."

"How can I convince you that I don't want anything but his name?" Allison looked helplessly at Gabe.

"At least tell him who Allison is," he suggested. "Let him make the decision about whether he wants her to know."

"If he had good sense, would he have gotten involved with Monica in the first place?" Sandra asked derisively.

"We don't intend to let the matter drop," Gabe warned. "It would stir up a lot less talk if you told us in confidence, instead of forcing us to question Monica's friends."

"You must have done that already," Sandra answered shrewdly, seeing through his bluff. "You've been snooping around here for two weeks. I can't stop your witch hunt, but I don't have to be part of it."

"Isn't there anything I can to do prove I'm not a threat?" Allison pleaded.

"You can leave and never come back." Sandra pushed roughly past her and almost ran up the path.

Allison's eyes were desolate as the other woman disappeared around a turn. "There goes my last hope."

Gabe tried to be consoling. "At least there's no doubt that you're Monica's daughter. Isn't that enough?"

"It only answers half the question. Now I'll always wonder who my father is. Although he wasn't any happier about me than my mother was," she commented ironically. "Why am I surprised at being considered unacceptable when my own parents didn't want anything to do with me?''

Gabe took both her hands in his. "You don't know that. Monica might have wanted very much to keep you, but I'm sure she wasn't given the choice. I knew Peter Van Ruyder. He was a very self-righteous man. You mustn't blame Monica, and certainly not yourself. Mary Louise is ready to welcome you into the family."

"I guess you're right," Allison said without conviction.

Gabe could tell it wasn't enough. "We aren't licked yet," he said with a confidence he didn't feel. "Sandra was never a promising source of information."

"She was the only one we had left."

"Not necessarily. I've been kicking around an idea. Somehow or other, we have to get invited over to her house tomorrow. Let's try to figure out how."

"Are you kidding? After what happened here, Sandra would have us arrested for trespassing!"

"She won't be at home. I'm sure Mary Louise can manage to lure her away if we ask her to. Just concentrate on wangling an invitation out of Pinky."

"What will we do when we get there?"

"Leave that to me. All you have to do is go along with anything I suggest." He took her in his arms and kissed her. "I haven't disappointed you so far, have I?"

"Never." Allison returned his kiss, feeling better in spite of herself.

That night at dinner, Gabe enlisted Mary Louise's help in carrying out his scheme.

She wrinkled her nose. "Two days of Sandra is a little much. Although I shouldn't talk that way, considering how friendly I am with her parents."

"Then make a date that includes her mother," Gabe suggested.

"I really want to help, but Sergei and I have a luncheon date. I've been looking forward to it." She smiled at the older man. "It's so seldom that he has a free day."

"Actually I have an appointment in the afternoon," Sergei said. "It would have been a short lunch. Why don't you go ahead and make plans with Sandra and Elinor?"

Mary Louise's smile faltered, but she tried to hide her disappointment under a joking manner. "All right, I suppose I can be patient for another day. But I warn you, I'll expect a very fancy lunch to make up for saddling me with Sandra again."

"I might have to give you a rain check. It's time I got back to work."

"I thought you intended to stay another week, at least!"

"It would have been nice, but all good things must come to an end." His smile was perfunctory.

"I hoped it wouldn't be so soon," she answered in a muted voice.

They were all a little subdued after that. When the evening ended, Gabe lagged behind for a private word with Mary Louise.

"Sergei doesn't really want to go," he said quietly.

"You aren't up on your psychology," she replied in a brittle tone. "Nobody does anything he doesn't really want to."

"Men have fragile egos. They have to feel needed."

"That's the whole problem. Sergei doesn't realize how badly I do need him."

"Have you ever thought of telling him?"

"I couldn't do that. It would put him in an awkward position. If he really loved me he'd tell me so. Evidently I want more from him than he does from me."

Gabe shook his head. "You two are unbelievable! You're both so cautious that you'll end up being alone and miserable. Take my advice and tell him what you just told me. Or better yet, say, listen pal, we aren't getting any younger so stop screwing up and let's get married."

Mary Louise laughed unwillingly. "Can't you just hear me saying something like that?"

"No, but I wish I could."

It was surprisingly easy to get an invitation to Pinky's house. Allison had prepared an involved story about dropping off something for Mary Louise. It wasn't very convincing and fortunately she didn't have to use it. Pinky invited them over without prompting.

"I'm so glad you called," she said. "Mother insists that I stay home today and wait for the pool man, so I have to waste the whole day here alone. Who knows when he'll show up? I'd love it if you and Gabe would come over and keep me company."

"We'd be glad to," Allison said. "I'd enjoy a nice, relaxing afternoon."

"Great! Come over anytime."

Just to double-check, Allison said, "It will be nice to see your mother again." She was fairly certain Sandra hadn't mentioned their meeting the previous day.

"She won't be here. That's why I got stuck. Mrs. Watkins, our housekeeper, could just as easily tell the guy that the pump isn't working right, but Mother is sure she'll get busy and forget to watch for him. Isn't that the pits?"

"Well don't worry. We'll keep you occupied."

The Gresham home was a substantial house set in lovely grounds, much like Gabe's former home. Pinky took them through a center hall and out the back, where a swimming pool sparkled in the sunshine. Chaises and chairs padded with yellow-and-white striped cushions were grouped along the decking.

"Do you have your bathing suits on under your clothes?" she asked.

"No, we decided to be lazy today. We've been getting enough exercise." Gabe's remark was innocent enough, but Allison's cheeks warmed.

"Well, if you change your minds, I've got lots of spare bathing suits," Pinky said.

Whatever Gabe was planning, he didn't seem in any hurry to put it into operation. They lounged on chaises and drank lemonade, chatting idly about mutual friends and their jobs in the city.

Allison's nerves gradually tightened when he continued to make small talk. Did Gabe really have a plan, or had he just said that to make her feel better? If he didn't make a move soon, Sandra might catch them there. Allison's stomach knotted at the thought of the scene Sandra would make. She was really a little paranoid.

"When will your mother be back?" Allison asked when she could work it into the conversation.

"Not for hours. Mary Louise shanghaied her to work on one of her endless committees. She's the only one who can make Mother do something she doesn't want to do." Pinky grinned. "I must ask her how she does it."

"It's a knack," Gabe said. "Mary Louise has been co-ercing people in that genteel way of hers ever since I can re-member—and I go back a long way."

"Come on, grandpa." Pinky laughed. "You're not that much older than I."

"You're a youngster," he scoffed. "You never knew what Newport was like in the old days when Monica Van Ruyder and her crowd was getting into mischief."

"I heard some of those stories. She was really outrageous."

"That's right, I forgot. She and your mother were good buddies. You probably heard the stories firsthand."

"Not from her. I don't know what happened between them, but she goes ballistic whenever Monica's name is mentioned."

"Monica was quite a femme fatale, even at seventeen. Maybe she tried to steal your father away from her," Gabe suggested.

"It couldn't have been that. Mother didn't meet Dad until after she graduated from college."

Allison saw what Gabe was driving at. If Monica had set her sights on Ted Gresham, it might have accounted for Sandra's almost pathological hatred. That evidently wasn't the case, though.

"Well, it's too bad their friendship broke up," Gabe said. "They had a good group in those days. It seems funny now that I thought a bunch of teenagers were so cool." He smiled. "I wish I could see what guys like Cokey Pembroke and all the rest looked like back then."

"Mother has a lot of old snapshots. I could get them, but it wouldn't be much fun for Allison. She didn't know any of those people."

"I'd love to see the pictures," Allison said quickly. "I've met Cokey and Danny and a few of the others, and I've heard so much about Monica. I'd like to see what she looked like."

"Mary Louise must have shown you pictures of her," Pinky said.

"Only one. I'd like to see more."

"Okay, I'll go get them. It might take me a few minutes, but I think I know where they are."

When he and Allison were alone, Gabe said, "I had to take my time leading up to it. Was I sufficiently casual?"

"About what? I don't even know what you're trying to accomplish."

"I want to know who else was in the crowd Monica and Sandra ran with. I can't remember every one of them after all this time. I figured old snapshots might give us some new leads."

"Will you recognize them so many years later?"

"With any luck, Sandra wrote down their names."

Pinky returned with a bulky scrapbook. "There were more—Mother must have taken photos of every living thing in Newport. I thought this would provide enough of a trip down memory lane, though."

She placed the album on an umbrella table and they all pulled up chairs to look at it together. Sandra had been very methodical. Each snapshot was dated and the people identified, although sometimes only by their nicknames. She supplied other reminders, however, like "birthday party at Ashley's" or "Tommy's new car."

"Aren't these wild?" Pinky chuckled. "Look at those weird hairdos."

"Your children will be saying the same thing about you in thirty-some years," Gabe said.

"Where is Monica?" Allison asked, trying to conceal her intense interest.

"There she is." Pinky pointed at a snapshot of a beautiful young girl surrounded by gangling youths.

Gabe read off the names printed underneath. "Danny, Cokey, Mark—that must be Mark Levinson. I remember him vaguely. But who's the blond kid?"

Pinky peered at the printing. "It says 'Cowboy Bob.' Does that ring a bell?"

Gabe shook his head. "I can't recall anyone with that nickname, and his face isn't familiar."

"Maybe he was visiting somebody. Did anyone you know have relatives out West? He didn't get that label around here. This is fun." Pinky grinned. "Like playing detective."

"As long as we're sleuthing, we might as well be professional about it. Make a list of all the people we can't identify," Gabe told Allison. "We'll call them suspects."

Allison took a pocket notebook and a pencil out of her purse and wrote down Mark Levinson. Underneath she put Cowboy Bob.

Pinky glanced at the entries. "Mark shouldn't be on the list. Gabe recognized him."

"Oh, that's right. He was somebody I hadn't heard of before, so I got confused." Instead of erasing the top name, Allison put a faint line through it.

She started to get discouraged as the list of suspects grew. How could they possibly question this many people? They'd have trouble just finding them all!

Pinky was having a great time. "This is my girlfriend Barbara's mother." She pointed to a plump teenager in white shorts that emphasized her generous hips. "She'd absolutely die if she saw this picture!"

They were all so engrossed that they didn't hear footsteps on the terrace. A moment later, Sandra was standing over them like an avenging fury.

"What do you two think you're doing here?" She was practically quivering with anger.

Pinky gave her a shocked look. "I invited them over."

"Go in the house!" Sandra ordered.

"You must be joking," Pinky said uncertainly.

"You heard me. Do as I say!" When Sandra noticed the scrapbook on the table her body tensed. "You have no right to come here and snoop through my private possessions," she told Gabe heatedly.

"*I* brought out the album, Mother. I didn't think you'd mind. We were talking about Newport in the old days, and we all thought it would be fun to see how you and your friends have changed."

Sandra turned on Gabe. "What did you expect to find out by prying into my personal life?"

"Mother, really! How can you—"

Sandra cut her daughter off in midsentence. "This doesn't concern you. Leave us alone this instant! I don't want to have to tell you again."

After opening her mouth to argue, Pinky thought better of it, realizing her mother was beyond reasoning with. "I'm sorry," she murmured to the others before going back into the house.

"I should call the police," Sandra rasped. "I will, too, if you ever come here to my house again. I won't be harassed this way!"

"I'm really sorry." Allison rose. "We never would have come if we'd known you'd feel this strongly."

"What did you expect me to do, roll out the welcome mat? I knew you were going to cause trouble from the minute I laid eyes on you. These past two weeks have been sheer hell!"

"I don't understand." Allison gazed at her in bewilderment. "What have I done?"

"Explain it to us, Sandra." Gabe was staring at her with narrowed eyes. "Why do you find Allison's search for her father so threatening?"

Belated caution made Sandra try for self-control. "It doesn't concern me personally, but nobody likes to see their friends get hurt. I'm simply outraged that she's being so selfish."

"What would you call the man who fathered her? I don't know why Allison would want to find him, but since she does, I'm going to track him down. With or without your help."

"You can't do that." Sandra's control slipped. "It wasn't his fault! Monica seduced *him!* It was just a game to her, another trophy."

"Is that what he told you?" Gabe asked softly.

"It's the truth. I knew what she was like. You didn't."

"So you've covered up for him all these years. Don't you think it's time he accepted his responsibility and met his daughter?"

Sandra's eyes took on a wild glitter. "He'd be just fool enough to do a stupid thing like that, but I won't permit it! Monica isn't going to reach out from the grave and destroy us all over again. Get out of my house and take that spawn of the devil with you!" Her voice rose hysterically.

* * *

Allison was thoroughly shaken. She trembled as she sat in the car next to Gabe.

"Take it easy, honey," he said gently. "I'm sorry things got so unpleasant, but at least we found out what we came for."

"We did?" She gazed at him uncertainly. "All we have is a long list of names from years ago. I don't think it was worth that awful scene we just went through. Sandra seemed actually unbalanced at the end."

"She was afraid we'd gotten too close to the truth."

"But we haven't!"

"She doesn't know that. Her apprehension has obviously been building for two weeks. Yesterday's conversation and our visit today finally blew the lid off."

"But why? It's so strange that the whole affair matters to her that much. The father of Monica's baby is evidently a friend, but does anyone get that worked up over somebody else's problems, even a very close friend's?"

"It doesn't seem likely, does it?" Gabe started the engine.

"Where are we going?"

"To the tennis club."

Allison stared at him in disbelief. "You want to play *tennis?*"

"No, I want to talk to a tennis player." He glanced over at her and smiled. "You can tear up that list of names you made."

Chapter Eleven

Gabe deflected all of Allison's questions on the drive to the tennis club. "Just be patient a little longer."

"Do you really know who my father is?"

"I think so. It's the only answer that makes any sense."

"Then why won't you tell me?"

"Because there's always the chance that I'm wrong. We'll find out together."

That was the most she could get out of him. Allison was plagued by conflicting emotions as she and Gabe entered the clubhouse. On one hand she was consumed by curiosity about her father, on the other was a strange reluctance to meet him.

Monica wasn't exactly the sort of mother anyone would choose. By all accounts she was selfish and heedless of other people's feelings. What if the man she was attracted to had the same traits? What kind of heritage was that? Allison was never more acutely aware of the old saying: you can choose your friends but not your relatives. Should she have left well enough alone? Well, it was too late now.

Gabe was glancing around the lounge, which was empty except for a group of women playing bridge in a corner. "Let's walk outside," he said.

It was late afternoon by then, and the tennis courts were deserted except for a pro giving a lesson. Two men had finished playing and were walking toward the locker room. One of them was Sandra's father, Curtis Mayhew. When Gabe called to him, the older man left his partner and came over to them.

"This is a nice surprise." He smiled at Allison. "Have you come to take me up on my offer of a guest card?"

"No, we just stopped by for a drink." Gabe was the one who answered.

"Capital idea. Would you like to go into the bar, or shall we sit outside on the terrace?"

"It's your call. Wherever will be more private."

After a moment's pause, Curtis said, "Let's go into the bar."

There were a few men playing liar's dice at the bar, and two couples sitting at a table close to them. Curtis led the way to a leather booth in the far corner of the room.

They made small talk until a waiter had taken their order, although Allison contributed very little to the conversation. She was totally confused and a bit disappointed. What could Curtis Mayhew know about Monica's affair? Did Gabe think Sandra might have confided in her father, of all people? It seemed highly unlikely. Even if she had, what reason was there to think he'd be any more cooperative than she?

Gabe waited until the waiter had served their drinks and left them alone. "We didn't just happen to drop by this afternoon," he said quietly.

"Were you thinking of joining? I'd be happy to sponsor you, but I must point out that it's a little late in the season." The older man seemed perfectly relaxed, but his eyes were like a poker player's, revealing no emotion.

"We came to talk to you about Monica."

"Mary Louise's daughter? Tragic about her death. Such a beautiful girl."

"There's no question of that, but you're one of the few people who have a good word to say about her."

"That's shameful! Monica might have been a trifle capricious at times, but the woman is dead. People should be more charitable."

"Your own daughter speaks very bitterly about her."

Curtis paused. "Yes, well, Sandra and Monica had a falling out a long time ago. I'm afraid my daughter doesn't have a very forgiving nature."

"What was the argument about?"

"Good God, man, how should I know? It was something that happened between two teenage girls over twenty-five years ago. A minor matter. How can you expect me to know what they quarreled over?"

"I don't mean to be rude, but I think you know very well. I believe you were the cause of it."

Allison made an inadvertent exclamation. Gabe couldn't suspect *Curtis!* He was old enough to have been Monica's father!

After the shock subsided she began to have second thoughts. Monica was always described as being very precocious. When Cokey and Danny said she was having an affair with somebody older, they inferred it was a college man. But suppose they both just assumed that?

Curtis didn't *act* guilty. He was looking at Gabe with incredulity. "I can't imagine what you're talking about. You think I took sides in a juvenile spat? That's utterly absurd!"

"A spat doesn't last a lifetime. Sandra found out you were having an affair with her best friend, didn't she?"

A fine sheen of perspiration broke out on Curtis's forehead, but he covered his uneasiness with indignation.

"That's slanderous! I could sue you for an outrageous accusation like that. I will, too, if you breathe one word of this shocking allegation to anyone else."

"You don't have to worry about that. This isn't a shakedown. All I'm after is the truth. I know part of it, and I can guess the rest, except for a few details. How did Sandra find out about your affair?"

Curtis seemed about to repeat his denial, when suddenly his shoulders slumped. For the first time, he looked his age. Even his voice sounded old and tired. "Monica told her."

That took Gabe by surprise. "Why on earth would she do a thing like that?"

"Something happened between Monica and me. It was a…an accident, but she blamed me. In retaliation, she told Sandra about us. Quite understandably, it irreparably damaged my relationship with my daughter. She has never forgiven me for my…indiscretion."

"Did your wife know about it, too?"

"No! Sandra never told her, thank God. Nobody knew except—" Curtis caught himself. "Nobody else knows, and I beg you not to rake up the sordid story now. I'm not asking for myself. I'm thinking of Elinor. She shouldn't have to pay for my transgressions."

"You don't have to worry, she won't hear about them from me. Or Allison," Gabe added when Curtis glanced at her. "Was Monica's pregnancy that accident you referred to?"

Curtis looked at him sharply. "How did you find out about that?"

Gabe didn't answer directly. "Her father discovered she was pregnant and took her to Philadelphia to have the baby. He was the other person you were alluding to. Was that why Monica was angry? Did she want to keep the baby?"

"Good Lord, no! She was merely furious that she'd gotten pregnant." Curtis stole an uncomfortable look at Allison. "Sometimes contraceptives don't work, but Monica was in no mood for excuses."

"Presumably you knew that could happen," Gabe said dryly.

"You can't blame me any more than I blame myself." Curtis sighed. "I've asked myself over and over again how I ever got involved with a teenage girl—the same age as my own daughter! You don't have to remind me."

"Monica was seventeen, and you were ... ?"

"Forty-two." His voice was barely audible.

He must have been very dashing, Allison thought. Curtis was still attractive to women. She could just imagine what a charmer he was in the prime of his manhood.

"I'd known Monica all her life," he continued. "She was just another one of the little girls running in and out of the house with Sandra. I never paid any attention to her."

"That couldn't have set well with Monica," Gabe observed. "She liked to be noticed."

"Maybe that's the way it started. One day Sandra had a group over for a swimming party. I was working in my den when Monica came in to use the telephone."

"Isn't there one out by the pool?"

"Yes, but I suppose it was too noisy out there. Or maybe she wanted privacy."

Gabe raised an eyebrow, obviously wondering how private the den was, with Curtis at his desk. He didn't interrupt, however.

"She was wearing a bikini, and for the first time I realized she was fully developed. Any man would appreciate a body like hers. I'll admit I enjoyed looking at her, but the thought of seducing her never entered my mind. She was like a lovely child in a woman's body. After she finished her phone call she came over and sat on my lap and put her arm around my neck. She called me Uncle Curtis and told me about some party she and Sandra were planning to give together."

"You didn't advise her that she was asking for trouble by sitting on a man's lap almost naked?"

"To tell the truth, I was ashamed of thinking of her as a woman. The way she climbed onto my lap was so trusting, not to mention the fact that she thought of me as her uncle. I was embarrassed enough at the effect she was having on me. I certainly wasn't going to bring up the facts of life."

"Didn't you worry about how it would look if someone came in and saw you like that?"

"It crossed my mind. As soon as I could get a word in, I told her I had work to do. I think she knew I was uncomfortable, because she laughed and put both arms around my neck and kissed me. I was alarmed, naturally. I stood up and said something stuffy like you should be ashamed of yourself, young lady. She merely said, 'Why? You aren't really my uncle.'"

"That sounds like Monica," Gabe murmured.

"I gave her a lecture and sent her back outside. It was an uncomfortable incident, but I thought that was the end of it. Then a couple of days later I went to get my car after playing tennis. Monica was sitting in it, waiting for me. I was really annoyed. When I asked her what she was doing there, she said she came to apologize. She said one of the boys had dared her to kiss me, and she hadn't realized what a dumb idea it was. She really seemed sincere, like a little girl who knows she's been bad and is sorry."

"She seems to have had that act down pat."

"I had no reason not to believe her. Even so, when she asked me to go for a walk with her, I said no at first. I'm not completely stupid, although you wouldn't know it from my behavior. She said I hadn't forgiven her, and what could she do to prove to me that it would never happen again? I didn't want to be unreasonable. I remembered the silly things kids do on a dare."

"So naturally you went for a walk with her," Gabe said sardonically.

"I didn't see any harm in it. We drove to the outskirts of town and walked through the fields. It was really quite pleasant. We talked about her school and she asked my advice on career choices. Monica picked wildflowers like any kid on a nature hike, and then we sat under a big tree while she twined them into a wreath." Curtis paused for so long that Gabe prompted him.

"And then what happened?"

"I honestly don't know. Monica was putting the wreath on my head and she lost her balance or something. Suddenly we were lying on the ground and she was in my arms. I kissed her. A man would have to be made out of stone not to. She was so alluring. I'd known a lot of women, but none as captivating as this innocent girl."

Gabe let out an inadvertent exclamation that he quickly stifled. Not fast enough, however.

The lines in Curtis's face deepened. "You don't have to tell me how loathsome I am. I've lived with it all these years."

"I didn't mean—never mind. Go on."

"She pulled off her T-shirt and she wasn't wearing a bra underneath. I wanted her—God how I wanted her!—but I still had a shred of decency left. I told her how wrong it would be for me to take her, but she said she wanted to become a woman in my arms."

With great self-control, Gabe forced himself to remain silent.

"It might have happened then and there, in spite of my rather dubious scruples. But a tour bus stopped by the side of the road and a load of tourists got out to look at the wildflowers. That gave me time to get a grip on myself." Curtis smiled cynically. "It turned out to be only a postponement. The next morning, Elinor received a telegram saying her mother was ill and wanted to see her and Sandra. They left immediately. I stayed behind to close up the house if it proved to be anything serious. We were concerned naturally, but Elinor's mother was a bit of a hypochondriac."

"Let me guess. Monica sent the telegram. It has her touch."

"I was asleep that night," Curtis continued woodenly. "I awoke to find her in bed with me, nude. Maybe you could have resisted her. I couldn't."

"So Monica did seduce you," Gabe mused.

Curtis was startled and chagrined at the implication. "I didn't mean to give you that impression. I accept full responsibility for our affair. I was a mature man. It was up to me to see that nothing developed between us, no matter how attracted I was to her. She was too immature to deal with her emotions."

But she wasn't, Allison thought, appalled at the cold-blooded purpose of that seventeen-year-old girl. Monica wasn't in love with Curtis. She'd merely wanted him, like she wanted a new car or a fur coat. The torment of guilt she left him with meant nothing to her. It was an emotion she'd never experienced personally.

"Monica was like a narcotic after that." Curtis sounded tired. "I knew what we were doing was bad for everybody. When I was away from her, I'd vow not to see her again. But every time she called I went running. And then it was over. Just like that. I didn't even know what had happened until she called me from Philadelphia in a rage."

"She didn't tell you she was pregnant?"

"Only over the phone."

"How did her father find out? Her condition couldn't have been apparent yet."

"She went to a clinic for a pregnancy test and they mailed the report to him. If you remember Peter, you can imagine his reaction. They must have had a terrible row. Monica wanted to have an abortion, but he wouldn't hear of it. He moved her in with his sister, whom Monica couldn't stand. I never met the woman, but if she was anything like Peter, the poor kid had a hard time of it."

"I don't imagine it was a picnic for Aunt Jane, either," Gabe remarked ironically.

"I couldn't marry Monica. It wouldn't have been in anybody's best interest. But I did offer to support the child.

Both Peter and Monica refused. Neither of them wanted to have anything to do with it."

Allison had experienced rejection before, but never anything this crushing. She was aware of Gabe's compassionate gaze, but she couldn't look at him.

"Monica told me she was putting the child up for adoption. Telling Sandra about it wasn't enough for her. Monica's final revenge was refusing to tell me who the adoptive parents were." Curtis sighed. "I never got to know my daughter."

Gabe waited for Allison to make the revelation, but she was reluctant. The poor man had been through enough. All she had ever wanted was to know the truth, and now she did.

"Maybe it's just as well," she said quietly. "Sandra would have been furious if you'd had any contact with the child, no matter how discreet."

"My daughter is a very unhappy woman. For a long time I thought it was my fault, but I'm not sure I'm solely to blame. If she concentrated on making her own life more satisfying she wouldn't be so fixated on my one mistake, horrendous as it was."

"That's true," Gabe said. "You can't keep on punishing yourself for something you can't change. If Sandra persists in carrying on a vendetta, then she's the loser."

"She won't ever accept the situation," Allison said. "Sandra really hates me."

Curtis stared at her in surprise. "Why should she hate you?"

"Take a good look at Allison," Gabe said. "Who does she remind you of?"

As comprehension dawned, Curtis said, "You think *she's* Monica's daughter?"

"There isn't much doubt. Allison was born in Philadelphia at the same hospital on the same date that Monica had her baby. I'd say that's pretty conclusive, wouldn't you? She even looks like her."

"There's a superficial resemblance, but Allison isn't Monica's child. I know that for a fact."

Allison's first reaction was a sudden surge of relief. It was illogical after her insistence on knowing, but even anonymity was better than a mother like Monica.

"How can you be so sure?" Gabe asked. "You just said that Monica wouldn't tell you who the adoptive parents were."

"That's correct. I accepted the situation because I was in no position to argue about it, but I couldn't get the child out of my mind. Was it in a good home? Was it being cared for properly? I've heard there's a waiting list of people wanting to adopt infants, but some of those couples might not be suitable. What if our baby was being neglected or abused? The worry wouldn't go away, so after a few years I hired a firm of private detectives to find her for me. It took a while, but they finally located her. She was adopted by a fine family who were able to give her everything. They named her Diane."

"You're positive about this? You have absolute proof?" Allison had to be sure.

"There wasn't a shed of doubt," Curtis said.

"Did you tell her who you were?" Gabe asked.

"No, I didn't want to intrude on her life. I didn't have that right."

"You must have been curious, though. Did you ever see her?"

"Several times while she was growing up, although I never spoke to her. I had the same detective keep track of her and tell me what was going on in her life. She was very beautiful, the image of her mother." Curtis's eyes were sad.

"Was?" Gabe asked, sensing the story had an even unhappier ending.

"Unfortunately Diane inherited Monica's wild streak. At fifteen she was expelled from private school for drinking. The same year she was almost jailed for malicious mischief."

"History repeats itself," Gabe murmured.

"At sixteen she was killed drag racing with her boyfriend at ninety miles an hour."

After a shocked silence, Allison whispered, "I'm so sorry."

"I am, too—for everything," Curtis said heavily.

Gabe and Allison were both silent as they walked out of the tennis club. The story of lies and betrayal they'd just heard was sobering.

When they were in the car, Gabe looked at her with concern. "Are you all right?"

"I honestly don't know how I feel. I was so convinced that Monica was my mother. Finding out she wasn't, kind of leaves me in limbo."

"I know it's a disappointment, honey."

"That's the strange part. I'm sorry for everybody but myself. I raised Mary Louise's hopes, almost drove Sandra over the edge and reopened old wounds for Curtis."

"It was an honest mistake. Mary Louise convinced herself because she wanted to, but you really believed you were Monica's daughter."

"You never did, though. Not truly. Why not?"

"Because you're such a thoroughly normal, warmhearted person," Gabe answered simply. "You couldn't have inherited any of Monica's genes."

Allison shivered slightly. "She destroyed everyone she touched."

"Thank your lucky stars she's out of your life—*our* lives. Let's talk about us. How soon can we get married?"

"I don't know, we'll have to talk about it," she answered vaguely.

"That's what I just said."

"I meant some other time. I can't even think straight at the moment."

"You're waffling and I'm not going to let you get away with it," Gabe said firmly.

"I just have a lot on my mind," Allison answered defensively. "It's unfeeling to think about ourselves when Mary Louise is due for such a disappointment. What am I going to say? I can't tell her all of the story. She's suffered enough because of Monica—Curtis, too. But she won't believe me unless I tell her how I know I'm not her granddaughter."

"You'll just have to clean it up, leave out the details about Monica climbing into Curtis's bed, things like that. She has to know about their affair, though."

"I suppose there isn't any other way."

Allison was relieved that Gabe had dropped the subject of marriage. After all, nothing had changed. She didn't want to argue about it right now, though. Her emotions were in too fragile a state.

Allison didn't realize they weren't going back to Rosewood Manor until Gabe drove through the gates of his uncle's house. He wasn't giving up on the argument. He'd just postponed it until the conditions were more favorable—for him. When they were alone and he held her close and searched out every hidden pleasure spot in her body, she would promise him anything.

"We don't have time for this, Gabe," she said quickly. "I can't put off telling Mary Louise."

He stopped the car in front of the house. "Relax, Angel, I didn't bring you here to make love." He was grinning as he opened the door and led her inside. "Did you ever think you'd hear me say that?"

She smiled in spite of her troubled state of mind. "I never had to be talked into anything."

He put his arms around her. "Of course, I could be persuaded."

When his mouth covered hers, Allison put up no resistance. Her love for Gabe was the one constant in her chaotic world. She clung to him almost desperately.

A man's voice startled them. "I presume this is Miss Riley?"

"Dad!" Gabe exclaimed. "What are *you* doing here?"

"Your mother and I decided to take a few days vacation."

"Mother is here, too? That's great!"

An older woman joined them in the entryway. She was attractive and poised, the product of an expensive finishing school and an exclusive college. The kind of person who would automatically expect her son to select a wife from the same rarefied atmosphere. Allison's heart sank.

Gabe went over to kiss his mother's cheek. "I'm so glad you're both here. I want you to meet Allison, the woman I'm going to marry."

"You promised you wouldn't tell!" Allison exclaimed.

"The agreement was, not until you met them. That's just been accomplished."

After politely acknowledging the introduction, Lily Rockford said, "Why don't we all go into the den and get acquainted?"

Allison sat stiffly on a couch next to Gabe, waiting for the inquisition to begin. His parents wouldn't be as crass as Bruce's had been, but that was cold comfort.

"This is quite a surprise," Lily began.

"Yes, we'd almost given up hope that Gabriel would ever get married," Burton agreed.

"*You* might have." His wife smiled. "I always knew that sooner or later some clever girl would make up his mind for him."

Allison tensed, even though she'd known this was coming. Gabe's mother was planting the seed—ever so innocently—that Allison had tricked him into proposing.

"That wasn't the way it happened," Gabe said. "I had a devil of a time getting Allison to agree to marry me."

Lily gazed at her without expression. "You have some doubts about marrying my son?"

"Not doubts exactly," Allison answered carefully. "You might call them reservations."

"*I* call them nonsense!" Gabe said forcefully.

"You've known each other a very short time," Burton said. "Perhaps Allison is being more realistic than you."

"Time has nothing to do with it. I knew we were right for each other as soon as we met."

Burton's smile was faintly derisive. "The old love-at-first-sight defense."

"I'm serious, Dad! Maybe you've forgotten what it's like to love somebody so completely that you can't imagine a life without her. When you find someone like that, you know in an instant."

Burton's gaze went to his wife. "I haven't forgotten," he said softly. "After all these years, I still can't imagine being without your mother."

"That's very moving, my dear." Lily's eyes held his, full of shared affection.

"All right, now you know how I feel about Allison," Gabe said.

"We haven't heard from her," Burton commented. "Do you love Gabriel?"

"Very much," she replied in a small voice.

"Then I presume the matter is settled," he said.

Allison was tempted to let it go at that. But she couldn't. "Not if you object to our marriage."

"We don't have anything to say about it. You and my son have made your decision."

"Not really. There was one possible stumbling block, and I'm afraid we've run into it."

"You're imagining things," Gabe protested.

"Am I?" She gazed at him steadily. "I haven't noticed the open arms you were counting on."

"I get the impression that Lily and I are the problem," Burton said. "Why would that be?"

"Gabe values your opinion highly. The three of you have a very special relationship," Allison said wistfully. "I've never been that fortunate myself, so I know it's a blessing you don't give up lightly. I told Gabe I'd never come between him and his family."

"You must not love him very much," Lily observed.

Allison couldn't let her use that excuse. "You don't know what this is costing me! I'll never get over losing him. It's *because* I love him so much that I'm giving him up."

"Then all I can say is, you're a very foolish girl," Lily said calmly. "My opinion shouldn't matter, nor Burton's or anybody else's. The only important thing is whether you two believe you can be happy together."

"How can we be if I've alienated him from the people he cares deeply about? Gabe doesn't think it would affect his feelings, but I know he'd grow to resent me."

"For one thing, what makes you think Burton and I object to your marriage?"

"It's pretty obvious isn't it?" Allison's eyes were bleak. "I understand how you feel. You hoped he'd marry somebody more suitable. Your husband must have told you I grew up in an orphanage."

"Yes, Burton told me the story on the plane. He also said there's a possibility that you're Mary Louise's grandchild."

"I thought I might be, but I'm not. We found that out this afternoon."

Burton looked quickly at his son. "You have proof of this?"

"I got it from the horse's mouth, so to speak. I'll tell you all about it later. Right now I want to settle this thing with Allison, once and for all." Gabe turned her to face him. "I don't know if my parents approve. If they don't I'm sorry. I love them very much, but not enough to give you up— ever. I can't imagine them even asking such a thing. The only way I'll get out of your life is if you tell me you don't love me."

Allison's eyes filled with tears. "You know I can't do that."

"I think that's pretty conclusive," Lily said with satisfaction. "I'm sorry if you got the wrong impression, my dear," she told Allison. "Our concern had nothing to do with you, personally. We were simply afraid that you were both confusing overwhelming attraction with something more lasting. You've more than convinced us that's not the case. Don't you agree, Burton?''

"Wholeheartedly," he answered with a warm smile. "Welcome to the family, Allison."

She found it hard to believe. "You don't mind that I don't know who my parents were?"

"Whoever they were, I'm sure they were a gorgeous couple," Lily answered. "You're very lovely. You and Gabriel should have beautiful children."

Gabe chuckled. "Aren't you being a little premature, Mother?"

"It never hurts to plant the idea," she answered complacently.

"Unfortunately I can't act on it." His eyes sparkled with deviltry. "You and Dad have seriously cramped my style. This was the only place Allison and I could be alone."

"Gabe!" Allison's cheeks felt fiery. "We came here a few times because I wanted to see where he spent the summers when he was growing up," she explained self-consciously. "It's a beautiful home."

"We enjoyed it, although it's nothing like that palace Mary Louise lives in. Rosewood Manor is magnificent, but I must admit I don't envy her the upkeep."

Allison was reminded of the unhappy task ahead of her. "We really have to go talk to her," she told Gabe. "I'm dreading the prospect, though. She was so sure I was Monica's daughter. It's going to be quite a blow to find out it was wishful thinking after all."

"Will it help if we come along?" Lily asked.

"You might be able to lend some support," Gabe said. "I'll phone and tell her we're on our way."

"I'll look forward to seeing you, Lily. And Burton, too, of course," Mary Louise added, concluding her conversation. She turned with a happy smile as Sergei entered the den. The smile faded when she noticed the suitcase he was carrying. "Are you going somewhere?"

"I told you I had to go back to work."

"I didn't think you meant immediately."

"It won't get any easier." He smiled, as if it were a joke.

"Couldn't you at least stay for the weekend? Gabriel's parents are in town. They'll be over shortly."

"I can spare a few minutes to say hello, but that's all. My plane leaves in an hour."

"We both know you don't have to go," she said quietly. "Why are you really leaving, Sergei?"

"It isn't like you to provoke a confrontation." His voice was gently teasing.

"Maybe that's been my trouble. I'm always so ladylike that I never say what's actually on my mind. And I never force anyone else to speak frankly, either. Just once I'd like to break all the rules of etiquette and be incredibly direct."

"I doubt if you could do it." He smiled. "You can't change the habits of a lifetime."

"I didn't think so, either, but I've suddenly realized that time is running out."

"I suppose it had to eventually," he said heavily.

She gazed at him impassively. "Are you in love with me, Sergei?"

For a moment he was too surprised to speak. "That's really laying it on the line," he said finally.

"You haven't answered my question."

"What difference does it make? It doesn't change anything." He thrust his hands into his pockets and paced the floor. "We have no future together."

"Why not? When two people love each other, it usually makes a difference in their lives."

"Are you saying—" He broke off to stare at her, afraid of misinterpreting her meaning.

"If you need it spelled out for you, I love you very much."

Sergei's eyes lit with dawning joy. "Mary Louise, my dearest, I don't know what to say."

"Perhaps I can help you." She smiled mischievously. "Sergei, my love, will you please stop screwing up and ask me to marry you?"

Mary Louise and the Rockfords were friends of long-standing. They all greeted each other fondly. For a short while the conversation was about mutual acquaintances and reminiscences of the last time they'd seen each other. Allison sat silently, reluctant to spoil their happy reunion.

Gabe knew how hard it was for her, so finally he squeezed her hand and said, "Mary Louise, we have something to tell you."

"You're getting married!" she exclaimed happily. "I *told* Sergei that things always work out when you're in love. Aren't you thrilled, Lily?"

"Well, yes, of course."

Mary Louise misunderstood her friend's suddenly sober expression. "If you're concerned over their whirlwind affair, don't be. Allison is a darling girl. You'll find that out when you get to know her."

"That's no problem," Gabe said. "What I want to—"

"I'd love to hold the wedding here. We can have the reception in the garden, and you can wear my wedding gown," Mary Louise told Allison excitedly. "If you want to, that is. Monica wasn't interested in tradition, but I've saved it all these years, just in case." Her voice had a wistful note.

Allison was close to tears. "I wish things had worked out that way. It would have been a dream come true."

"Allison is trying to tell you that she isn't your granddaughter," Gabe said gently. He related a highly edited version of Monica's affair with Curtis.

Mary Louise was surprised and troubled by the story. The haunting sadness in her face at its tragic conclusion broke Allison's heart.

She put her arms around the older woman. "I'm so sorry. If I'd never come here you'd have been spared all this pain. Can you ever forgive me?"

"There's nothing to forgive. You've given me more happiness in two weeks than Monica gave me in a lifetime," Mary Louise said quietly. "When I dreamed of having a granddaughter, she was someone exactly like you."

"It can still happen. Maybe someday Martin and Laura will have a child, and you'll get your wish."

"That would be nice. I hope they do, but I've already gotten my wish. I have a grandchild to love and cherish. Our relationship is based on mutual caring and respect. That's a lot more important than heredity. In every way that counts, you are my family."

All the women were misty-eyed, and the men had lumps in their throats.

"Well, now that that's settled, how about telling them *our* news," Sergei suggested.

"Sergei has asked me to marry him—after I insisted on it." Mary Louise laughed like a young girl.

"You didn't!" Gabe exclaimed. "I wouldn't have believed it."

"Not only that, I used your exact words," she said proudly.

Congratulations were exchanged all around, and the subject of weddings was discussed. Mary Louise was as excited about the young couple's as she was about her own.

After a while, Gabe said, "Allison and I have something to talk about. We're going out for a little walk."

"Why don't you go over to Uncle Herbert's? We'll be visiting here for an hour or so," Burton said casually.

Gabe grinned. "It really pays to have an understanding father."

Allison felt a twinge of apprehension. Gabe's expression had been serious when he said they had to talk. What new problem had arisen? Whatever it was, he wouldn't discuss it until they reached his uncle's house. By then, his refusal had set off all kinds of alarms in Allison's head.

Gabe led the way into the den. "Can I fix you a drink?"

She stood in the middle of the room, regarding him warily. "Am I going to need one?"

He gave her a puzzled look. "I don't understand."

"When everyone was discussing our wedding, you didn't join in. Are you feeling pressured now that it's official? Do you want to wait a few months until we get to know each other better? You can be honest with me."

"I always have been." He came over to take her into his arms. "How can you possibly doubt my commitment? If it were possible, I'd like to get married tonight. That's the only kind of pressure I feel."

Allison flung her arms around his neck. "Oh, Gabe darling, I love you so!"

His kiss was deeply reassuring. They clung to each other murmuring words of endearment. In the beginning it was an innocent affirmation of their love, but the sexual attraction that was always present between them became insistent.

Gabe's caresses grew more sensual, his need more evident. Allison moved against him in mounting anticipation. When he whispered something in her ear she smiled seductively and tugged his shirt out of his slacks.

They walked up the stairs slowly, undressing each other as they went. By the time they reached Gabe's room, they were both completely nude.

As they stood by the bed he cupped her breasts in his palms and kissed each rosy peak. "My beautiful bride," he said in a husky voice. "What did I ever do to deserve you?"

"I'm the lucky one." She traced the lean triangle of his torso down to his taut stomach.

When she continued on, he tensed and drew in his breath sharply. "Not yet, sweetheart. I want to make this special for you."

"You always do." She clasped him around the waist and carried him with her as she fell backward on the bed.

Gabe was powerless to resist when her legs circled his hips invitingly. He plunged deeply, joining their bodies. They were welded into one person, sharing the molten excitement that zigzagged from one to the other.

Allison welcomed his driving masculinity. She arched her body to return his thrusts as the throbbing ecstasy mounted to unbelievable heights. They reached the pinnacle together in a fiery burst of sensation that reverberated like thunder inside of them. The storm subsided into a satisfying glow of pleasure that left both utterly contented.

Gabe stroked her hair lovingly. "That was a lot more gratifying than what I planned."

"You expect me to believe you had something else in mind?" she teased.

"Actually I did. I wanted to have a private talk with you." He levered himself up on one elbow so he could watch her reaction. "Everything turned out pretty well today—with one exception."

"What do you mean? It's been a fairy-tale day! Your parents are happy for us, Mary Louise and Sergei are going to get married. What more could we possibly ask?"

"You still don't know who your parents are," he answered quietly.

A look of surprise crossed her face. "I didn't even think of that!"

"Does that mean it won't bother you anymore?"

"I guess I'll always wonder about them," she said slowly.

"That's what I was afraid of." Gabe suppressed a sigh. "Okay, honey, it won't be easy, but this time we'll leave it to the professionals. I'll hire a top-notch private detective and let him take it from here. If you'll just be patient, we'll find your parents sooner or later."

"You don't have to go to all that trouble. It doesn't matter any longer."

He gave her a puzzled look. "You just said you'd continue to wonder."

"That's different from needing to know. I suppose it sounds strange after my insistence on ferreting out the truth, but these past two weeks have changed my whole outlook. I'd like to leave things as they are."

"Because you're afraid of what you might find out? It's understandable. The possibility of having someone like Monica for a mother would scare anybody off."

"I'm sure my real mother wasn't anything like her. I have a feeling she gave me up out of love, hoping I'd have a better life than she could provide. That's what really matters, not bringing up memories that might be painful for her. It took me a while to realize what an unselfish gift she gave me. I never would have found you, otherwise."

"My beautiful bride." Gabe held her so tightly she could feel his heart beating against hers. "Whoever your parents were, they must have been wonderful people to have produced a jewel like you."

Allison managed a watery smile. "The best part of all this will be having a name that really belongs to me."

"The best part?" Tiny flames lit his gray eyes as he raised his head to gaze at her.

"Unless you can think of something that will make me feel even better." She smiled enchantingly as she lifted her face to his.

*   *   *   *   *